Ben Okri is a Ni͟ ͟ ͟ ͟ ͟ ͟ ͟ ͟ ͟
in London. He was nineteen when he completed
Flowers and Shadows, which was received with
critical acclaim. He has since published a second
novel, *The Landscapes Within*, and two volumes
of short stories, *Incidents at the Shrine* and *Stars
of the New Curfew*.

Ben Okri studied at the University of
Essex and was Poetry Editor of *West Africa*.
He has also worked as a broadcaster with the
BBC. In 1984 he was awarded an Arts Council
bursary. In 1987 he won the Commonwealth
writers' prize for Africa and was awarded the
'Paris Review' Aga Khan prize for fiction.

FLOWERS
AND
SHADOWS

Ben Okri

with an introduction by
Adewale Maja-Pearce

Longman

DEDICATION

To my father and mother, with love;
to Henry Atenaga, with affection;
and in the inspiring memory of
Victor Omodia.

Longman Group UK Limited,
Longman House, Burnt Mill, Harlow,
Essex CM20 2JE, England
and Associated Companies throughout the world

First published in Longman African Classics 1989

Produced by Longman Group (FE) Ltd
Printed in Hong Kong

ISBN 0-582-035368

Contents

Introduction

The corruption of modern Nigerian society is the dominant theme of this novel, first published in 1980 when the author, himself a Nigerian, was just nineteen. The action takes place in Lagos, the capital city, and centres on the person of Jeffia Okwe, the only child of well-to-do parents whose entry into adult life, a sort of rite of passage, is effected in the course of the book.

The Plot and Characters

Flowers and Shadows opens with premonitions of disaster, hence the title of the first section, 'Presentiments', which effectively sets the tone for everything that happens in the course of the novel. Walking home after visiting a school friend Jeffia comes across two boys torturing a puppy:

> 'One held the dog by the legs, while the other, it seemed, tried to stick a piece of wood up its anus. Indifferently they watched it struggle. The bigger of the boys held the dog's mouth to prevent it yelping.' (p. 4)

Jeffia rescues the dog and takes it home with him. No permanent damage has been done. A few days later Jeffia's mother points to an advertisement from its owner in the local newspaper. He returns the puppy to its mistress, an attractive woman who lives in a well-appointed apartment nearby. What Jeffia does not know is that this woman, Juliet, is one of his father's former mistresses.

His father, Jonan Okwe, is a successful businessman who all his life has been driven by the fear of poverty. It was poverty that killed his own father when he was still a child:

> 'From the day he was old enough to know what impossible things money could do, from the time his father died

consumed by a mysterious plague, from the moment he realised the truth of his father's words that poverty was a curse, he always dreamt of the big time.' (p. 11)

It is this dream that haunts him and that makes his success possible. But hard work in itself is not enough to make the kind of money he wants. To succeed he must himself become corrupt. In order to take control of the paint factory that makes him his fortune he frames his half-brother, Sowho, on a trumped-up charge which lands him in prison. The second of the premonitions with which the novel opens is the arrival, early one morning, of a telegram from Sowho announcing his imminent visit. This is followed by a series of mysterious phone calls in which Jonan is threatened with a revelation about his past: specifically, the supposed existence of a photograph showing him and Juliet in bed together. Enraged at what he supposes to be Juliet's duplicity – how else could they have got hold of such a photo? – he calls on Juliet. Faced with her denial he beats her up. In his anger he also kicks out at the puppy:

'The dog barked at his feet, pulled at his trousers, and bit him on the ankle. Jonan turned round and kicked it savagely. The dog howled, landing near the door. It gave a short sad whimper. Then fell still.' (p. 156)

The murder of the innocent, in this case the puppy, is paralleled by the much more serious murder by Jonan, through thugs employed for that purpose, of his longest-serving employee who is about to leave his company to set up on his own. The man knows too much about Jonan's illegal business practices and so must be stopped. The death is itself an accident; he had only meant for the man to be taught a lesson. But – and this is the point the writer insists upon time and again – corruption is an evil which can only result in tragedy. When, in the penultimate section of the novel, 'Darkness', Sowho finally makes his appearance, Jonan meets his nemesis. Giving chase he collides with Sowho's car and both perish in the ensuing flames. He has killed his brother. But he has also, thereby, effected the reconciliation that could only be achieved through the ultimate sacrifice:

> 'His tormented spirit struggled out of the reluctant wreck of his body and soared away from the ruins it left behind.
>   'Two souls joined in one and blood burned on metal.' (p. 176)

By sheer coincidence it is Jeffia, driving home from a party late at night, who happens upon Cynthia, a nurse from the nearby clinic, kneeling over the body of his father's dying employee. Such an unpropitious meeting contains the seeds of a new beginning. Cynthia is the personification of goodness, the triumph of life over death and, ultimately, Jeffia's salvation. In terms of the novel this is a heavy burden for her to carry. It is one of the many strengths of the book that the author succeeds in creating a character equal to the task.

Cynthia's life to date has been dogged by hardship, specifically the wrongful imprisonment of her father and the ensuing death of her mother. When her father comes out of prison, broken and bitter, it is Cynthia who nurtures him back to life. To do so she must develop her own resources. Jeffia glimpses her inner strength on that first day when he drives her home and then watches her help her drunken father into the slum that is their home:

> 'There was a charismatic defiance in her gesture, a fortitude in the face of pain that aroused his profound respect.' (p. 67)

Ben Okri is particularly good at creating female characters. Like Cynthia, they almost all serve as protectors of the life-force, the foils to the corruption of men. Jeffia's mother, for instance, although a weaker woman than Cynthia, is constantly contrasted with her husband, always to his detriment. Throughout the novel her love of flowers is at odds with Jonan's contempt for anything that can't be of immediate use to him at a purely material level:

> 'He didn't particularly like flowers. They never did a thing for you, never solved one of your problems. It was

the same with religion, he reasoned, a thing people did because they were stupid creatures of fancy, of fear.' (p. 135)

It is important for the author's purposes that Jonan has never developed his aesthetic feelings. He doesn't see beauty. He even despises his son for sharing with his wife what he considers unmanly, here used as a term of abuse. The relationship between father and son is an important sub-theme.

This is not to say that Jonan is necessarily wicked. Such an interpretation would be too simplistic. He is a man driven by an idea, but it is an empty idea because it militates against his proper growth as a human being. In so far as he commits evil he does so because he has wilfully killed that part of him that one would recognise as his moral centre, the moral imperative being the definition of a human being. It is the same part that can see the beauty in a flower, an otherwise insignificant object of no material value. When his life begins to fall apart, what is revealed is a man who no longer understands what is happening to him, or why. A truly evil man would have possessed foreknowledge; Jonan is simply confused.

His father's death is the final stage in Jeffia's coming of age, his emergence into the world as a man in the fullest sense. The moment is pinpointed to one specific evening on the beach when he is suddenly given an insight into the nature of the world and his place in it:

'At first the great ocean, the great spaces, the engulfing sky, seemed to crowd on my senses, filling me with an intense loneliness and smallness. But I got used to it. Here I had learnt that everything had its time and place, strange as they might be. I had learnt too that I was an infinitesimal part of nature and that I could not possibly understand all the strange ways of life. Such moments alone enabled my soul to soar and experience a joy that rose above the torments that I had suffered.' (p. 196)

Flowers and Shadows is finally a novel of great optimism. The cycle of corruption and evil has been played out and Jeffia can begin all over again. This belies the refrain running throughout the novel, articulated most vehemently by Sowho, that ' "The sins of the father are visited on the children . . . ' " (p. 167), unless we are to interpret this only at the level of Jeffia's reduced circumstances: deprived of his father's material protection, Jeffia and his mother are forced to move down the social scale and rent some rooms in one of the poorer areas of the city. But to Jeffia, with a larger conception of what life is, his material circumstances are of little consequence. More important than money and what it can buy is the love he and Cynthia have for each other. This alone makes him complete:

> 'I felt warm and free. Cynthia had that power of making me feel whole again. Just standing there with her made me joyful. As the pleasure of her presence glowed in me, the inner world where I had been hiding seemed to recede far into the background. And all I knew then was that I could be happy again.' (p. 193)

Corruption

The theme of corruption is not new to modern Nigerian literature in English. In many ways it can be said to be the dominant theme of Nigerian writing of the last thirty years or so. To understand why this is the case one has only to experience the scale of the corruption in the country since it became independent from Britain in 1960.

Corruption was endemic in the political structure from the very start, partly because of the way that power was transferred by the departing imperial masters, partly because of the nature of Nigerian life itself. The one ensured instability; the other permitted the growing use of patronage as the dominant style of politics. It would be out of place to elaborate on them here. It is enough to say that the results quickly assumed tragic proportions as two successive military coups were followed by a bloody civil war within the first decade of independence. By the end of the civil war in 1970 Nigeria's most celebrated writer, Wole Soyinka, the recipient of the 1986 Nobel prize for literature, was able to write:

> 'Militarist entrepreneurs and multiple dictatorships: this is bound to be the legacy ... The vacuum in the ethical base – for national boundary is neither an ethical nor an ideological base for any conflict – this vacuum will be filled by a new military ethic – coercion. And the elitist formulation of the army, the entire colonial hangover which is sustained by the lack of national revaluation will itself maintain and promote the class heritage of society. The ramifications of the alliance of a corrupt and rapacious Mafia in society are endless and are nearly incurable. The war means a consolidation of crime, an acceptance of the scale of values that created the conflict, indeed an allegiance and enshrinement of that scale of values because it is now intimately bound in the sense of national identity.'
>
> (Wole Soyinka: *The Man Died*)

This is precisely what happened. Throughout the 1970s Nigeria became legendary for the scale of its corruption, made worse by the growing revenue from its huge petroleum resources. The ramifications were horrendous. In a society where money replaces the vacuum in the ethical base, where money becomes the ethical base, brutalisation is the end result. If there is no God, anything goes. On the streets of Lagos, for instance, it was possible to witness, on a daily basis, the forces of law and order demanding bribes from passing motorists and whipping innocent civilians for no readily apparent reason.

This is the world of *Flowers and Shadows*. One of the most effective scenes in the novel is the description of soldiers beating people inadvertently caught in a traffic jam:

> 'They shouted at the motorists. The jam eased up bit by bit. They flogged the bonnets of cars, screamed at drivers as though they were partially deaf. One of them pounced on a motorcyclist who was without a crash helmet. The soldier lashed him three times on the back.' (p. 97)

Later we learn that the motorcyclist is reduced to 'a whimpering, groaning, crying mass of respectability'. At a technical level what is interesting here is the author's use of language. The soldier, uneducated and brutish – by no means synonymous – can only manage pidgin English: ' "Where your helmet, eh? Where am?' "; ' "Fuckin' man. Where you licence?' "; ' "Where your insure?' ". The use of pidgin in a novel otherwise written in a simple, straightforward style not only helps to define the characters but to stretch the resources of the available language. All Nigerian writers have made use of pidgin to a greater or lesser extent. Ben Okri, who has a good ear for dialogue, captures the rhythm of pidgin exactly.

What is chilling about the soldier's brutish behaviour is the way this is presented as perfectly normal, as are the descriptions of the filth and squalor in which most of the city's inhabitants live:

> 'There was a terrible stench in the air. The roads were bad, filled with ugly potholes, dirty. People who looked sickly and limp milled past us and I couldn't help being revolted by some of the sights I saw. There was a man under the Ijora bridge who had no legs. He was sleeping beside the spot people had habitually used as a urinal. There was a boy no more than fourteen lying on the side of the road with flies dancing all over his swollen body. He was dead. There was another group of children all crying round their beggar mother.' (p. 187)

Wole Soyinka's vision had been realised and Ben Okri, along with the other writers who came of age during this period, immediately took it on board. The list of novels published in the late 70s and early 80s is a long one, but they all belong to what can be clearly identified as a single school of writing. They include: Festus Iyayi's *Violence* (1979) and *The Contract* (1982); Kole Omotoso's *Memories of our Recent Boom* (1982); Ifeoma Okoye's *Men Without Ears* (1984); Lekan Oyegoke's *Cowrie Tears* (1982); Bode Sowande's *Our Man the President* (1981); as well as Ben Okri's own later novel, *The Landscapes Within* (1981).

An interesting feature of all these novels, Ben Okri's no less than the others, is their literal identification of corruption with evil. In *The Contract* a man becomes initiated into a secret cult involving 'eating the meat of snakes, lizards, and, he was later told, vultures'; in *Cowrie Tears* human sacrifice is used to appease the dark gods; in *Flowers and Shadows*, Jonan Okwe, sensing the impending chaos, calls on the power of juju:

> 'Jeffia was drifting into sleep when the sinister clanging of sacrificial bells and the mysterious chuckling of cowries reached him.
>
> 'It was a long time since he had heard those sounds in the home. They were like a funeral dirge, charged and distorted in the mind by echoes of the supernatural.
>
> 'His father was calling on the spirits of his forefathers and invoking his juju.
>
> 'To Jeffia's troubled mind the ritual seemed like a last resort as if whatever evils were lurking about in realms of pre-manifestation had to be countered.' (p. 75)

The unremitting sense of lurking evil pervades the novel like a bad smell. Cynthia's father, for instance, assumes as a matter of course that his wife was killed by witchcraft. This powerful presence of the other-worldly is the essence of tragedy. The knowledge that Jonan Okwe is finally destroyed by forces greater than himself, forces which exact their vengeance without pity, raises the novel to the tragic dimension.

Adewale Maja-Pearce

Suggestions for Further Reading

Books by Ben Okri:

Novels: *Flowers and Shadows*, Harlow: Longman, 1980. *The Landscapes Within*, Harlow: Longman, 1981.

Short Stories: *Incidents at the Shrine*, London: Heinemann, 1986. *Stars of the New Curfew*, London: Secker & Warburg, 1988.

Background to the Nigerian Novel:

Berth Lindfors (ed.): *Critical Perspectives on Nigerian Literatures*, London: Heinemann Educational Books, 1979.

Lewis Nkosi: *Tasks and Masks: Themes and Styles of African Literature*, Harlow: Longman, 1981.

Ulli Beier (ed.): *Introduction to African Literature*, Harlow: Longman, 1967, rev. 1979.

Shatto Arthur Gakwandi: *The Novel and Contemporary Experience in Africa*, London: Heinemann Educational Books, 1977.

James Booth: *Writers and Politics in Nigeria*, London: Hodder & Stoughton, 1981.

Oladele Taiwo: *Culture and the Nigerian Novel*, London: Macmillan, 1976.

David Cook: *African Literature: A Critical View*, Harlow: Longman, 1977.

Reference:

Hans M. Zell, Carol Bundy and Virginia Coulon (eds): *A New Reader's Guide to African Literature*, London: Heinemann Educational Books, 1983.

Presentiments

Chapter One

It was a scorching day.

But the heat did not bother everybody alike. For some it was a menace. For others it was just another hot day to be tolerated. For a few whose minds were occupied with good thoughts, it didn't exist. One of these few was Jeffia Okwe.

He was returning home from a visit to his childhood friend and his mind was filled with the satisfaction that comes from having been helpful and understanding. On his way back he had rescued a dog, a jumpy brown and white puppy which he now carried.

He walked through the open gate, and waved to the aged watchday who sat in the shed keeping awake with difficulty.

'Welcome – O, Oga. Today be like fire.'

'True,' Jeffia said. He stopped and tossed the man a ten kobo coin.

'God go bless you. This go buy me cigarette.'

Jeffia smiled and went to his room through the back door. He put the dog on his bed and changed into a towel. Then, taking the dog along with him, he went to the bathroom.

Climbing into the bath, he sighed as he immersed himself in the delightfully cold water. He splashed some on the puppy. It barked playfully. *I never had a bath with an animal before*, he thought.

While he bathed, he thought about the events that had brought him and the dog together.

He had been coming home from Ode's place. He had been there all morning playing table tennis and Monopoly, having endless arguments and discussions with his friend. That day they discussed their exam results and what they would each do when the results came out.

'Daddy wants me to study in London,' Ode said. 'If my result is good . . .'

'Which you are sure it will be . . .'

'Why do you say that? The results are not even out. You're giving me false hopes, you know.'

'Come on, Ode. Stop pretending. The mock was excellent, and all the teachers said that from what we did we should have good results.'

'But I want to be *sure*. What will you do when your result comes out, if you do well?'

'Go to a university here.'

'Don't you want to go abroad? To London or America?'

'No. Mum thinks it's best to go there after getting my first degree, when I'm a bit older.'

'I've got three provisional entries already. In five years' time we will see who will be better, you with your local education and me with my international . . .'

'You'll be too westernised then. I'll be a man of home, and we won't take back prodigal sons.'

'The greatest Africans first had to be men of the world.'

'No, first they had to be men of the land.'

'Five years will tell,' said Ode, getting up. 'Let's go and have another round of table tennis.'

'Okay, but it's terribly hot,' complained Jeffia.

'Have a *terribly* cold bath when you get home.'

They laughed and went out into the garage where the table tennis board was kept when it was too hot. That was how they spent the day. Ode was one of the few friends with whom Jeffia was really intimate. Their parents often remarked what great friends they had always been.

The day passed slowly and Jeffia said he must be going. Ode saw him off. They walked down the streets and lanes together.

'Did I tell you I am taking a temporary job?'

'No.'

'Well,' Ode said, hitting Jeffia playfully, 'I am going to be a reporter on the *Everyday Times*. Dad said it would give me experience of the world and how tough it is to make money.'

'Great idea. Mum said the same thing too. She said when a vacancy comes up at the school where she teaches, she would help me get it. Maybe I could do some part-time teaching of juniors.'

'A reporter's life is a million times more exciting than a teacher's.'

'But without teachers you would be a lazy illiterate.'

'Just think of it, I will attend press conferences, go places, meet people . . . '

'Not too soon, mister . . . so stop your dreaming. When do you start?'

'The editor said next week. He's a friend of Dad's.'

'Well, you can write about me for a start.'

'You? Nobody knows you! Nobody wants to read about you!'

'That's what makes a good writer.'

'What?'

'The ability to make people want to read about the ordinary.'

'Nonsense! Not for a reporter.'

They walked on in silence. They were both sweating profusely. Soon Ode spoke.

'Jeff, I will have to go back here. I've seen you far enough.'

'Yeah. Or it would turn into the rat's escort. To and fro.'

'When are we going to meet next?'

'Any time. I'm always in. Ring, call – you are a friend, not a stranger.'

'All right then.'

'See you, cub reporter.'

'And you, village headmaster.'

They went their different ways, back to back. In the distance Ode turned and waved. *Great friend*, Jeffia thought.

The sun shone furiously, its rays flushing everything around with a vivid tinge. The asphalt road ahead gleamed and in the distance gave the illusion of a puddle. The street was lined with tall whistling pine and Indian almond trees. Shadows from the trees crossed the road here and there. The air was heavy, hot, and sweet-smelling.

Jeffia brought out his handkerchief and wiped the sweat from his face. Harassed by the heat, he could only think of what he and Ode had talked about. *Ode has strong views on the ills of society. Maybe that's why he is going to be a reporter. But doesn't it strike him that by getting the job through his dad, he's also contributing to the ills he talks so strongly about?'* He turned into Park Avenue.

That was when he first heard the howls. Then he saw the two boys. They were at the corner of the road, under a whistling pine tree. One held the dog by the legs, while the other, it seemed, tried to stick a piece of wood up its anus. Indifferently they watched it struggle. The bigger of the boys held the dog's mouth to prevent it yelping. It was a small brown and white puppy, too small to fight back.

Jeffia stood and watched them. Not many people kept puppies. The ones that were usually about in the streets were lean, ugly strays. This puppy was too small to be a street dog, and its fur was beautifully groomed. *Maybe it belongs to some rich person, maybe it got lost or stolen*, he thought. *But why are these boys being cruel to it like that?*

The two boys looked like the new breed of small boy conductors of the Kunbi buses. They were ill-dressed. Their khaki shorts were dirty and in tatters. Their shirts were buttonless and too small. Their hair was unkempt and their faces were very serious.

Ajegunle boys! Jeffia thought. And when the puppy whimpered, he felt it. All the pain, the condensed cry, communicated itself to him.

'Why don't you leave that puppy alone? What do you get from punishing it?' he said, moving towards them. They turned round, startled. Expressions of surprise and resentment alternated on their faces.

'Mind your own business! Go your own way, you hear?' It was the bigger one that spoke. He couldn't have been more than fourteen years old, but his voice was husky and tough. He glowered as though if angered further would fight.

'Abi you dey find trouble?' He relaxed his hold over the dog's neck, and paused to sum Jeffia up, looking at him from toe to head. He took in Jeffia's white Adidas canvas shoes, his well-cut, moderate-bottomed trousers, his rich-looking blue polo-neck, and the Polaroid sunshade on his face.

'Abi you go buy di dog sef ?' the dog's tormentor added, smiling at the suggestion. The smaller one, who had been pulling the dog's leg, spoke.

'We don't eat dogs. Since morning we have eaten only garri. If you give us three Naira, you can take the dog. You be like big man pickin. My father was jailed – they say he thief, what can a poor man do? If man no die, he no rotten.' The boy stopped, coughed and spat out. He threw away the stick he was holding, wiped his mouth and went on, 'It's not that we are wicked. We don't care no more. You go give us di money?'

There was a soft and bitter quality to the boy's voice. He began caressing the dog, his eyes dull and distant. A heart in pain from little corners of society's lowest depths seemed to be reaching out from that voice. Jeffia, who had all along stood watching them, was moved to the warmer end of the scale of feelings where other people's suffering registered more strongly. He understood. But it was an understanding born not of experience, but of instinct. He understood that people who knew pain lived pain. They were like weeds that spread the offensive odour of their lot wherever they went. That was why a hungry man is an angry one.

Brings home what me and Ode keep discussing. He brought out his wallet from his back pocket.

'I give you two Naira, eh,' he said, coming down to their level. The smaller one nodded, the bigger one broke into a self-satisfied smile. Jeffia gave two Naira to the smaller one who in turn handed the dog to Jeffia.

'Where una find the dog?' Jeffia asked.

'We was returning from our mama message when we see am dey run for corner of road. One car nearly jam am. I pick am up but the foolish dog bite my hand, so I am vex, then you come.'

He walked away and left them staring at him. An ineffable joy bubbled within him. He was well tuned to feelings as they were. These young people were capable of violence. It was one of the few languages they could speak quite clearly. In an age of plenty there could be no consolation in living off the crumbs of the land. *The worst thing a person can experience,*

Jeffia thought, *is helplessness. It's like being in a dark room in a wilderness, not knowing what to do, where to go.* His joy was that in his own way he had lit up a small light in that room.

He branched off Park Avenue into Rundle Crescent. The trees were fewer and the sun shone down undisturbed.

'Excuse me, mister.'

Jeffia stopped and turned around. The smaller boy ran up to him and stood there panting.

'I want to say we are grateful for the money,' the boy said awkwardly. He had particularly soft features and there was a sparkle in his eyes. It was as if they had suddenly come alive.

'We will always remember it,' the boy added, staring into the distance.

'Always remember, too,' Jeffia said, 'that you must work for whatever you get. Don't punish others for what you don't have, you hear?' The boy nodded and smiled.

'God be with you.'

The young boy turned and ran back. His tattered shorts flapped behind him. Jeffia felt happy. He scratched the puppy's head, and walked home.

The bath was half full and smelt of Badedas. Jeffia smiled at the memory of the incident. The puppy was on the bathroom floor, running about and barking. *I don't know if Badedas is good for dogs*, he thought.

He soaked himself in the cold, sweet-smelling water and let peace run through him. He shut his eyes. He thought about his results and whether he would perform better than Ode. Competition at exams was an integral part of their friendship. He rubbed soap over himself and scrubbed his body. *Ode is lucky to get that job as cub reporter. I wish I could get a job too. Dad is always against my working. I will ask Mum about that teaching vacancy.*

His thoughts ran on. *Strange how some things come into your life. You meet a person once and soon it's as though they had been there all along. That was how I met Ode, in the college fields. We began talking about many things, and became friends. That day.*

The puppy, in the way it wagged its tail, the luminous glow in its liquid brown eyes, did not behave as if it scarcely knew

Jeffia. He dried it carefully with the extra towel he used for his feet.

He spent the rest of the evening looking through some of his school books, reading Chinua Achebe's *Arrow of God* and listening to jazz. His parents didn't come home early. He wondered why.

Soon, he fell asleep. The puppy lay on a cushion. He slept peacefully and dreamlessly.

He had been asleep for some time when a piercing scream cut through the sacred early morning hours. Jeffia woke up, and listened. Hearing nothing more than the disquieting ring of silence, he fell back gratefully into the carefree world of sleep.

2

For Mrs Okwe it was a fine day. The winds, eavesdropping messengers of gods, rushed by, propelling her towards a cliff–edge. The sun was locked behind a mass of blue clouds. The sky was the fabric of yellow dreams.

Suddenly the weather changed. The day darkened. The winds, as if in pain, moaned. And the clouds turned grey. She stared down the side of the cliff, and didn't recognise where she was.

Then a car came hurtling towards her. She shouted but her voice stuck in her throat. It was her husband's car. He was at the steering wheel, a fiendish look on his face. On seeing her, he swerved, hit the sidewalk, and lost control. The car turned sharply right and headed for the edge of the cliff. She tried to scream, and ran towards it. But too late. It went over, bounced twice on jutting rocks, and finally exploded on the ground below. The winds swept her over the cliff, down to the vortex of the disaster. But she didn't hit the ground. She was spared the experience. Instead she woke up, trembling, sweating. The moment she realised that she had been dreaming, a vague premonition settled upon her. But somnolence flowed over her, carrying her back into a dreamless state.

When she woke up again the sun had risen in the sky and light filtered into the room.

Staring out of the window, she pondered the nightmare. She didn't particularly believe in dreams as auguries, but she couldn't deny a feeling of impending chaos that her dream had given her.

She tried not to think about it. She tried to think of something else. She had come a long way from her past, from the loneliness and quiet despair she had known; the concessions and compromises she had always had to make to the world about her; the suppressed memories it always pained her to recall.

She had security and relative happiness now, a great contrast to her life before she got married. When she was very young her parents went away, nobody knew where, and she was taken to an orphanage. Life there was tedious and sorrowful. Then by some good fortune a certain rich widow came and took her away. She spent most of her time in this woman's house, doing the housework, going to the market and cooking. In return she was allowed to attend the secondary school nearby. Yet her life in this house was worse, in some ways, than in the orphanage. As a housegirl she was treated with condescension and contempt, and as an orphan, which the other housegirls never let her forget, she was tortured by self-pity. The house was large and there were always too many people. In its largeness and confusion she had to fight to retain her identity.

When the rich widow died, her life took another turn. The various men who frequented the house before the widow's death now thronged it to select wives from the horde of housegirls. It was at the widow's funeral that she met Jonan. He often came to the house on social calls but his face was unknown in the throng of other incessant visitors. Not long afterwards they got married. Her life still had its ups and downs, but over the early years they were cushioned by Jonan and by her own peculiar responses to its uncertainties. Things ran smoothly: life had been generous. She had reason to be happy. She had reason to worry.

The dream gave her an elusive glimpse into the mirrors of her worst fears. Yet the reflections didn't make sense to her. They only deepened the worries that always lurked behind her everyday living.

She left the window and looked at herself in the mirror. But for the puffs under her eyes and the lines on her mahogany-complexioned face, she could easily have passed for an ageing model. Her lips had not lost their sensuality, and her delicate nose served to emphasise the chaste structure of her face. The eyes which stared back at her from the mirror were slightly reddened from sleep. They were frank and trusting. They stared out into the world with a pathos that was appealing.

Still in her nightgown, she went downstairs to the sitting room. There was a note on the centre table. It was from her husband. She could guess its contents. He was going somewhere and wouldn't be back till night. As usual. It was either a meeting, an inspection, a tour or something. Business always came first with her husband, it was an obsession. He had only just recovered from a heart attack that had nearly claimed his life and now, barely weeks later, he was back into business activity with force.

Basically we are two of a kind, she thought. *It's only that we react differently.* She remembered how in their early days together, he would tell her about his village and how he got his obsession with work. A plague had attacked the village and people died like poisoned flies. Those who were wealthy got their people out, the ordinary folk died miserably. When his father was dying, his father spoke six words to him, and didn't finish the sentence. They were the words behind his life, Jonan said.

'*My son, poverty is a curse . . .*'

He was terrified of falling back into the poverty from which he had risen.

She shook her head, and deep down in her heart she prayed. For on Jonan hung her secret fears.

She opened the front door. A rush of warm wind swept her, the sun shone in her eyes. The air was fresh and the sky looked as if it had just been washed by a conscientious cleaner. Distant houses, distant trees and fields crowded her vision. She looked into the letterbox for mail. It was a telegram, addressed to Jonan Okwe. A telegram! She wondered who would want to send them an urgent piece of news.

They had not received any telegram for a long time now. She had a horror of them. While she pondered it, Chema, the cook, stepped forward to greet her.

'Morning, madam.'

'Morning, Chema. How are you? Just waking up?'

'No, madam. Even sef, na me sign for the telegram,' he said indicating the telegram in her hands. He was smiling meaninglessly.

'Oh, thank you, Chema. Did you see your Oga when he left this morning?'

'Yes, ma. But he dey for hurry.'

'Okay. I think you have some cleaning to do in the kitchen and later you will go to the market?' He nodded. The uncalled-for smile on his face had gone. Seeing that she had nothing more to say to him, he scratched his neck, and went away.

She stood there at the door, thinking about all the homework she had to mark. She taught literature at a secondary school. She loved her job as a teacher. They called her 'ma' at school. She was a favourite with her Form One students because she not only taught them, she took a personal interest in their lives: she never found it too tedious coming down to their level, nor was she too tired to answer the many questions they put to her.

She thought about the flowers she and Chema had transplanted a few days ago. She thought about the painting she was going to do next. None of these things were what she really wanted to think about. She knew.

The kindly rays of the morning African sun flushed her face with their golden radiance. For a moment she let her eyes take in the serene Ikoyi surroundings that were exclusively for the rich. She could see in her mind's eye the many ornamented and expensive houses, with large tennis courts, large swimming pools and well-kept gardens. She vaguely wondered how leaders of the country could claim to be in touch with the people's spirit when they were so far removed from their guttered worlds. Despite years of comfortable living, she still felt uneasy with the luxury around her.

Her mind wandered to the present. She thought about Jonan. She thought about the dream.

She sighed, her hands holding the telegram trembled slightly. Whatever news the telegram carried might not be pleasant. She felt a shiver run through her, and closed the door.

She vaguely felt she was on the threshold of an indefinable experience.

It was not a comforting feeling.

After so many halcyon years she suddenly felt troubled . . . uncertain.

3

Jonan Okwe's offices were in Wilm Street. This street is the big business street of Lagos, essentially for those whose names resound through the business world with ceaseless echoes. Jonan's offices had all the trappings that befitted movers of the economy: large as tennis courts, oak-panelled, soundproofed walls with filigree designs and rare art pieces hanging on them.

As the managing director of Afioso Paints he was entitled to it. And that was the way Jonan had always liked his life. He called it big time. From the day he was old enough to know what impossible things money could do, from the time his father died consumed by a mysterious plague, from the moment he realised the truth of his father's words that poverty was a curse, he always dreamt of the big time.

He had worked ceaselessly, even ruthlessly, towards it. And when he arrived it still looked to him a distant thing.

It had been a long, chequered ascent. Things had not worked out in the beginning, but as he gradually climbed up he began to master the harsh, ruthless, unwritten rules of business survival in Nigeria at the time. He soon acquired that implicit sense of power and satisfaction of being able to say 'I told you so' to those who always doubted the things he always believed strongly he could do.

But the satisfaction and sense of power reached a stage when they turned into a paranoia, into an obsession, restless and uncompromising, to possess and subjugate. They became pillars of his one-track life-style.

Now the time had come, with the cold inexorability of fate, when his authority and power had begun to wane. It was as though all along he had been creating problems by his own attitude, and concentrated all his strength upon solving them.

That explained why after many years his business success had nearly come to a standstill. But as always, he was the only person who did not see it.

Now the edifice was shaking, and the tremors were unmistakable. The picture emerged gradually: staff resigning, sharp drops in profit, clamouring shareholders, and other strange and unforeseen happenings. Like the heart attack.

He was at a board of directors' meeting when his heart chose to fail him. He had lost consciousness immediately and was confined to bed for months.

His doctor suggested that he go for a trip abroad, away from the tumult of business life for a while, to lighten the strain on his heart. He went but came back after a month.

Jonan couldn't bear the thought of not working; of being considered too infirm to handle his business; and of being away from the hub of activity. Nevertheless the attack had been a severe shock to him. It filled him with the numbing realisation that his efforts were futile. He had always prided himself on being tough and unbreakable. He always saw himself as riding out in waves of unfailing energy; but the attack drove home to him the fact that he was only mortal.

And now that he was better, he didn't think about it any more. The disconcerting implications diminished in his mind as he resumed his old life. He no longer considered the threat serious.

But hovering at the back of his mind was a different kind of fear: that his control over the company was weakening: that the company was having a life larger than that which he had infused into it: but, more, that his energy for ruthless activity was failing.

Then came the telegram. He had been returning to the office from a meeting with some German contractors when he decided to call in at home, change his suit and maybe have something to eat. His wife told him he had a telegram and gave it to him. He didn't notice the tone of her voice and the intensity with which she stared at him when he opened it.

The telegram was from Sowho, a half-brother. And it simply said he was coming.

He couldn't control the spasms of emotion that ran through him. His wife became worried, which didn't make it easier for him to think. Half in anger, half in distress, he left her and returned to the office.

The drive had helped to cool the spasms of emotion. He could think a bit more clearly.

The seeming harmlessness of the telegram's wording was all the more disturbing. *Why* was Sowho coming?

Jonan remembered Sowho all right: in fact he was one of the unacknowledged fears somewhere in Jonan's mind.

Jonan smiled wryly as he remembered the early days when Sowho had slavishly helped to establish the company. Sowho poured his life and hopes into the company, and with time Jonan thought he was becoming dangerously ambitious, even treacherous. A clash was inevitable, and Sowho got the worst of it. Jonan remembered only too clearly how the clash had concluded for Sowho. In jail.

That was a long time ago.

It was also a long time now since they met.

But why had Sowho sent a telegram to say he was coming?

Jonan vaguely remembered Sowho shouting in court that he would have his revenge. The audience in the court had laughed. Even the judge smiled.

It was all a long time ago now. That matter had been settled. Relatives had stepped in, and Jonan took some steps back. They had a small party to celebrate the forgiveness, and Jonan and Sowho had rubbed wine and native chalk on each other's foreheads.

But Sowho was not to be trusted. He was a snake, silent and deliberative. Had he come to fulfil his shout of revenge?

Why, after all these years when the wounds must have healed?

What could he be planning to do?

Jonan shook his head and with an effort dismissed the thoughts.

He directed his gaze to the large portrait of himself that an artist had painted three years ago. It hung on the wall facing his table. The artist had put a flattering calm, confident expression on his face. It reminded him of Daniel staring into the lions' den. Whenever he had a difficult problem, a trying situation, one look at it would stir some power within him, and he would feel an inner strength. But looking at the picture now stirred nothing. Instead it seemed to stare down at him with a mocking frown that he hadn't noticed before.

He got up and poured himself a stiff whisky and tossed it down his throat. There was a tingling burn as it rushed down and exploded in his stomach. But it didn't change anything. The feeling was still there.

He got out his snuff-box and inhaled a pinch of the brown, powdery stuff. He shook his head violently as it sent its burning pungency to the brain. He got out his handkerchief and blew his nose into it. His head was slightly cleared.

Now he picked up Gbenga's letter of resignation. What was the reason behind it? Gbenga was a pioneer worker, Jonan's right-hand man and stooge who helped him with important information about people. He also carried out Jonan's ruthless operations.

Why was he leaving? Where was he going? Why resign in such a hurry? Could the rumours Jonan heard about his wanting to start his own paint business be true?

Whatever it was, he was dangerous to Jonan. He knew too many of Jonan's secrets just to throw in a letter of resignation and walk off. Did he think he was untouchable?

We will see, Jonan thought. *We will see.*

He picked up a blotter and began punching holes into it with a letter opener.

There was a tension all around he could feel: that deceptively peaceful tension that preceded a storm.

14

Where had he gone wrong? He had built his success on so many wrongs, so many that they became normal, insignificant.

Was this the payback?

Something was wrong somewhere; he was too old in the racket not to recognise the red light. It reminded him of the supposed restlessness of goldfishes before an earthquake.

Just where was it coming from?

The questions scattered all around him like seed thrown off when a rubber pod bursts. But all he could hear in his spacious office was the hushed hum of the air-conditioner.

Chapter Two

Jeffia's mother was washing some clothes in the back-yard. She had soaked them for most of the morning and was now washing them with warm water.

She wore a pair of trousers and a yellow blouse. She had on a hairtie. She liked doing the washing herself. It gave her time to think and to review the events of the past week. She had woken early and set about the cleaning of the house and the tending of the flowers.

It was a bright morning, the perfect washing-day of abundant sunshine. The lawn spread before her, green and close-cut. She looked at the flowers. The cluster of roses looked bowed. The hibiscus with their bright red petals made her want to paint them. A few birds flew past low, and perched on the tree near the garage.

'Morning, Mum.'

She turned round with a smile.

'Doing the washing yourself?'

'Morning, Jeff. That's a funny question to ask your mother on a Saturday morning. You know I always like to do the washing myself on Saturdays. Jeff, is there anything on your mind?'

'No, nothing. I was only wondering why you don't let Chema do the washing, sometimes.'

'Chema can't wash a napkin clean enough. Besides it's good exercise.'

'Yes,' Jeffia said. 'I've not seen you for two days. You were late home last night.'

'Oh yes. I had to arrange the children's party I told you about. It was a nice little party. The kids enjoyed it.'

Jeffia was silent. He stared into the distance. His face was flushed with the sun's rays. He looked tall standing beside his seated mother. The birds that earlier on had perched on the whistling pine tree, flew off, flapping their wings and casting swift shadows on the lawn.

'How is Ode?'

'Oh, he is all right. We were together yesterday morning.'

He was silent again. His mother had stopped washing to wipe the sweat off her face.

'Mummy, you know Ode has got a temporary job as a reporter on the *Everyday Times*?'

'That's nice. So you want a job too?'

Jeffia smiled. His mother had a way of reading his thoughts.

'Yes, I was thinking of that teaching vacancy you told me about.'

'You see, the teachers have not left yet. They are from the training school. They will go any time now. Be patient. Have you talked it over with your father?'

'Father?'

'Yes, your father.'

'He would say the same old things. Besides, I hardly see him. It's as if he doesn't live here any more.'

His mother laughed at that.

'When your father gets up for work, you are still sleeping, and when he returns from work, you have gone to bed.'

'Yeah.'

'Anyway, I will speak to the headmaster of the junior section to see what he can do. Take it easy, Jeff.' There was a glint of fondness in her eyes. She went on with her washing. It made her happy to talk to Jeffia about his plans.

A cloud obscured the sun. A gentle darkness suddenly came over the sky. Then it passed. The sky turned bright, was traversed by clouds of stunning aesthetic shapes. The expanse was blue and grey and beautiful. There was a slight wind, and it rustled the leaves of the plants around the lawn. The flowers swayed gracefully.

Jeffia's mother got up and picked up the basin.

'Let me help you, Mum,' Jeffia said, taking the basin from her. He helped her change the water from the tap near the kitchen that was used to water the plants.

'Thanks, Jeff.' She sat down and began washing again.

Some time passed before Jeffia spoke. His voice was unusually calm.

'Mum?'

'Yes, Jeff darling.'

'Why is Daddy the way he is?'

'How do you mean, Jeff?'

Jeffia mumbled. He finally came out with something that wasn't really what he wanted to say.

'He doesn't seem to have very many friends.'

A moment passed before she replied.

'Jeff, your father is a very functional man. He doesn't trust people. His few friends are those who know what they want from each other. He is a tough man. But you know that, don't you?'

'I was only thinking. He seems to live all his life in the office.'

'And that is why he is as successful as he is. That is why he is able to provide for us and do all he does.'

'He must be very unhappy . . .' He didn't complete the sentence. At that moment he felt it was an unnecessary thing to say.

'I have not seen him for a week now. I met him on Thursday morning when I went to the toilet, I wanted to talk to him about school but he said it could wait till the evening.'

'Don't worry. You'll see him tonight.'

'You want me to help you, Mum?'

'No. Don't worry. Thanks, my son.' She said the last bit with a smile. Jeffia smiled too, and looked towards the flowers. Neither of them said anything for a moment. Jeffia excused himself, mumbled something about the puppy, and went to his room. She looked at him as he went. She smiled and shook her head. He's such a tall, nice son, she thought.

She loved Jeffia not just as her only son, but also because she was proud of the kind of person he was turning into. She attributed it partly to the sheltered upbringing they had given him. He had attended the best schools, and had done well all along. But what pleased her more about him was that he did not seem to be turning out like other people's children. Some fought with their parents. Some had run away from home. Others went out and came back when they liked. She even had some friends whose sons had gone to prison for crimes they had committed. Others were ill-dressed, ill-behaved, and smoked and drank.

But Jeffia was different.

He was gentle and intelligent. Tall and bright for his nineteen years, he had developed a sense of maturity that never failed to amaze his mother.

On his side, too, a closeness had developed with his mother. It seemed to Jeffia that she was always there, that she had always been there.

But with his father there seemed a gulf between them, they were not at ease with each other. Though his father had given Jeffia the best education and a good life, Jeffia was resentful that he put so much of himself into the business at the expense of his family.

One thing about Jeffia's life was that somehow it seemed too good to be true. Too straight. In nature nothing grows straight. And to be untouched by the strong winds of strife was not something that lasted for ever. The threat was always there.

In parts this was what his mother was thinking about. The threat. Thoughts of the dream she had had flitted through her mind. A disembodied fear grew within her, making her shiver as if at a cold wind.

'Mummy, was it you who screamed last night?'

She started. Engrossed in her thoughts, she hadn't heard Jeffia come back.

'It was only a funny dream,' she said hurriedly.

'A funny dream?'

'It was nothing. Just a dream. Forget it. It was nothing.' The words came out unnaturally. She tried a smile but it didn't quite work, so she bent down to do some rinsing.

Jeffia sensed she wanted to be alone. He sidled towards the gate. The shed was empty. The watchday was not on duty; he would come in the afternoon. Jeffia stood in front of the gate and looked at the road and at the people passing by.

The sky had darkened. A cluster of clouds, magnificent and melancholy, passed beneath the sun's direct rays.

There was a mango tree on the other side of the road, in front of another big house. Jeffia noticed that birds were building a nest on its branches.

He thought about what his mother had said. He wished he could ask his father some questions about his mother, and about many other things. But his father would be too tired. His father always seemed to him either too tired, too much in a hurry or too something else. Ode's father was not like that, he thought. Last Saturday, he, Ode and Ode's father had been to the beach and then later to the National Theatre. Ode's father was a friendly, humorous man. He was the director of an engineering company. He liked making jokes and made Ode and Jeffia laugh a lot. *My father's not like that*, Jeffia thought. *It's months since I went out with Dad. He always seems to be thinking deeply about something, he always looks serious and business-like.*

A few birds flew past him to the mango tree. *They are making a nest*, Jeffia thought. A car drove past. There was a whole family inside it, laughing. They were perhaps coming back from an outing.

The birds chirped and twittered, happy in their work.

Then suddenly someone threw a stone, wounding one of the birds. Then came another stone, which caught the nest. It came tumbling down. The other birds flew away in confusion. Jeffia turned to see who had thrown the stones. It was a muscular man who wore a khaki shirt and 'jump-up' trousers. He laughed gleefully as he picked up the nest and the wounded bird.

'Great throw, eh? First time I take stone kill bird,' the man said more to himself than to Jeffia. He went, laughing down the avenue.

Above, the other birds flew wildly around the tree. They flapped their wings noisily and made strange twitterings.

Chapter Three

She had finished the washing and had hung the clothes on the line to dry. Chema had returned from the supermarket; with little rest in between she went into the kitchen to get things ready for the afternoon's food. Chema usually did the cooking, but she liked being there to oversee everything.

'Rush dey for supermarket today,' Chema was saying as he put the pots on the cooker. She merely nodded.

'This supermarket good – O,' he commented to himself.

'Chema, get on with the warming of the oils, I don't want the meal to be late, you hear?'

'Yes, ma.'

She stood there watching him for a few minutes, then went to the sitting room. She wondered what Jeffia was doing in his room. She had no reason for wondering. She just wanted him to be around.

The phone rang. She picked it up expecting it to be a call from her husband.

'Hello, Mrs Okwe here.'

'Mrs Doye here. Hello, Lizzy.'

Mrs Doye was one of the few close family friends.

'Ah Grace, is that you? How's everything? Quite some time, eh?' They chatted about a number of things and made jokes about each other. Mrs Doye soon came round to the reason for her call.

'Lizzy, I would like you to come to the small party we are having.'

'What are you celebrating?' Whenever the Doyes had a 'small' party they always had something to celebrate. From her husband winning a big contract to her daughter passing her examination, from any member of the family escaping an accident to a birthday, they loved making a ceremony out of anything they considered important. In the past Mrs Okwe had been exasperated by the number of minor things turned into celebration.

'Nothing really. I just remembered that it's our anniversary. Our twentieth, you know. We just want to have a small get-together.'

'Your twentieth! What a lucky woman you are . . .'

'You too. We are both lucky. We should be thankful to God for giving us good husbands.'

'Yes. We should be thankful.'

'You know, Lizzy, I know many women who have married over three times in the past five years. I know some who are dry like bunga fish because their husband beats them and maltreats them. I know some who do not even have children. One must be thankful to God.'

Mrs Okwe was silent for a minute. Then she changed the topic.

'So how is the job? And how is the man? and Adama?'

'Ah ha, Lizzy. Three questions in one? Well, the job is fine. My husband is doing very fine and taking good care of the family or else I would not be here talking now.' She laughed and went on, 'And Adama is all right.'

'Adama hasn't come to see us lately.'

'Don't mind her. She is growing into a woman now, goes out the way she likes, even borrows my wig. That's how these children are. So how is our fine young man Jeffia? Has his result come out yet?'

'Jeff is all right. His result has not come yet, we are all waiting. I tell you what, Jonan and I will come round during the week.'

'All right. We'll be expecting you then.'

'Have a nice anniversary, Grace.'

'Okay. Bye bye.'

She put the phone down, and went to the window. *Grace doesn't change*, she thought smiling to herself. Except for the hissing sounds of frying that came from the kitchen, everything was quiet. The sitting room was darkened; not all the window blinds had been drawn. There was a sweet smell about. The sitting room always had that sweet smell. The furniture was expensive and new, the thick carpet looked clean and felt nice under the feet. The shelves, the grandfather clock, the air conditioner, the colour television, the paintings hanging on the walls (some of which were her creations), the cabinet-built hi-fi, all these gave the house a look of elegance and luxury. The richly cushioned sofa and easy chairs and Jonan's favourite reclining chair gave the room character. Yet there was a loneliness about the elegance and the luxury. Nobody sat in the sitting room long, and for most of the day it retained its lonely quality. Everybody in the family spent their time in their various rooms and it was not often that the family got together. Visitors seldom called these days.

As she stood there in the sitting room, too many uninvited worries crowded into her mind.

Jonan had become withdrawn and touchy recently. The telegram had brought this out more than anything else. She remembered the look on his face when he tore it open and read it. The controlled expression he always wore slipped off. There was a confused look on his face. His hands trembled slightly.

'Is anything wrong, darling?' she had asked him. For anything to disturb her husband so visibly, it must be something that went deeper than surface emotions.

'Is it bad news?'

After a time he spoke. Before then, his forehead was creased in thought, his eyes were hard and distant. She recognised these signs. His voice was hoarse when he finally spoke.

'No. Not really. It's only Sowho, he says he is coming. But I think he is already in town. This telegram took a week to get here. See the postmark?'

'Did you say Sowho?'

His eyes flashed upon her.

'Who else did I say? Better be careful ... now what could he be looking for in town? Why bother to send me a telegram?' He fell into a thoughtful silence, got up from the chair, and started walking up and down the room. Mrs Okwe, who didn't like the violent way he answered her, got up and made for the kitchen.

'Did I tell you that Gbenga had resigned, just like that?' he said across the room to her. She stopped and turned round, surprised. Gbenga had been very loyal and trustworthy. It had been impossible to think that one day he would leave. He was the typical faithful servant.

'Well, wipe that foolish look off your face, because he has.' Then he seemed to speak to himself, but still loud enough for her to hear. 'Now the fool is gone I might not be very secure . . . that goat knows too much about me. He can't just leave like that, ah ha! Can't just wake up one morning and resign like that, wetin.'

'Why do you have to be worried if what you are doing is clean? You don't need to worry, do you?' Her voice was challenging.

Jonan gazed at her the way a father would at a son who did not understand the harsh things of life. He smiled. But it was a dry, humourless smile. Then he said in a voice that frightened her, 'That goat knows too much about me and Afioso. That's all there is to it. You read the papers every day – don't you know about blackmail cases and other dangerous things that people do nowadays? You should know better. Let me tell you before you begin to preach, if anything goes wrong because one fool wants to resign, everything I have been working for all my life would sink with me. You are a woman, you do not understand these things. There are some things about myself and my business that people shouldn't know about. You hear?' He said all this with a finality weighing on his voice.

A sudden fear came over her.

'Jonan. Jonan! You have not been doing anything wrong and shameful, you haven't, have you? What is happening, Jonan? All these years . . .'

His eyes were cold, his mouth smiled. He said rather quickly, 'There is nothing to be afraid of. I can handle it. There is nothing. Don't you worry.'

With that he walked slowly to the staircase and climbed up the stairs hurriedly. When he came down again, he had changed into casual clothes.

'Aren't you going to eat before you go out again? You've been out since early this morning.'

He didn't say anything. He waved his hands irritably, opened the door with exaggerated energy and went to his empty office. He needed to be alone, to think.

She listened as the car started and drove out of the compound. Loneliness swept over her in a relentless tide. Sadness filled her. She couldn't help crying a little.

Many years ago she had persistently quarrelled with Jonan about his business. People had been telling her all sorts of things about her husband and she couldn't ignore them any further. It was all driven frighteningly home when suddenly one night policemen banged on their door, stamped through the house and roughly detained Jonan in connection with an alleged fraud. The whole event, which had lasted less than ten minutes, was traumatic. Though, strangely, the case never came to court and he was soon released, her fears had been triggered. She was frantic. She talked and cried to him about it. She called in relatives to help advise him. She begged him to think about their son. If he went on like this, didn't he realise that he was spoiling her son's future? In a rage he beat her up and turned her out of the house. Later, when he had recovered himself, he begged her to come back again.

Eventually after many similar quarrels, Jonan promised to be more careful. The strange people who used to crowd their house at odd times and have endless secret meetings with Jonan stopped coming. She had never understood what her husband's activities were all about. It was a relief when the strange comings and goings ceased. But they were replaced by his unpredictably protracted outings; his notes on the table; his cryptic messages to her through the houseboy.

'He has another woman, somewhere,' her friends told her. But she didn't altogether mind. What really mattered to her was that he was clean in his business and that the space they had carved out so far should not be violated.

'*God, I beg O,*' she prayed by herself in the lonely sitting room. '*Whatever good things you give us, God, let us keep.*'

The memory made her feel sadder. The room was darkened. She was troubled. That name: Sowho. What was he doing in town? *Why send a telegram?* she thought, echoing her husband's questions.

The name swirled around in her brain and struck something deep in there – a nameless fear, an association with some kind of numinous horror.

'No, no, no! I don't want it!' she cried out suddenly.

Jeffia, who had been reading in his room, heard the cry. He was momentarily terrified. He ran out into the sitting room.

'Are you all right, Mum? What is it?'

There was silence as she emerged from herself. Her face was pallid. She stared at Jeffia as if she were somewhere else.

'I'm fine. I was just thinking aloud.'

Jeffia stared at her unconvinced.

'Are you sure? Don't you think you should go and see the doctor, Mum?'

She gave a forced laugh.

'I'm all right. I feel like this sometimes. Everybody does.'

'Does what?'

'Everybody wants to shout out sometimes,' she said in a near whisper.

There was another awkward silence. She rubbed her eyes and then she stared curiously behind Jeffia, at something on the floor. He followed her gaze.

'Who brought that dog in here, eh?'

'Oh, it's only a puppy I found some boys ill-treating. I'm taking care of it till I can locate the owner.'

She had regained her calm. After what seemed a long time she spoke again.

'I think I saw an article or advert in yesterday's paper or so about a dog. I'm not quite sure, but I remember it struck me because I have never seen advertisements about dogs before. Except security dogs. Why not check yesterday's and today's papers? They are in my room.'

The puppy had run to Jeffia's side and was playfully trying to climb up his legs. Jeffia bent and picked it up.

'You are sure you are all right, Mum?' he asked awkwardly again, studying her face.

'Quite all right, son.' She had turned again to the blurred scenery outside the window, her eyes distant, apparently submerged in thought.

Jeffia stood there for a moment. He wanted to say something more, but he sensed that she wanted to be alone. Knotted up with worry, he went slowly up the stairs.

Chapter Four

He saw the ad on page two of the newspaper. It was in a corner, at the bottom of a column.

DOG MISSING
Did you find a brown and white coloured puppy? If so kindly return to the owner at No 7 Rowland St. Apapa.

What made it all the more conspicuous was its oddity. Such advertisements for missing dogs were rare in Nigerian papers. Nigerians are not great lovers of animals, except those on higher social scales who have been to Western countries and want to look 'civilised' and different.

When Jeffia read the ad, he couldn't help feeling sad. He was just getting fond of the dog. It jumped and wagged its tail and pawed his shirt. *The crossroads are always there*, he thought. *People and things have to go their different ways in life.*

The puppy had jumped down from his lap and was running about the room. He put the newspaper on the centre table and went out of the room. The puppy followed him.

He went to the kitchen where his mother and Chema were doing the cooking. 'Mum, I think I should go and check that ad out.'

His mother coughed. There was oil smoke in the kitchen. 'That's all right. Will you be long?'

'I don't know. I might call on a few friends I haven't seen for some time.'

'Are you taking the car?'

'Yes. The Datsun.'

'I done wash am shine for this morning,' Chema put in.

'Thanks, Chema. I'm off, Mum.'

'Okay.' She coughed again. 'Have you got the key?'

Jeffia nodded.

'Drive carefully then. Bye.'

He reversed the car. It had been parked outside the garage. Jeffia's father had two cars: a Mercedes and the Datsun, and his mother had a Mazda. The garage had room for two cars, so the Datsun had to be parked outside the garage door.

The watchday opened the gate for him as he drove out.

'Afternoon, O – Oga.'

'Afternoon, mallam. I go see you when I come back.'

He turned off the Avenue and drove towards the Kingsway. *It will be quite a drive to Apapa*, he thought. *Hope there won't be any go-slows today*. His father let him drive the car mainly because he had done well in his School Certificate exams and had passed his driving test. Besides the car was unused most of the time.

The sun beamed brightly. The sky was clear and open like the soul of a saint. It made him happy just to look at it; as though for that brief moment it invited his spirit to partake in its resplendent dream. Jeffia pulled down the sun-visor. The puppy lay quiet on the seat next to him.

He drove past big, stylish houses and tourist hotels, down streets and avenues lined with tall, shade-spilling trees. They stood with silent dignity, swaying in the gentle wind. The area was quiet, rural, superior. Everything about had that stamp, from the clean streets, to the tall trees, from eye-resting green fields to the houses hidden behind exotic plants. Yet, somehow, it unsettled his soul. There was an elusive feeling of tension in the atmosphere.

He had been driving for twenty minutes. There had been slight go-slows on the bridge. At the residential area near the wharf, he had stopped to ask pedestrians about Rowland Street. He had been directed and mis-directed numerous times before he finally located the street. It was not far from the Roxy Cinema. He drove down the street slowly, looking for number 7. It was at the other end next to number 15. *What a strange way of numbering a street*, Jeffia thought as he parked carefully.

It was a two-storey building. The dull stench of its overflowing garbage bin combined with the smell of the over-running gutter. The wall in front of the building was broken, as if a drunken driver had reversed into it.

He went to the apartment on the ground floor, and rang the bell. The imposing door was chestnut-coloured and it smelt new. Inside the apartment could be heard soft strains of Barry White and the occasional clanking of plates. He rang again.

'Hello, who are you looking for?' a woman asked through the narrowly opened door. When she opened the door wider Jeffia caught his breath. A pleasant sensation ran through him. He hadn't expected to meet a woman as beautifully-complexioned and as poised. He was overwhelmed. There was a half-formed smile on her lips. Her attractive face was almost the kind you saw idealised in face-cream advertisements. Her hair was in curls, and her eyes held mild amusement at Jeffia's reaction. He surreptitiously glanced downward, noticing how her figure curved out into shapely hips and ended in smooth, long legs. The skirt she wore gave her a girlish look. Her head was cocked sideways. Her eyes went to the puppy fussing under his arms. She smiled, her eyes widening in delight.

'Well ... I ... eh, am Jeffia. I saw a little ad in the papers ...'

'Oh yes,' she interrupted eagerly. 'I should have guessed. You have found my Joey! How wonderful of you! Oh excuse me,' she said. 'Do come in.' She stepped into the sitting room. He hesitated.

'Come in!'

He couldn't refuse; not with her using that persuasive tone of voice. He followed her into the sitting room and stood there uncertain whether to sit down. The puppy wriggled under his arms. She stretched out her hands, smiling, and took the puppy. Wagging its tail, barking delightedly, it jumped into her hands and licked her face. She scratched its head and stroked its fur.

'Won't you sit down? Sit anywhere,' she said.

Jeffia sat down on the sofa nearest the door. He felt himself sink into its softness, and he relaxed.

'Joey's a lovely little dog,' he remarked.

She gave him a proud, assenting smile, then came and sat next to him.

'Where did you find it?'

Her proximity made him uneasy. The fragrance of her perfume pervaded the room. He guessed she had just taken a bath. He felt himself getting embarrassingly warm.

Briefly he told her how he had met the boys ill-treating the dog. He omitted to mention that he had given them some money. He didn't want her to think that it was because of a refund that he had returned it.

'I don't know how to thank you,' she sighed. 'I had almost given up hope of ever seeing Joey again. I went to see a friend and left it in the car. I didn't know I had left the window open. By the time I came back he was gone.' Her voice lowered. 'You see, Joey is a part of me.' There was a faraway look in her eyes.

'Dear Joey . . . still the same . . . only God knows what he's been through.' She scratched the dog's head again, her face glowing.

'When I was coming I wondered how you could get the advert in the paper so quickly. It usually takes about five days.'

'That's true,' she said. 'But, you see, I have some good friends in the advert section. They helped.'

Jeffia could not think of anything else to say.

'Excuse me a moment. Let me go and put him in . . . he must be starving now.' To the dog she said, 'What happened to you, Joey? Did you think of me?'

She got up and went out into the corridor.

Jeffia felt it was all very strange. The only time he had seen people make so much sentimental fuss about dogs was on the screen or on television when watching some Western movie. It was almost as if the dog were her child or something. He liked animals but what he had witnessed struck him as being a bit excessive.

He took a deep breath and looked round the room. It was elaborately furnished, the floor so well carpeted, so comfortably yielding, that his feet kept sinking into it. There were two fans, working full-time, in the room, and an expensive-looking four-piece stereo system in a mahogany cabinet. Her tastes were shown in the paintings and carvings that adorned the room. Suddenly he felt he was being watched.

He looked round.

'Like the place, don't you?' she said, chuckling. He nodded.

'Hope Joey wasn't naughty?'

'Not really. He urinated on my floor, but then he couldn't help that,' he replied. 'He seemed to know I was a stranger who liked him. He was jumpy sometimes, and sometimes quiet as if homesick. But he enjoyed the meat I fed him.'

'Yes, he would like that.' She paused. 'My mother gave him to me last year when she returned from England. Two weeks later the poor woman died in an accident. Joey helps me remember her. He comforts me and is more a companion in many ways than human beings can ever be.' Her voice was sad. There was silence. She got up.

'Stupid of me not to have offered you something,' and before Jeffia could protest that he wouldn't be staying long, she went into the kitchen and was soon back with a tray. On it were nuts and pieces of cake, a bottle of orange drink and a jug of water.

'What did you say your name was?'

'Jeffia. Jeffia Okwe.'

She nearly dropped the tray. But the slip was brief. The next moment she calmly put it down on the centre table and pushed it towards him. It seemed ages before she spoke again.

'Are you Jonan Okwe's son?'

He turned and looked at her. People were always asking that question whenever he mentioned his name. It often made him feel exposed, vulnerable. And it sometimes frightened him the ways people responded when he said yes, he was Jonan Okwe's son. Some would immediately lose interest in him, some would give him intense, malicious looks; others would make a fuss of him. He remembered once when he went to a bank in Wilm Street to cash a cheque for his mother. At the counter they asked his name and he told the cashier. When he had finished, the man behind him – a short, glassy-eyed, large-foreheaded fellow, asked him if he was Jonan Okwe's son. Jeffia paused before answering. Then the man looked at him for a long minute and said, 'So this man get pickin wey big so, nai he dey do wetin he dey do, eh?' Then he hissed and went to another counter. Jeffia was bewildered.

When he told his father afterwards his father said, 'Maybe he is a poor man. Poverty makes people bitter about successful people. Don't let it bother you.'

But now it was something different. There was something indefinable about the way she asked the question. Something vaguely cool. He tried not to analyse it.

'Yes,' he said. She was silent and when she spoke again her voice had dropped. 'I used to know your father.'

'I see,' he replied, his voice dropping as well.

'I didn't know he had such a big son.'

Silence passed over them. She poured out a glass of orange juice and pushed it over to him. He picked it up and took a long drink. She chewed on a cake, her eyes on him in a silent scrutiny.

'You didn't tell me your name,' he said.

'Juliet. Simply Juliet. What do you do? Work? School?'

'I have just finished my higher school. I am waiting for my result. Meanwhile I stay around and read, go places and think. Not much, I'm afraid.'

'At least you are free. No unnecessary restraints, no struggles, no suffering .'

'I don't know about that. I have my own troubles.'

They chatted on for about fifteen minutes. She made him feel relaxed and asked questions about himself and the books he was reading. In turn he asked her about the paintings and carvings in the room. All along he wanted to ask her when and where she had known his father, but decided against it. He wondered if this was the 'other woman' his mother often said his father had outside. But he doubted it.

'So what do you do?' he asked her.

'Oh, me? I'm a businesswoman,' was all she said. In the silence that followed, a key was heard turning in the keyhole. The door opened. A man walked in, said 'Good afternoon, darling' to Juliet and went through to another room. He was a tall man with a walking stick. Because of his position Jeffia had only a brief glimpse of the man. Yet there was something familiar about him. It was more of a feeling than an actual recognition.

'Is anything the matter?' she cut into his thoughts.

'No, but I think I should be going now. It's been wonderful being with you but I have to get around to seeing a few friends.'

She understood.

'Has his coming anything to do with it?'

'No. I just remembered other things, that's all.' He stood up.

'It's all right,' she sighed, following him to the door.

'Whenever you feel like it, come and say hello. It's been nice talking with you. And thanks again for finding Joey.'

'Thanks too for the nuts and cakes. So long.'

He went down the small flight of stairs. He opened the door of the car, waved to her, and drove off.

She stood there alone. She stared sadly at the deserted road, into the dust and smoke Jeffia's car left behind.

Chapter Five

He drove around aimlessly.

He simply couldn't explain it. Any of it.

Who was she? Why did she nearly drop the tray when he mentioned his name?

Who was that man? Why did he seem vaguely familiar?

He still couldn't explain it.

As he turned into Wharf Road, he tried to remember what she looked like. *Could she be one of Daddy's girl-friends?* he thought, then soon put aside the thought as it seemed to complicate things further.

There was a go-slow in front. A Peugeot car and a Kunbi bus had become entangled in an accident. The Kunbi bus driver had tried overtaking the car in front; as he didn't have a side mirror, he didn't know that the Peugeot was driving past. The owner had already got out of the car and was shouting the inevitable. 'You don jam my car!'

A crowd had gathered and there was much shouting and quarrelling.

'You must pay for the car! I swear to God!'

'You no get horn? Why you no horn when you dey pass? Na so una dey find trouble!'

Jeffia saw from the mirror that the other cars were reversing and taking the narrow space in the middle of the road. He reversed too and took that way. He drove up the bridge. Just then he remembered that he had promised to visit a friend who lived around Surulere. He changed gear and increased speed. The sun had dipped behind a cloud. It wasn't so hot. He drew up the visor. Cars sped past him, horning challengingly, tearing away.

Mad people, he said to himself.

He took the way down and drove into Western Avenue.

A policeman waved him to stop. He slowed down, parked neatly, and waited. *What now*, he thought.

34

The policeman walked over and peered through the glass at Jeffia.

'Open this door, will you?' the policeman bawled. Jeffia wound down the window.

'Is there anything I can do for you?' he asked, without opening the door. The policeman gave him a malevolent look. He seemed to be in a bad mood. He didn't bother to reply. He reached into the car, pulled up the lock, and jerked the door open. It was all done in one swift, angry motion. He glared at Jeffia.

'I no answering nonsense question from people like you. Now where your licence?' The gruff voice had the practised authority to frighten. Jeffia ran his fingers through his pockets. Then he opened the glove compartment. It wasn't there. He searched his pockets again, more patiently. All he came out with was a piece of paper on which he had written his friend's address.

'You dey play nonsense games with me?' The voice was heavier, more frightening. The policeman knew.

Jeffia ransacked the glove compartment again. *It must be here somewhere*, he thought. Then he remembered that it was in the jacket he wore on Friday when he and Ode went to the cinema. He cursed silently. His father's words came to his mind.

'Never forget to carry your licence with you when you are driving. We are in a sick society where nobody would hesitate to exploit you if you gave them the slightest chance. Once you are caught without your licence, you might as well be in a boxing ring with your hands down. They will hound you till you grease their palms. Watch it, son, you still have a lot to learn.'

He sat back in the car. He felt hot. He sweated. He took a deep breath and turned to face the policeman.

'You dey fool around with me, boy? You heard of me? Big Joe, heh?'

'Please mister, I think I forgot it at home. If you would be kind enough to follow me home I would show it to you.'

'You dey crase,' The policeman glowered. A crooked smile crept onto his lips giving them a sinister leer. He got into the car and banged the door.

'Suppos'n instead,' he continued, 'you follow me to the nearest police station and tell them the foolish cock and goat story that you left it at home. Let me tell you one thing – they wouldn't believe it.'

'But please . . .'

'Please my yash. Move!' he shouted.

What kind of people are these? Jeffia thought angrily. He started the car and drove on slowly. They had barely gone a few hundred yards when the policeman told him to stop. A slightly bewildered look crossed his face. There wasn't a police station anywhere around.

'How much you get?'

Jeffia's mouth went dry. The policeman was staring at him placidly, contemptuously.

Was this the 'palm-greasing' his dad had told him about? So shamelessly direct?

He had read about such things in the newspapers. But reading it in the papers made it seem like fiction. Something to be read. Here was reality. He looked at the policeman's face to see if by any chance he was joking. From the black, dry face, two small red balls of fire glared back at him.

'Did you hear me?' the voice rose threateningly.

'Eh, I did. I think I have ten Naira here.'

'Let's have it then. Save you trouble, eh?' Sensing Jeffia's hesitancy he went on with practised smoothness, 'You want to hear what you buying? Dangerous driving, failing to produce licence on request, driving without a licence on the highway, resisting arrest, molesting a police officer on duty. I could add more if I wanted to. You no want embarrassment, abi. I am a good man.' His eyes twinkled bemusedly. His breath smelt as if he hadn't washed his mouth for weeks and was covering the smell with cigarette smoke.

Jeffia brought out the ten Naira note from his back pocket. It changed hands between them. The policeman chuckled.

'We be friends, eh. That's how we get on. Part of the system. Man can't live by . . .' he struggled for the word. 'Can't live by uniform alone.' He chuckled again. It seemed funny to him.

'Don't forget to carry your licence around with you next time, if you have any. Some of my colleagues would take three of this.' He got out of the car and closed the door gently. His eyes still twinkled. He winked, and strode off in the opposite direction.

Jeffia sighed. Just like his father said, he had a lot to learn. Too much.

He hoped he would learn gently.

2

'Take it easy, Jonan. Easy. That used to be your principle. Take it easy, and eat.'

'Why don't you leave me alone for a moment? Leave me alone! I've got enough to think about without you waving "easy, easy", over my head as if it were a magic wand.'

Jonan was in a bad mood. The food lay cold on the table. His face screwed in concentration, he clenched and unclenched his fists. Now and then he would get up and pace the floor. He wore a long wrapper and a singlet. He went to the sideboard, poured himself half a glass of whisky, and drank it all at once.

'Aren't you going to eat?'

'No. I'm going upstairs. I don't want to be disturbed. If anyone rings tell them I don't want to speak to anybody.' He blew his nose, put the handkerchief on the table for his wife to wash, and with his face still screwed in thought, went upstairs to his room.

It was from that moment that she began to feel something was wrong. She started to sense what had been there all along, things that hadn't emerged from the shadows. It began with the phone call.

The work for the day had all been done. Chema had gone to his quarters. She had taken a bath and retired to the sitting room to relax. In the background a Mozart piano concerto was playing. She sat still and let her thoughts wander through her mind.

Sitting alone, pondering the events of the day in the blue lights of the room, was something she looked forward to in the evenings. She relaxed in her room upstairs. That night she intended to wait up for Jonan.

She had earlier received a call from Jeffia. He said he'd been held up by his friends, that there was to be a party, and he would be late. She felt weighed down by a maternal fear. She asked him to come home as early as he could. It was seven o'clock.

'I'll try, Mum,' he said. 'Though I doubt it.'

She gave up pressing him. But the fear persisted.

Jeffia had begun asking troubling questions. *He doesn't seem too happy. Maybe it's growing up,* she thought. *He likes telling me about his outings with Ode. He likes Ode's dad a lot, says he is a humorous man.* With a pang she thought about the phone call from Ode's mother. *How is he going to feel when I tell him? Poor boy. Maybe I shouldn't tell him. They were such friends. What a tragedy.*

She felt more desolate than ever. A strange atmosphere like the ghost of an old man, had been hanging over the house lately.

She turned her thoughts determinedly to her work. She had two classes to teach, Forms One and Two. There weren't enough teachers for Form Two classes. Teaching both classes was hard work. The students were nice but dull and some were quite unwilling to learn. The Form One students were even more difficult to teach. Their minds were like the proverbial monkey, jumping everywhere. They ate bread under their desks, had fights with one another, daydreamed. But she was fond of them. She wondered how they would like *The Smugglers* when they got around to reading it. Maybe they would like Oladele Taiwo's collection of stories better.

Her thoughts returned home. She thought about the painting she was going to do next. She thought about her new vase. Jeffia hadn't seen it yet. *He hasn't even seen the flowers I transplanted. I wonder what he will think of them.* At the sound of a passing car she wondered for a moment if it was Jonan or Jeffia. She got up and looked through the curtains. The car had gone. Outside it was darkening. A sombre tinge hung over everything. The big tree swayed in front of the compound opposite. She shut the curtain. The Mozart record had finished playing. She went and changed it. She put on Beethoven's Pastoral Symphony and lowered

38

the volume.

Another car approached. She looked through the window again. It drove past.

Jonan. Every night for the past few days, he had been coming home late. He was sullen and withdrawn and his face wrapped in deep business worries. He seldom spoke to her over dinner and as soon as he had finished eating would go upstairs to his room. Business was doing badly. It showed.

Jonan. He used to love telling her about his business experiences in the evenings. They would end up laughing happily and would go to bed together. Now he greeted any question about the office with a sharp wave of the hand and a curt 'I don't want to talk now'. Then he would lapse into his grim thoughts.

After the night when he told her of Gbenga's resignation they had seen relatively little of each other. Not much had been said between them. She was angry that he allowed his business to affect a marriage that had endured for over twenty years. She was angrier that despite everything he wanted to go on possessing, go on fighting and fighting as if he still had the vigour of youth. *Why can't he face the fact that he is getting old and tone down wisely?*

She had endured and adjusted. Being uncompromising never made things easier, and she had her son to think of. Besides where had she to go? Her whole life had been built around Jonan. She had learned to live with him, and had begun to understand him. But she knew one never fully understands another, never completely knows another. And she didn't pretend to. But she hoped at least that whatever he did was for the good of the family.

All through the years she had never stopped having fears about him and about the life she was living. She couldn't explain her fear. It was always there and as the years passed with apparent serenity, she gave up anxiety for prayerful watchfulness.

Now things seemed to be coming out from the shadows. Hazily at first, then more definitely. Jeffia's becoming rebellious. Jonan's heart attack; her nightmares.

A car's sound came up. Probably just another passing car, she thought. But she got up and looked through the curtains. It was Jonan's Mercedes. The watchnight had opened the gate and he drove into the compound. She heard him telling the driver to be there early the next morning.

The door opened, he came in. Without saying anything he dropped his briefcase on his reclining chair and went straight to the sideboard. He poured himself a quarter glass of whisky, put in an ice-cube, and swallowed. He chewed on the ice-cube. It crunched in his mouth. He often did that. He said it cooled him inside.

'Welcome J. How's the office?'

For a moment he said nothing. He cracked the last bits of the ice-cube in his mouth, his face screwed, his eyes distant. He pulled at his tie and removed it from his neck. The room was silent.

'Somebody is poking sticks at me in the dark. Somebody is trying to breathe down my neck.' He paused and removed his coat and loosened some buttons on his white shirt.

'I had a note from some anonymous person,' he continued. He went to a drawer in the cabinet and brought out a small bottle. He put some snuff into his hands and inhaled it deeply. His wife looked on with disapproval. He never gave up his snuff-taking. It was a habit he had retained from youth which she had never liked.

'What did the note say?'

His eyes took on a strangely reddened intensity in the blue room as the snuff hit his brain. He shook his head vigorously and then let out a noisy sigh. His countenance seemed to brighten.

'It said I should remember ten years ago. That history repeats itself but with the tables turned.'

'What is that supposed to mean?' Her voice became agitated.

'How do I know what crazy people who would do a thing like that, mean?'

'Who could have written a thing like that and why anonymous, Jonan? Why?'

'Ah . . . don't you worry about that . . . it's probably some stupid fellow who is jealous of my success . . . ah, don't you

40

worry about that . . .'

He brought out his handkerchief and blew his nose. An offensive noise followed the action. He snatched up his coat, walked past her, and picked up his briefcase. He went into his study, was there for a few minutes, then came out.

She watched him. He had removed his shoes and began padding about in his socks. His stomach was like a pillow under his shirt. His trousers, without the shoes, looked baggy. He looked shorter than he actually was.

When the telephone rang, they were both startled. The clanging went on as if with a calculated intent to disturb.

'Why don't you go and set the table for my food?' he said to her. She got up. She looked lovely in her long light dress flaring gracefully to the ground. There was a pathetic look on her face, that patient, suffering look. When she had disappeared into the kitchen he picked up the phone.

'Jonan Okwe here!' he shouted into the mouthpiece. 'Who is phoning at this time of night and what do you want?' His voice was impatient in its authority.

'You had better keep your voice down if you want to hear what I want to tell you,' a muffled voice said impersonally. Jonan stole a glance at his wife who was carrying in a tray of food to the table and watching him.

'Who is speaking?' he asked, lowering his voice.

'That should not concern you.'

'What do you want?'

'I have a picture here that might interest you. It is the picture of you . . . listen to this . . . you naked on bed with a certain lady.'

Jonan said nothing. He gripped the phone a bit harder.

'It's quite a nice picture. Does it ring a bell with you?' The disembodied voice laughed coolly. 'Amazing how things hidden comes to light, abi?' The laughter became fiendish.

'I don't know what you are talking about.'

'Honest to God you don't? Not until the newspaper gets them or until your wife and relatives and the whole of Wilm Street becomes pasted with enlarged copies of them? Honest to God you don't know what I am talking about?'

Jonan felt hot and sweaty.

'You are lying, there are no such pictures. You are lying. Now who are you? Who are you? I could get you arrested for this, you know?'

For a moment there was a deadly silence over the phone.

'Is that so, Mr Okwe? You want me to send you more than an anonymous letter? You want me to send a free copy of this shameful picture to all your associates and enemies and publish it to the whole world, eh?'

Jonan lowered his voice further.

'What do you want? What's the price? Wetin you want, eh?'

'That's the problem,' the disembodied voice said maintaining its sinister dignity. 'That's the problem.'

'Wetin you want? You madman, what do you want?'

'That's the problem,' the voice chuckled. 'I don't want anything. I want you filled with dread. That's all.'

'What's this? You mad ...' Jonan shouted, unable to restrain himself. It was no use.

The phone was dead in his hands.

Chapter Six

The party went well. At first. There were plenty of drinks, food, young men and women, and good music. The music was mainly the heavily vibrating rock and reggae beats with an occasional cool record. It was one of those occasions when after a period of separation old friends came together.

Jeffia saw many of his former schoolmates. Above the vibrating music they talked and joked about each other and laughed a lot.

'You remember teacher Shapiro?'

'Ah, that great yawner?'

'I hear he's sold that bicycle of his.'

'Man, that bicycle is older than my father.'

'They say he doesn't wear his large-bottomed knickers any more.'

'Yeah, now he wears a khaki trouser that is one foot from the ground.'

'That man sef, eh!'

They talked casually about their plans and activities. From time to time one of the people talking would suddenly get up and say 'I am going for a drink' and disappear into the party. Those who got fed up of being in the dance hall and wanted fresh air would go outside with their drinks and tell stories.

'Oh boy, is Ode around?' Koko asked Jeffia. Koko was another good friend and classmate.

'No. Did he say he was coming?'

'Yes. We rang him up yesterday. He said he would come with a chick.'

'We were together yesterday.'

'Maybe he will come later. He's always doing that. Coming late.'

'Where's Simon?'

'Ah, as if you don't trust him. He's in there with some chick. Booh, I am going in for a drink. See you later.'

43

He went in. Jeffia approached a girl who was sitting outside alone. They went in and danced together. But soon the girl said she was tired and wanted to be with her boyfriend. Jeffia let her go. *Terrible coming to a party without a girl,* he thought, looking around for one that was unattached. He didn't see any, so he too went for a drink. Unlike many of his friends, Jeffia was an abstainer from strong drinks. This made a few of his friends mildly cool towards him. They said they could not trust someone who stayed sober while they got high.

'He fit go sell us, you know,' they said. But Jeffia thought it was better that way. He didn't want to be in the same disgusting state some of his friends were, vomiting and misbehaving.

As Jeffia had come to the party without a girl, he found himself lonely most of the time. Occasionally a girl who knew him would dance up to him and pull him on to the dance floor, but would soon leave him when her partner came looking for her.

When the party was coming to an end, Simon, another of his former classmates, staggered up to him.

'Hey, man, Jeff. You looking like you're at a burial ceremony, man. Cheer up, fella. There's a girl who says she would like to meet you. Boy, she's a live wire, so watch her.' His big red eyes appeared crossed. He stared at Jeffia as though he were looking right through his head at something behind him. He had a foolish grin on his face. Without waiting for a reply from Jeffia, he went into the noisy dance room and came back with a thin girl. She took pains to emphasise her hips when walking. Her face was covered with lipstick, mascara, eye shadow, and an indiscreet use of rouge.

'Hey, man, Jeff, meet the smashing Marge. Marge, this is Jeffia, son of a tycoon and you know what that means. You don't have to look far to see what's in him that gets everybody. Well, eh, now you two have met, suppos'n I go in for a drink and leave you both to . . . you know what.' He bounced back into the dance room winking at Jeffia, who was mildly surprised. Marge smiled, a naughty look in her eyes. She was too much of a social climber not to be in control of a situation like that.

'Well, suppos'n we get seated first. I have never been a good soldier if anything.' She dragged a fallen chair nearby, dusted it, and sat down. He too drew up a chair and sat next to her. For a moment they were silent.

From where they sat they could see people jumping up and down in the dance hall. It was the latest Frog dance. At the entrance of the dance room several young men stood around. They were desperately looking for girls to dance with and make advances to. Near the window were a couple of lovers, standing close together, kissing, and laughing. Near the other entrance, one of the guests was having an argument with some gatecrashers. A few chairs from where Marge sat, a boy slept drunkenly in a chair. Spittle dripped from his mouth. A mischievous character passing by kicked the chair's leg and the drunken fellow crashed to the ground. He muttered a few curses and continued with his drunken sleep on the floor.

'This one don drink die.'

Suddenly from one of the kissing couples standing near the window a fight started. A boy had come up claiming the girl was his girlfriend, the chap with her said otherwise. A fight erupted. The girl dashed into the dance room and was soon seen leaving in another fellow's car. The two fellows flung each other to the ground and kicked and punched each other.

'The girl una dey fight for, don run with another man, fools,' someone said from the dance room. The fighters broke up. Their shirts were torn, their faces bleeding and swollen. They felt foolish and went home, different ways. Jeffia looked at Marge out of the corner of his eye. She knew he was watching her. She smiled coolly. She held her head in an attempt at sophistication.

'Now what does Jeff stand for? Jefferson, Jeffery or Jeffoman?' she said, affecting a poor imitation of an American accent. It was the fashion among youths wanting to give the impression of being 'cool'.

'None, try again.'

'Jefftomac. Jefferosandissonism . . .'

'Lord have mercy,' he said, smiling. 'It's not that jaw-breaking. Simply Jeffia, you see it's an African name.

45

An Urhobo name. And does Marge stand for Margarine, Margenometes or could it by any chance be Margenotheisis? I'm curious.' He wore a mock-curious expression.

'No, it's Margaret. And it's an English name. If that makes any difference.' She gave him a sidelong look. He smiled and said nothing.

Not far from them another mischievous boy was pouring some beer into the fallen drunk's open mouth. Others were laughing behind him.

'Put salt and cigarette for he mouth,' someone shouted.

'No he fit go swallow them, then die – O,' some other person replied.

'He don die already, sef.'

The mischievous fellow went a little further. He stuck the bottle into the drunk's mouth, so it looked as if he were still drinking on the floor. The fellows at the back laughed again and made drunken jokes. The gatecrashers, who had pretended not to want to enter the party again after being accosted, had sneaked into the dance room and come out with beer and food.

'That fool thinks he is wise and tough,' one was saying to another.

'I don duck enter party when big and heavy pass this ten times,' the other replied.

'I go pick up one chick for this party, you'll see.' They laughed.

The record was changed into something gentler. It was hold-tight time. The fellows standing by the door itching for girls were in a frenzy.

'I must find one girl dance this record. Oh God.'

'The music has melt my soul.'

'I must dance this with a chick.'

They stood there, frustrated, staring into the dance room where people were glued to their partners. Somebody put the lights out. There was now an on-and-off blue and green light. Somebody screamed ecstatically. Marge smiled at Jeffia.

'I like your type,' she was saying.

'True?' He wondered why women were particularly friendly that evening.

46

'Yeah, true. You're kind of different, you know.' She paused and looked sharply at him. 'Other boys would want to know what I have got under this dress and would pester me with silly questions. "Where do you stay?" "Where do you work?" "Do you mind if I visit you some day?" this and that. Some would blow their dirty trumpets, others would fiddle keys as if wanting me to know that they had cars. Stupid, vain men. What I usually do is dismiss them. Petty men move with petty girls. I'm not petty – I'm not cheap.'

'I wonder why you are telling me all this?'

She looked at him. Her eyes seemed to flare up.

'Just why on earth did you want to meet me? People had told you that I was a cheap thrill, not so? You imagine I am a pick-up, not so?' Her voice was hard, her eyes were bright. Her indignation and aloofness surprised Jeffia.

'Hey, what are you getting at? It was you who wanted to meet me. Hey? Sorry if righteous indignation is among your latest tricks, I'm not playing.' He got up and without another word, went into the sweaty dance room. The off-and-on disco lights and the ear-busting music in the place was just right to excite a person out of turn. There was a hot record on now. Most of those dancing did so tiredly and trance-like, as if they were zombies at some rock-voodoo festival. There was that necessary atmospheric madness that got into one's head. Making his way through the dancing crowd, he bumped into a couple locked in an out of harmony hold-tight dance. They cursed him for disturbing them.

'Idiot . . . jealous . . .'

He managed to make out where Simon sat fussing over a stiff-looking girl who reminded him of receptionists at private clinics. Jeffia dragged Simon by the hands.

'You, Quarter-past-four-eyes, I want to talk to you about something.'

'What the hell, Jeff ?' His breath smelt of booze. 'Get on with your chick, man. I'm necking, can't you see?'

'Quarter-past-four-eyes, I want to talk to you,' Jeffia insisted, holding on to Simon's hands.

'Okay, what is it?' he said, reluctantly following Jeffia outside. 'Did you call me outside to play games?'

'No. I want you to straighten something your big mouth made bent. Wait, I'll be back.' He went in search of Marge and found her talking with another young man. Simon went over. The fellow began to raise trouble, thinking Jeffia had come to steal the girl he'd just discovered.

'Look, man, they are together, you see they had a little misunderstanding.' Simon lied to the young man who melted back into the party.

'I must have caused some misunderstanding. The thing is I wanted both of you to meet. Now you know, settle yourselves, be nice to each other, enjoy the party . . . my throat is itching for some booze, man.' He was gone.

After that Jeffia and Marge became steady partners for the evening. When it was eleven-thirty, he said he was leaving. He went round to say goodbye to his friends, but they were mostly drunk or in some room somewhere doing some secret thing. He saw Koko.

'Nice of you to stay with us, brother. So Ode didn't come again? When I see him, I will yab him. See you, Jeff, and take care of that chick,' Koko said, winking suggestively.

'Tell the rest I've gone. See you some time.'

Marge joined him in the car, and he dropped her off on the way home.

2

Alone in the car he drove slightly faster. He turned into the expressway. It would help him get home quicker.

The time was crawling to midnight. Once away from the party, its noise and excitements, he felt the loneliness that came after. The contrast produced a certain hollowness within him.

The lugubrious blackness of night with its attendant fears and horrors, engulfed him. The only things to be seen were a few slanting streetlights shedding their ghostly light on the sinuous road. His car lights cut through the darkness ahead. It stretched out before him like a wilderness of ectoplasmic shadows. The dismal silence, ringing in the ears, was disturbed by the purring of the car. The silence unrolled itself upon his senses.

He thought about the events of the past few days, touching upon them briefly, trying to find a connecting thread. This was something his mother had taught him: always to ponder on the day's experiences. In that way, she had told him, the lessons that experiences have to teach will not be lost. In that way the mind is able to find coherence in the drift of events.

His mother had taught him many things. She said that since his father was a very busy man, she would tell those things that would help him understand and adjust to the demands of living.

She taught him to look to his father for the examples as to how a man should stand on his feet in a hostile world.

And in profound moments she would tell him seriously that the real meaning of living was not to possess but to express one's self in the noblest endeavours, and to improve one's self in one's own way. He loved those moments he spent with his mother.

But now when he thought of his mother, he remembered the way she had behaved that morning. He remembered her screaming. He remembered the way she stared unfocusingly ahead, as if through an open curtain to some terrifying event. There had been something momentarily trancelike about her that still baffled him. Then there was the early morning scream, a funny dream she called it. There was the lady who knew his dad, the disturbingly familiar man, his encounter with the bribe-thirsty policeman . . .

Too many things were being compressed into one day. Things were all of a sudden moving too fast.

At that moment he remembered something his mother told him a long time ago.

'*Experiences, son, are the stuff our lives are made of. Learn to face them. Never be afraid of the unpleasant. Never forget that you are a man.*'

His mind came back to the present.

He drove past shadowy trees, newly erected office buildings, and farmlands. Occasionally one or two people walked down the dark road. The sky was blue-black and starless. The thick blanket of night covered everything. The thinning forests on both sides of the deserted express road had fearful outlines. They were like moving shadowy souls. They took infinite shapes in his mind.

Then, suddenly a large frog hopped across the road.

He tried to avoid it. He swerved slightly. But he felt his back tyre run over it and he heard a muffled sound as it burst. He held the steering wheel tighter and increased speed.

Deep down inside him he felt as though someone had stepped upon his quiet life.

Chapter Seven

Somewhere in the distance, a young nurse was preparing to go home from the clinic where she worked. The night had been unusually long. She should have gone home long ago but someone had telephoned late in the evening that a wounded person would be brought in. She had to wait. But no one brought in any emergency case. It was a few minutes to midnight already and she had a particular horror of night shifts. It was then that men would lurk about in the darkness waiting for one nurse or the other, like people waiting their turns at a prostitutes' den.

The van that usually took them home hadn't come. She wondered how she was going to spend the night in the clinic. From experience she had discovered that the doctors were used to making passes at the nurses. The last time one attempted it on her, she walked out and managed to get a lift home. She later threatened to resign if it continued. For that she lost favour in the eyes of some of the doctors. Her progress was affected. She was picked on to do the nasty jobs.

That night, Cynthia was much inclined to take a walk in the dark till the van came. She wanted to be alone. She wanted to go out there in the silence around and be with her memories. They were her closest and most reliable companions. They spoke to her truthfully, they comforted her. She had endured a hard life. She believed that when a life goes peacefully along and then is suddenly thrown to the ground, little is left of the wreck but scars and memories. They were the only true touchstones. Even in picking up the pieces and weaving them into newer patterns and attitudes, she believed it was her memories that served as the connecting link.

She put down the novel she was reading. She went out to look for her companion. The emergency ward was empty. The walls were high and painted a light blue. The vacancy of the long benches and chairs in the ward had something unnatural about them. It made her feel quite lonely, and the night, coupled with the knowledge that the clinic was in a desolate area, accentuated the feeling. But it was a loneliness she was used to and even welcomed sometimes.

The reception area was also empty. The door was bolted. There was a notebook and a ballpoint pen on the table. Beside them, looking slightly ominous, lay Jane's rimless glasses. The walls there were white and shining. It often gave Cynthia an uncomfortable feeling to stay in the reception too long.

'Jane!' she called, going out of the door.

'Yes? What?' came the reply. Cynthia opened the diagnosing room door.

'What is it?'

Jane was arranging the medical chest. Cynthia remembered the doctor giving her the instruction when she came in late. She had finished cleaning it, and was now neatly putting the various bottles and equipment back. Jane whistled a Millie Jackson tune to herself, as if at peace with the world. The ever-pungent smells of antiseptics and disinfectant rose to her nostrils. Jane stopped putting in the bottles and looked at Cynthia.

'Why are you calling my name as if you saw Dracula?'

'See who's talking about Dracula,' Cynthia said, smiling. 'You think when you invoke names like that, your neck cross would save you?'

Jane looked at the arrangement she had done so far, then shifted a few bottles sideways.

'I wonder what Baldhead is going to do with all these empty bottles?'

'Are all of them empty?'

'Only the ones on the top shelf.'

'I'm going out for a walk, Jane. I want to be by myself a bit.'

'I wouldn't advise that,' Jane said, looking up.

' "Things that love night love not nights as these". That's Shakespeare, not so?' Jane always prided herself on being able to quote at length from English literature, even though she had failed it in her School Certificate exams.

'Yes, it's Shakespeare. But I am going for a walk. I hope you have Dracula as company.'

'He'll be my guest. But he's afraid of me and my neck cross.'

'I'll be back soon.' Cynthia opened the door behind her.

'Cynthia!' Jane called.

'Yes. What?'

Jane put down the bottle, rubbed her hands together, and came towards her.

'I know how it is, Cynthia. I know.'

Cynthia stood staring at her.

'But, Cynthia, remember Lot's wife — never look back.' Satisfied with the silence that followed, she went back to the medical chest. She had said what she wanted to say. She went on whistling the Millie Jackson tune, as though at peace with the world.

Cynthia stood there for a moment, then silently went out into the chilly night.

She walked up the dirt track that led from the clinic to the express road. The incessant drone of mosquitoes and the occasional piercing cries of nocturnal animals were the only sounds to be heard.

The nightmarish shapes of objects, distorted by darkness, in some strange way only served to heighten her calm. In the distance, a few street lights shone dimly.

She walked on slowly.

She was one of those people who had been forced by circumstances to learn to be at home with the futility of things. The events of her life had taught her to leave a little mental gap for the unpleasant and the unexpected. She had experienced more downs than ups, the downs only succeeding in pulling her lower than the ups could raise her. But she had fashioned an attitude of quiet courage and resilience: she had learned to live with herself and with life as she found it. At heart, Cynthia was a lover of life, a warm-hearted optimist for whom the sight of a sunset, or a moving song, or a sincere smile from a friend held untold promises of future joy. But she kept these feelings to herself. Outwardly she expected little, for she had learnt that this attitude sharply reduced her feelings of disappointment.

In her relationships she was warm and gentle and only smiled enigmatically when men with their various transparent tactics tried to break through the aura of aloofness she had built round herself.

From the bushes near her a cricket thrilled sharply. The sound was like a faulty, shrill whistle. It reminded her of her schooldays when they used to catch and roast crickets at night. Those days were gone now, those childish, happy days. She remembered the night her dormitory prefect sent her to kneel down outside on the lawn. She was in Form Three then. She had been kneeling down, feeling drowsy, when she suddenly saw a snake dropping from the branch of a tree nearby. She screamed and ran indoors. The snake had got away by the time the school gardeners arrived. The prefect who had punished her was suspended from school.

She smiled in the darkness.

The clumps of bushes on both sides of the dirt track were a dense mass of shadows. The air was fresh and cool. The wind blew with a gentleness that was almost loving. The sky was an exposed, dark blue photographer's plate dotted with stars and stretching out endlessly.

The night didn't bother her much. Rather, she experienced a feeling of freedom and closeness with herself and a joy that the company of other people seldom offered. In moments like this, she felt she was her own best friend.

She kicked a stone in the dark. It was with her left foot. She stopped. Bad luck this night? No! It's all superstition, she said to herself, and walked on. She had now reached the beginning of the track. By the side of it, looking dark and undignified, stood the slanting signboard of the clinic. She smiled. Baldhead often had the funniest ideas.

'A slanting signboard,' the doctor had said, 'makes people bend their heads to read it. There's a secret psychology involved that even PhDs don't understand.'

Baldhead. She wondered who first called him that name. Maybe it was Jane or Cecilia. Jane had such a jumpy mouth, just the type to manufacture nicknames like that. Baldhead! Imagine calling him that!

The express road was dark and clear. She took the bend to the right. She decided to walk to the lamp post and back.

She stopped suddenly.

In the distance she saw the outlines of several people. There was a car near them. As it all became clearer, as her eyes grew more used to the sight, she could make out that the people were holding weapons. They seemed to be beating up someone. The man fell to the ground. His shouting and pleading came faintly over the air.

It all happened too quickly for her to be sure of what she was seeing. She froze. The first impulse that ran through her was concern. Then came anger, and then fear. Just as quickly as it unfolded to her, the people dashed for a waiting car which sped off past her. She waited for a minute. The Peugeot car had become two specks of red light in the distance. Soon it vanished. The man who had been beaten up lay on the asphalted road, whimpering.

. Her mind worked swiftly. Without another thought she ran to where he lay. She gently turned him over and examined him. The dim street light revealed a bloody wreck of what was once a human face. His nose was battered to blood and bones. There was a huge cut at the back of his head, the handiwork of a blunt matchet. His body was covered in vicious wounds and cuts. She could not altogether suppress the feeling of nausea that crawled to her stomach at the ugliness of it all.

. There was little she could do immediately. The clinic was too far. She tried shaking him, but he didn't stir. By now his agonised groaning had stopped and unconsciousness had taken over. All through she was so engrossed in how to help the wounded man that she seemed totally unaware of her surroundings. The possibility of danger didn't occur to her.

Then she was startled by the purring of a car. But she was more angry that the driver hadn't the good sense to dip the headlights that were shining directly into her eyes.

2

Jeffia had mixed feelings about what he saw. The fear that had been growing in his mind made him unable to think straight. His mind clung to all sorts of fantastic possibilities.

Is it an accident? *A hit-and-run kind of accident? Some jealous husband's revenge? Or probably a set-up of armed robbers?* His mind clung a little longer to this last thought. It looked just right: a girl dressed in white to be conspicuously in apparent distress; a man feigning being injured; at that time of the night and along a deserted highway. The thought grew into a fear. It magnified in his mind.

But at the back of his thoughts he felt differently. *Maybe they need help*, he thought. *Maybe it's an accident. Maybe that's his wife.* He see-sawed between the two possibilities. He didn't notice the girl approach the car.

'Are you afraid or something?' came her voice. He started. 'What . . . ?'

She laughed, nervously. (Her mouth, her face, laughed. He knew they did, even though he couldn't quite make them out in the half-darkness.)

'I don't know whether I am or not.' He felt more at ease now. 'Or shouldn't I be?'

She had her back to the dim street light. He wished he could see her expression as she replied:

'I don't think so. The man there,' she indicated pointing, 'was beaten up by a couple of crooks and he is badly injured. I need help to carry him to our clinic not far away.'

'Is that so?' Jeffia said, eyeing her suspiciously. His hand lingered cautiously on the gear lever. *Got to be careful*, he thought, *this is the way it happens on television. Got to be watchful.*

'What are you doing here at this time of night?'

She laughed again at that. It was a soft, almost personal laughter.

'I don't think my reason would satisfy you. I wanted to be alone. My clinic is not far from here. I decided to walk a bit. Then I saw them beating him up. Then they ran away. He's badly wounded and needs help. Believe me.'

It was only when she added the 'believe me' that she realised how odd it was for her to be there at that time of night and with a man whom she knew nothing about. It sounded all the more odd to her that she was trying to persuade the young man to believe her. *Why should he believe me?* she thought.

'You see,' she continued, 'if he could get some treatment for the night, tomorrow we would transfer him to our main hospital. The important thing now is for him to be somewhere, to be treated.'

Jeffia felt he could trust her. *That voice has to be sincere*, he thought. The abandon of instinctive trust swept through him. He said, 'It's all right. It's all right.' He opened the door. 'Where did you say your clinic was?'

She smiled. He immediately felt he had been right to trust her. He smiled too. In the distance some nocturnal creature made a series of hooting and shrill noises. As if in response, some frogs croaked continually. Other noises followed. Soon they all died down and a brooding silence hung over the land.

She described the place to him. He went over and looked down at the injured man.

'Looks terrible,' he said at length.

'It is terrible,' she replied. 'Let's carry him to the car, if we can.'

He noticed that he was a bit taller than she was. She was slim. Her face under the dim street light was fresh and beautiful. He noticed further that her breasts cut a nice, round shape under her white dress.

Both of them, after initial difficulties, lifted the injured man into the back seat. He was still unconscious.

'Odd place to have a clinic,' he muttered aloud as he started the car and drove on.

'Baldhead is an odd man,' she said, laughing lightly. 'Baldhead is the nickname of the doctor.'

'Sounds an ingenious nickname. Straight out of a secondary school imagination.'

'He thinks that in a couple of years this express road will be an industrial centre, with factories all around. He wants to prepare for it, and cash in on it.'

'He sounds more like a businessman than a doctor,' Jeffia said, turning into the dirt track.

'He's both.'

'Very quaint. Hope he doesn't give injections with nails and recommend a full day's work for a complaint of headache.'

'Sometimes he does worse,' she said, laughing along with him, 'he prescribes Nivaquine for toothaches, and surgery for a sense of humour like yours.'

In the waiting room, to their surprise, they found that Jane was busy with a man. They were on the bed reserved for emergencies and night shift nurses. As soon as Cynthia and Jeffia burst into the room Jane disengaged herself from her lover, who got off the bed to make way for the injured man.

For all they cared, Jane had been disturbed from a fine sleep. She had about her that air of self-assurance and casualness usually found in those who taste generously from the nectar of living. Cynthia told her what had happened. She quickly dropped sensuality for efficiency and helped carry the man.

'Maybe he's the person they telephoned us about this evening,' Jane suggested.

'Could be. It's a weird coincidence,' came Cynthia's tired reply.

They carried the man into the emergency ward. Jeffia washed his hands of the bloodstains and went to the waiting room. Beside him sat Jane's lover. He looked embarrassed. He was good-looking, looked well fed, and was well built. He had a moustache and a responsible air about him. He looked like a man with a wife and kids. He fiddled with the key he held in his hands.

Jane came out from the emergency ward. She sighed, and smiled at him.

'Well, Jero, time is up. You'd better be going now. Business before pleasure, abi?' She went over and pecked him on the lips. He got up stiffly.

'When will I see you next?' he asked, his voice shaky.

'Come and pick me up tomorrow evening. You'd better be going or you-know-who will get worried.' There was a mischievous smile on her mouth. He hurried out of the room awkwardly.

'Goodnight, darling,' Jane called after him. Jeffia wasn't sure whether she said that mockingly.

Cynthia came into the room. Her hands were wet.

'That's that for the night. Tomorrow he will be taken to the main hospital,' she said. 'See that your fears were not . . . well . . .' she said this to Jeffia. He didn't say anything, only smiled.

'By the way,' Jane said, eyeing Jeffia, 'who is the handsome young man you brought along? Aren't you going to introduce me to your, you know . . . ?'

'Jane, for God's sake don't embarrass him! He's the one who brought us down here in his car. Why, we don't even know each other's names! Must you be so nasty anyway?'

'I'm sorry. Forgive my erring mouth.'

Jane looked from one to the other and laughed. Jeffia stood up. Cynthia sensed he wanted to go.

'Would you like to have a look at the man?' she asked him. 'We've managed to make him look human, but he is still unconscious.'

Jeffia didn't feel like it. He wanted to go home. It was getting very late. But Jane had stopped laughing and was looking at him. Cynthia was also looking at him. He felt he couldn't say no.

'All right. Let's see if he is all right.' Jeffia followed Cynthia into the emergency ward. He could feel Jane's stare boring into him.

One look at the short, stocky frame was enough. The inexplicable feeling he had all along reached its unpredictable climax. It didn't make sense at all. Jeffia couldn't think. His heart pounded with a sense of terror which he could not explain.

Lying there on the bed, possibly dying, was Gbenga.

'Is anything the matter?' Cynthia asked.

'Yes,' he said quietly. 'Things are happening too fast, too mysteriously.'

Chapter Eight

The grandfather clock beside the television struck one o'clock. Jonan stole a glance at his wife. She had dozed off on the sofa next to him. In her sleep there was something defenceless about her.

Both of them had been waiting for Jeffia.

She had started it when around midnight she went to Jonan's room to tell him that Jeffia hadn't come in yet.

'Why don't you leave me alone? Can't you see I don't want to be disturbed? Ah ha,' he had replied at first. He hadn't been able to sleep. Grim thoughts and grim fears haunted him. He had turned over and over on the bed. At one stage he got up to smoke and drink. He paced the room. Having gone back to bed again the thoughts came with the dark intensity that the relative stillness gave. Then his wife came into the room. He was irritated.

'Don't you hear? Jeffia hasn't come in yet. He's never stayed out as long as this!' Her voice had risen.

'Oh, you women sef. Why do you bother yourself. Jeffia is going to be twenty, you know. He is not a baby any more.' He didn't want to be disturbed. He was still thinking about other things. The mysterious telephone call he had received. The anonymous note. In his long business experience, he had never come across blackmail. It was something he did, but rather more subtly. It was a facet of his business hold over the people he dealt with. Business blackmail was one of the unwritten rules of the survival game which only the proficient played with commanding skill. But naked blackmail was something he had never bargained for. It was a thing usually attributed to fiction or to aspects of Western life. To happen here seemed a remote consideration. Pictures of him and a woman in bed! Unbelievable! Unthinkable! To make enlarged copies and paste them on walls!

Who was this character? What did he really want? Was there some kind of Nigerian-style mafia?

Whoever it was wanted Jonan to be on the rack and resign himself to whatever would come next. That was one thing Jonan had no intention of doing. He had been thinking seriously. *How could this person have got a picture of me and a woman naked in bed? Do such things happen here? Are people's minds so criminal?*

But suppose it is true . . . ? No! There's no telling its harmfulness. No!

Even by himself, he had been very uncomfortable with the thoughts.

Things just don't happen like that. All he had done seemed right and normal at the time. *Now it could all be fatal.*

Suddenly he became aware that his wife was still standing in the room. She was looking down at him. He wondered uneasily whether she had heard his thoughts. He got up from the bed.

'Jonan.' Her voice was low, her face pathetic. 'What have you been thinking about that is more important than our son? What is happening, J? What is happening?'

'It's all right. It's all right. Nothing to worry about. It's going on twelve already. Let's wait till twelve thirty, if he doesn't come then we will ring the police. Is that all right?'

They both went down to the sitting room to wait. Tiredness soon made her doze off on the sofa.

Jonan looked at her, and shook his head.

Women, he thought, *women. One moment they are devils prying into your mind trying to divine secrets that's bound to upset them. The next moment they are like children.*

He often thought to himself how far he could have gone without her. She seemed like a guiding light to him. A bringer of luck. She was a hardworking woman who had survived the rough journeys with him. When things were hard she was compassionate, understanding and helpful. At one time she had even been his secretary. That was a long time ago. She always reminded him of his mother, who had died young. He smiled when he remembered how in the early days of their marriage she was afraid and nervous of everything. She used to be shy to go out and coy in bed. He remembered also how some of his relatives had been thoroughly against the marriage.

'We don't even know the kind of family she comes from.'

'Her family might even be a witchcraft family.'

'All these fatherless women, sef.'

His relatives openly voiced their protest. But Jonan went ahead and married her. Sowho had wanted to interfere and had even tried to take her from him. They had a small quarrel over it, then settled. Those early days. She had been a wonderful wife.

My father always prayed that I should marry a good wife, he thought. *My father used to say, 'My son, a good wife is what a man should pray for. Have a good wife, and you will have a happy life.'* His father had told him a lot of things. Things that guided and helped him. He often believed that his father's spirit still helped and guided him.

Jonan stared at the blue light. He reached under his wrapper and scratched. He looked round the room. *The house is kept well. Everything is neat.* His eyes rested on the sword in its fanciful Hausa scabbard. Its colours looked dull in the blue light. His wife had bought it for the sitting room some time ago. She was always buying one thing or the other. He thought again about the telephone call.

Then the telephone rang. At first he started. His wife made some movements on the sofa next to him. His heart beat slightly faster.

'Jonan Okwe here.'

'It's me, Amazu sir. We don do am.'

'Done what?'

'We don give G the treatment.'

Jonan paused and looked at his sleeping wife.

'A clean job? No one saw you, eh?'

'Yes sir, I mean, no sir. No one see us, sir.'

'If any of you did a clumsy, stupid job you will feel sorry for yourselves O. I don't have to tell you that.'

'It's all right, sir. I ring the clinic, everything. They go see am, I sure.'

'Okay.'

'When he better, he go get sense.'

'Okay.' Jonan slammed the phone down. There was a wicked glint in his eyes.

'Now who is next?' he asked loudly. His countenance had brightened. He made for the sideboard.

His wife still slept on the sofa, waiting for Jeffia. The same child-like expression was still on her face.

Chapter Nine

Despite all Jane's attempts at persuading Cynthia to stay, she was determined to go.

'Suit yourself. You will have my sympathy if anything happens to you,' Jane said finally.

'I wouldn't need it then.'

'Eh heh?'

'Yes, you would have the cynical satisfaction of being able to say "I told her so!"'

As for Jeffia all that was being said didn't reach him. He sat in the car, all knotted up, trying to understand what he had seen. Gbenga's battered face came back to him. He kept asking himself questions he couldn't answer.

Who could have done such a thing? Who would want Gbenga dead? What harm would he do anybody?

Cynthia got into the car, startling him. She had changed from her white dress into trousers and a green blouse. Jane came over. Her breasts rested on the car's lowered window seemed to point at him like accusations. There was a sensuous half-smile on her lips. Her eyes were narrowed, her face had a calculating expression.

'Thanks, mister, for the help you gave us. You are a nice guy. Not many men I know would do a thing like that without asking a special favour in return. But don't take advantages, just take her home.'

'Thanks for the advice,' Jeffia said, starting the car.

'Get out from the window, baldface,' added Cynthia, smiling.

Jeffia drove off. They turned into the express road.

'She's like that. Always saying things. I like her though. She's a nice and helpful person when she wants to be.'

'I'm sure. Where do you live?'

'At Marine Beach.'

They drove on silently. The road before them was dark and ominous. The purring of the car was a solitary and unnerving sound in the silence around. It was as if in the great mass of primordial darkness they were alone in the world.

The purring sound continued. Jeffia occasionally wished it could be a little less loud. The car swallowed up the road. Dark trees, stretches of bushes, factory buildings, farmlands, flew past.

'What's the time?'

'Fifteen minutes to one. It's late.'

He glanced at her and smiled.

'No. It's early.'

She looked at him and laughed softly.

'Nice attitude, that.'

He said nothing for a moment. A silence that he didn't like came over them. He thought of a reply. Her voice did things to him. It drew him out of himself. It made him want to say nice things. It made him feel good.

'And it's attitudes that matter, isn't it?' he soon said.

'Quite true,' she said, then added, laughing, 'Though one's attitude doesn't make any difference to the pain of a toothache – without becoming a mockery.'

'Well, what makes the difference then?'

'The toothache. It's already its own difference.'

Jeffia enjoyed the drift of the conversation.

'I don't think I agree with you.'

'Well, why not?'

'The difference is always in how we respond to things, toothaches and all. We could sit down and let the pain rage, or we could do something intense and not be aware of the pain.'

He had driven up the bridge and taken the branching off to the right. There was a policeman on the bridge, but he was busy with a defaulting motorist on the other side of the road.

'I mean,' he said, 'it's attitude that determines how experiences affect us. I believe that depending on ourselves, we could be unscathed by experiences, at least we would not be essentially damaged by them.'

'You wouldn't be the person you are if you had someone else's experiences. Besides arguing the point would not resolve it. Life is the supreme test.'

They lapsed into silence. They had reached Ijora Causeway. Besides a few cars passing the bridge above at top speed, the place was deserted. Under the bridge were several Mallams sleeping on tattered mats. There was the stench of goat dung. The sight reminded him of what their cook, Chema, had told him: that when he first came to Lagos from his village, the Carter bridge was his first roof. He used to go about looking for work by day, and would sleep under the bridge at night.

'People dey go through conditions, but man pickin go always thank God the next morning, even when food no dey man belle,' Chema had said, ending his story.

'Turn at the next road, on the right,' she said. He slowed down and turned into the road.

'Life is the supreme test,' he repeated. He had no sooner said it than a man staggered across the road, a bottle of beer in his hands. The man tottered forward, and fell. Jeffia had been lucky to see him in time. The road was so winding that the headlights barely illuminated him.

Jeffia quickly applied the brakes.

'This is too much for one day,' he muttered. He got out of the car and rushed to where the man lay. There was a cut on his arm. He had fallen on the broken bottle. He was drunk. A crowd had gathered quickly. It was surprising how in such moments crowds seemed to come from nowhere like materialised shadows. The man mumbled and made all sorts of noises. His breath smelt of beer.

'Is he all right?' Cynthia asked Jeffia.

'Only a little wound on the arm. And he's drunk.'

'Turn him on his side so I can see the wound better.'

'Is that all right?' he asked her after turning the man. There was no reply. He half turned and looked at her.

She was pale. Her mouth was half open. It was as if she had seen a familiar ghost. She stared down at the fallen man.

'Is anything the matter? What's wrong?'

She clung to him for support. Finally, in subdued tones, she said, 'He is my father.'

66

2

There was a spooky silence. One by one the crowd dispersed as if their hunt for sensation had turned into something sour. Back into the sombre shadows they disappeared. That was the way it was. In trouble one is alone. Sorrow is one thing a crowd shares little of.

Cynthia soon regained her composure. She turned to Jeffia.

'Look eh . . . '

'Jeffia.'

'Forgive me for not asking all along. Thanks for the help you gave me. It's very kind of you but I think you should be going now.'

'But . . .'

'Don't bother about my father. I can take care of him. I hope we will see each other again.' She began lifting her father by the shoulder. There was a finality in her voice that Jeffia knew he couldn't argue with. Jeffia helped to put her father's arms round her shoulders and moving slowly they went towards their house. Her father buckled and mumbled beside her.

She didn't appear frail any more. There was a certain strength and self-reliance in the way she handled the situation. He didn't have to be told that here was a girl who had learnt to stand on her own feet.

'Don't forget to come and check on the man, if you can,' she said when they reached the door. 'And safe journey.'

He waved and turned reluctantly to the car. The night was bleak. The moon, like an old man's face disgusted at his children's evils, looked gloomy. Clouds took intriguing shapes.

On reaching the car, he stopped and took one more look at Cynthia as she and her father entered the house.

He felt a strange shiver run through him. He couldn't explain the emotion that glowed within him. There was a charismatic defiance in her gesture, a fortitude in the face of pain that aroused his profound respect.

As he drove home, it struck him that many strange and unrelated things had happened in just that one day.

But he felt also that he was not the only one that things happened to, and this brought him a measure of rather selfish relief.

He thought about Cynthia. It made the journey easier.

Chapter Ten

'Jeffia! Jeffia!'

'Yes, Dad?'

'Come to the sitting room, now!'

'All right, Dad.'

'Not "all right", come *now*. You hear? Now!'

Jeffia had driven into the compound quietly. He first had to bang on the watchnight's shed. The watchnight was asleep. The gate was opened. Jeffia parked the car. He went to his room through the back door. When his father called him, he was surprised. He had no idea that his father was awake. He quickly changed into his pyjamas. He hurried to the door, then paused. He didn't have to be told that his father was angry at his returning so late. But the surprise soon turned to resentment. He braced himself and went into the sitting room.

His father was pacing the floor with the dramatic intensity of a lawyer faced with a formidable criminal case. There was a cigarette in his mouth. At first he didn't pause or look up when Jeffia came in. Then he turned and faced him.

'Why are you returning so late, eh? Why are you coming back from wherever you went so late? What is the matter with you, eh? You keep us worried and you disturb my sleep. Now where have you been?' his father shouted taking a few angry steps over to him. Jeffia said nothing. Even if he had wanted to say anything, his father's shouting made him sullen.

'That is how you children grow up and turn into something strange,' he added, his manner sharp and impatient. Jeffia looked down at his mother.

'Jeffia, I am talking to you.'

'I know, Dad.'

Silence fell over them. It was not often they talked like that. Generally they had a rather silent relationship. They seldom met in the week and when they did there seemed little to talk about. It wasn't that his father wasn't nice to him. But that paternal spark of affection, which went above a mere sense of duty, was not always manifest. There was between them the forced and strained air of people who were thrown together. People who had long faced the fact that though they don't vibrate in harmony they just have to get on: 'Good morning, Dad.' 'Oh good morning, Jeff. Are you all right? See you in the evening, eh?' was all that seemed to pass between them when they met in the morning. In some strange way his father never inspired in him a strong sense of love. He was more like the embodiment of a great institution that had catered for his wants through life.

The silence in the room hung like gloom. His father sighed.

'How was the party?' was the next thing he said. His voice had lowered.

'It was nice,' Jeffia replied. The silence descended again. His father made for the sideboard. Jeffia heard him pouring a drink.

He shook his mother, who was still sleeping.

'Mum?' She stirred. He had seen sleep-walkers several times on television and always felt something frightening about them. They disturbed him. He felt the same way now as his mother stirred as if from a coma.

'Mum, are you all right?'

She smiled at him and held him in a loving embrace. She fondled his hair.

'Jeff, where have you been? I have been so worried. We were just about to go to the police.'

'There was no need to worry, Mum. I was all right.'

'That's what you say. Don't you read about all those kidnaps, highway robberies, and killings every day in the papers? You are all I have got, eh, I don't want anything to happen to you. The country is getting worse and worse every day. Things are not as they seem. You've got to be careful, eh?'

'It's all right. I'm fine. There was nothing. The party went on longer than I thought it would.'

She stroked his hair. He didn't altogether like it when his mother treated him as if he were a baby. But it was always comforting to be near her, knowing that she loved him and showed it.

'Oh God,' his mother said suddenly, straightening up. She had remembered the phone call from Ode's mother. He felt her tense. He quickly glanced at her. She went pale. She looked downwards at the carpet.

'What is it, Mum?'

She still didn't look at him.

'I don't know how to tell you.'

'What is it? Is it something bad?'

The silence that followed deepened his anticipation. His mother's eyes suddenly seemed withdrawn: a shadow fell over her brow.

'I had a telephone call this evening, just after you called.'

'What was it?'

'Ode had an accident.'

There was a strange silence.

'Ode? Accident? Which Ode?' His voice was incredulous.

She looked at him sadly.

'Ode, your friend.'

'An accident?'

'He's dead, Jeff. He died in a weird accident.' It came out almost as a whisper. Her voice was tearful. For a moment there was silence. Then the dreadful impact of what she had said hit Jeffia. His eyes opened wide, his mouth fell open, then he began to scream.

'No!!' he shouted. 'Mum, no! It can't be true. It just can't be true, Mum, no!'

'Take it easy, Jeff. Take it easy,' she said, putting her arms round his quivering neck.

He wrenched himself from his mother's embrace and fell face forward on the sofa. His body shook uncontrollably.

'It can't be true, Mum. No, not Ode, no!'

His wailing, passionate and deeply felt, was a lone sound in the night. She sat helpless, blaming herself for having told him. She had never seen Jeffia so upset. She felt his grief. After what seemed ages, his spasms subsided and an occasional tear ran into his mouth. His eyes were dazed; but his voice suddenly became calm, almost too calm.

'How did it happen, Mum?'

'His mother told me that he was urinating at the back of a stationary trailer, into a gutter, when another trailer which was reversing to park crushed him from behind. It's unbelievable. How did the trailer driver not hear the boy when he was shouting? How could the driver not hear when passers-by shouted at him? The trailers make so much noise, the drivers are so stupid, and the trailers are so long that the driver did not see what was going on at the back. Ode was rushed to the hospital but he died before he got there. His poor mother was sobbing when she told me. Oh, the poor woman . . .'

Jeffia was horrified at what he heard. It didn't seem true, couldn't be. Ode was like a brother. People often said that they were twin souls. They had grown up together. Their friendship, with its ups and downs, quarrels and challenges, had endured the many years of schooling. They were an inspiration to one another, setting goals, arguing, having big dreams about the future. They were also great companions in various amorous adventures. It was their silences he remembered most: those moments when the two of them were together, after watching a memorable film, when alone with their girlfriends, or just walking down the length of the beach. Ode had always wanted to be a writer and always had new theories about writing. Jeffia remembered something.

'Mum, Ode once wrote an article about the menace of trailers!' *Wicked irony*, he screamed to himself, *wicked irony*.

Ode always had strong views and in class he used to challenge the teacher when he thought the teacher was wrong.

'That boy too forward!' the teacher would mutter.

Now he was dead.

Jeffia slumped further into the sofa. Ode had died, and died so nightmarishly.

Jeffia felt as if something vital and intangible had dropped out of his soul. He felt empty. *It's the same failures in our society that Ode had always wanted to write about that had become responsible for his death*, Jeffia thought bitterly. He felt very bad.

'Take it easy,' his mother said, holding him close to her. 'Things like this happen every day. Worse things will go on happening. Life is full of them, and there is little anybody

72

can do. The best you can do is face them bravely.'

Her voice was hollow with emotion. Jonan moved about the room uneasily like an unwanted spirit.

'At some time or another one is alone. But what happens after depends on the individual. May Ode's soul rest in perfect peace.'

The grief had now sunk deeply into Jeffia and he could vaguely contain it. The memories came and went and the emptiness deepened within him with every memory. He wanted to be left alone.

Through all this Jonan had been moved. Ode's parents were family friends. He had seen Jeffia and Ode together a lot, and he liked their companionship. He said:

'A man's greatest battles are the ones he fights within himself. It happens to all of us, son. But we pass through somehow.'

Jonan had spoken more from a sudden fear than anything else. He had the unsettling guilt that he had failed his only son, that he hadn't informed him enough of the facts of life. It was like a moment of truth. In the earlier years he hadn't wanted to be bothered with the intimate side of bringing up his son. That was a woman's job, he had insisted. He had always been too involved with the establishment of his business. Jeffia grew up and spent most of his time at boarding school. Over the years, father and son had spent so little time in each other's company that they didn't really know one another. The personal touch had always been lacking.

Standing there and hearing Jeffia's mother talking to him like that had driven home Jonan's sense of failure. The anger he had felt earlier dissipated.

He wanted to make up for his lack of personal touch. He wanted to say all the words of wisdom he should have said long ago.

'Jeffia, you are becoming a man now. There are a few things you ought to know.'

Jeffia was only half listening. He was irritated. He wanted so much to be left alone.

'The society in which we live is a complex one. To get anything out of it you have to rise above the system. You might not know what I mean, but some day you will. Today, one is either big or small, you either clutch at the straws or you swim. The choice is yours. We are in a large entangled web of law and disorder, power, waste, and misuse. And in this crazy society it is the power people that really count. All the rest are means to an end. My choice was wealth and power. I have had my share of the people who passed through my fingers. But the price is an uneasy head that trembles at every creak in the edifice, a disturbed mind that remembers the threats of life-long enemies. My advice to you, son, is . . .' The words fell from his lips weightily, with an accord of their own. It was as though the words were wrenching themselves mechanically from him.

Jeffia was still only half listening. His irritation was becoming unbearable.

' . . . is to go your own way into life. Stand on your feet. Find your own blueprints. Be a tough, unshakable man. But do not follow my example. I have made many mistakes and have many enemies.' He paused. 'You know your uncle Sowho, eh? Well, watch out for him. He is dangerous, you hear?'

Jeffia, who had all along been thinking of Ode, shifted irritably on the sofa. 'Why are you telling me all this now?' he shouted suddenly. 'Why don't you just leave me alone, eh?'

'Jeffia!'

His mother got up from the sofa and gave Jonan a deep stare. Her eyes accused him.

'What are you looking at me for, eh?'

She didn't say anything: she just went silently upstairs. They heard her door open and shut.

Jonan stood there in the middle of the room, a glass in his hand, his cigarette burnt out, frozen in an uncompleted gesture. He pondered his wife's strange behaviour.

'Is Mum all right?' Jeffia asked. The next moment he wished he hadn't spoken. His father ignored Jeffia. He thought about his wife, his eyes misty. It was a lurid world that both of them shared, but responded to in different ways. While she reacted by having nightmares and being ill and delicate, he reacted by being more energetic and all-consuming in his business life. She was too preoccupied with her fears, too disturbed by them. He was too preoccupied with succeeding more and more, that he had no room in his mind for such depressing thoughts.

'She'll be all right,' he said after a while. 'The trouble with your mother is she is too sensitive to her fears. Don't let that worry you. That seems a better pastime for women . . . Men simply smile at their unfounded fears.' He smiled wanly at Jeffia. 'Don't be late next time, you hear?'

Jeffia got up, nodded, and silently, slowly, as if walking under water, went out of the room.

The melancholy quality about the room settled on Jonan. He felt a curious sharp pang in his soul as he watched Jeffia leaving the room. He felt as if he were allowing the sacrifice of his only son. It was an ill-defined sensation. He felt that he had done his son a grave but indefinite injustice. He could not place how.

Then the nightmare his wife had told him about jumped vividly into his mind, as if to shock him with its directness. It seemed to be forcing itself into the very crevices of his soul. A nameless fear stole through him. He shuddered.

Jeffia was drifting into sleep when the sinister clanging of sacrificial bells and the mysterious chuckling of cowries reached him.

It was a long time since he had heard those sounds in the home. They were like a funeral dirge, charged and distorted in the mind by echoes of the supernatural.

His father was calling on the spirits of his ancestors and invoking his juju.

To Jeffia's troubled mind the ritual seemed like a last resort; as if whatever evils were lurking about in realms of pre-manifestation had to be countered.

The chuckle of cowries, the beatings on gongs, and the loud chanting of incantations continued, exaggerated by the silence.

But their hollow echoes reverberated through the house, solitary and pathetic in their futility.

Shadows

Chapter Eleven

That night Cynthia had to carry her father to his bed, change his drink-sodden clothes, and clean up his vomit which gave off a stench that would have embarrassed a pig.

What happened that night was an unusual development in her father's drinking habits. He did drink a lot. Though she had tried her utmost to make him stop, he continued in one form or another. But he had never gone to such an extreme. She had often tried to stop him by restricting the money that reached him. But he got hold of money somehow. Besides, his other drinking mates always seemed to provide.

She wondered what made him do it. Did his drinking mates come around? She didn't think they would. She had warned them off, had even threatened to call the police if she saw them around again.

Could it be those stupid boys? There were a group of boys that liked taunting him. They called him names like 'crazy man' 'drinker man' and these often made him sink deeper into his gloom.

'Ah . . . ah . . . I'm a . . . big . . . yeah . . .' he muttered.

She looked down at him. His face was unevenly complexioned, unshaven, and his mouth was still opening and closing as though he were still drinking. He looked harassed. His forehead was like wrinkled khaki, deeply creased and unwashed. His face, bloated and blotched, had an unclean look. With his head resting on the shining white pillow, he looked the perfect picture of a man who had just been released from prison, too tired, too angry and too harassed to do anything else but sleep.

Poor man, she thought. She re-arranged the cover over his upper body. Even in his sleep he still looked haunted.

He turned over again, and muttered something about being 'big'.

He seemed to have nothing to live for and was plunging drunkenly down a miserable drain of life. Cynthia had done everything she could to help him find himself again, but he seemed relentless in his self-destruction.

Occasionally he would sink into such moods of utter gloom that his wrinkled brown-paper face would resemble a death's head in its dry boniness. Other times he would suddenly fly into a rage. It wouldn't be at anything in particular. Just an empty rage. He would let out a vehement stream of abuse at the social system. Other times he would sit down at the front of the house and broodingly watch the life about him, stewing in bitterness.

People had long been avoiding him. Old friends seldom came. Relatives cut him off completely. Neighbours regarded him with dark contempt. Nobody could, they concluded, go so deeply into themselves without touching veins of insanity.

He was plagued by a bad conscience. He blamed himself for all the misfortunes that had befallen him and his family. It was his way of punishing himself.

He had been jailed for his alleged conspiracy in the embezzling of some funds and the theft of a thousand cans of paint. He served two years' imprisonment and two weeks after he came out his wife died of spinal meningitis. It was enough to make him insane.

For Cynthia it was traumatic. Though she and her mother did not get on well, Cynthia felt her loss deeply. But what shook her most was her father's imprisonment. It was months before she knew the truth. At first her mother had tried to deceive her by saying that her father had travelled. But the newspapers got hold of it. The first time she heard was when her classmates mocked her with the newspaper report in class. Life for her took its first major tumble. But she pulled through with a combination of will, an ability to forget the unpleasant, and her books. When she went to visit him, he was optimistic and would talk about all the things he would do when he came out. His sentence was reduced for good behaviour. But when he came out things took another plunge with his wife's death.

Cynthia saw herself through. In standing alone she learned to be self-reliant. She found a way to adjust to her life. All along, deep within her, she knew that somewhere in the future was a brighter day. It was this belief which made the painful days promises of things yet to come. It was this attitude that pulled her through. She read various books, mostly inspirational books, and found some passage or quotation that seemed to speak to her and console her. She stood by her father, taking care of the house, cooking, and bringing in money for food and rent.

She stood by his bedside now and the memories coursed through her.

Tomorrow was his day off. Let him sleep well, she thought. He had a job as a labourer in a construction company and usually worked the whole day. He had worked over the weekend. Maybe he's got his pay, she thought, maybe that's why he went drinking.

The room was small for both of them. But they had managed to squeeze in two beds. His was a four and half foot bed while hers was a three-footer. They rented a room and parlour. The landlord had long been trying to evict them. The walls were a peeled glossy blue and there were no windows. There was a small space at the foot of the beds were people could pass up and down the room. There was also a little shelf beside her father's bed. It contained many old books. Her father treasured them and wouldn't let her look at them. On the other side of the room, beside her bed, was a table on which stood some of her things; ear-rings, bracelets, hairpins, a couple of books and a little square mirror.

Her father turned over again. He faced upwards. His mouth made some noisy movements and he muttered to himself again, like a faulty record:

'Me ke? . . . ah . . . heh . . . I be . . . big . . . yeah . . .' he seemed to smile, then the harassed look came over his face again.

'It's not so bad, Dad,' she whispered. She tucked his feet back into the blanket and again arranged the cover cloth over him. She looked at his face. Those features on which age and pain seemed permanently stamped never failed to depress her. Before all this, he was a man to love. He used to be strong and funny, often at the same time. He used to love coming to her school and would say to her jokingly, 'That's going to be my wife, and that, and, yes, that lovely one,' pointing to the girls playing in the field. He was known as the funniest dad on visiting days. He used to poke fun at her by asking if her boyfriend was half as handsome as he was.

She stroked his greying hair fondly.

As she stood up, she accidentally hit the bookshelf behind her. A couple of books fell out. Some looked rusty, others had been eaten by cockroaches, some had a thick film of dust over them. She bent down and picked them up and arranged them back on the shelf.

'I wonder what's so secret about these books,' she said to herself. From one of the books she had picked up some pages fell out. They were torn-out pages of a diary. She looked through them, curious. They had her father's scratchy, hurried writing on them.

They read:

13 December

Today we were arrested. They say it was because 1000 cans of paint are missing which we were supposed to have taken to Acomo. My wife and a few friends arranged my bail. I know I am innocent but nobody believes me. Even my wife. Our Oga did it to me . . . I know : . . the man hates me . . . because I . . .

20 December

My lawyer advised me to plead guilty. He say I have no chance against our Oga. I am in great confusion. My daughter. How can I tell her the truth that she will believe me, eh? Life has changed for me.

10 February

Today I was sentenced. The judge gave me two years. Okwe has done his worst. My wife cried in the courtroom. People were shaking their heads. Na so life be.

Cynthia stood petrified. A bleak sensation crawled up her spine. Her legs felt suddenly weak, her hands trembled. She made for the stool in between her bed and her father's, and sat heavily on it.

All along she had resigned herself to her father's crime. It was not even called a crime. An unfortunate fast deal. Everybody in business did it. The unlucky ones were caught. This is what her mother drummed into her. But she had long learned to live with the consequences. She hadn't attempted to blame her father as her mother had done. She only took it as one of those inexplicable impulses that occurred in a person's life. She had found a way to walk her own emotional tightrope, and to live with her mother who dwelt constantly with morbid thoughts. She found a way to steel herself against the silent accusations from society. All this without being too bitter. It had happened, nobody could do anything about it. That was her attitude.

Now this was a different story, with a heart-wrenching twist.

Had her father been framed?

Involuntarily tears streamed down her face. The flow filled her with a bitter relief. Two years had gone by since his release. They had long moved from their old home. The wounds had healed on the surface, but the memories lived on in their minds. Bitterness festered in his bizarre actions.

Her father had been innocent all along!

The thought staggered her. *How would Mummy feel if she knew this?* she thought wildly.

She let the tears flow freely, and she let all she had been enduring, all she had been suppressing, flow with them.

Her father turned and grunted on the bed. The harassed look on his face had now turned into a sleeping leer. There was the wetness of spittle on the pillow where his face had rested.

Cynthia soon stopped crying. She felt a weight lift almost mystically from her mind. It was as if metaphysical lead had been removed from somewhere inside her. She felt a lightness spread and engulf her being. She cried again, with joy. It was now more than ever that she realised how much she had been carrying, how much grief and tears she had steeled up within her. Now more than ever she could appreciate what her father was going through. The little hells he dwelled in. She felt with the lightness, a strong sense of injustice, an intense indignation that soon smothered into a feeling of futility. The futility, relief, and sadness, mingled inside her. She wept, smiling. Then her optimism, her courage, swept over the inner minglings like an over-riding chemical. She got herself under control and soon became calm.

It was all in the past now. It was all cinders now. Nothing could be done about what had happened. Nothing, she thought. Some day, somehow, he would have to come out of his hellish hibernation and face life again. Face life as he always had done, and partake in its challenges.

Who was that Okwe?

The name rankled in her memory but she could not place it.

Such people who press other people down are the world's real enemies. For them only a disgraceful and wicked end would be fitting. But she knew it was a hopeless wish. *Somehow it is people like that who sail on, crushing people, and weathering the storms to a comfortable old age. In the end they get eulogised as philanthropists and great men.*

Where is justice? Where is it?

Again she felt depressed. She put back the torn-out pages of the diary in the old book and, still thinking, she went to bed.

She slept easily, and dreamt about Jeffia. It was a pleasant dream.

2

She woke up feeling refreshed. The house was in a bad state. There were several empty bottles of beer all over the place. A combined odour of beer, Ogogoro, and vomit hung stubbornly over the room. Her father's bed was rough and untidy. It looked as if two wrestlers had fought in it. A number of fat black flies buzzed about the room. They had come in from outside through the open door. The peeling wall-paint only served to deepen the gloom.

She wondered why the home resisted all her attempts to make it moderately decent.

Where was her father this morning? Maybe out drinking already! The thought depressed her. She had her bath and dressed, taking a last look at the small mirror before going out. She was pretty and smart-looking. Her eyes were gentle, strong and frank. Her face was smooth and fresh. Her nose was slightly pointed and gave a sharpness to the general impression of her face. Her lips looked soft, small but determined. She never used make-up. Little of what she had gone through showed on her face. She always looked relaxed and fresh. She had matured along with the past. Her maturity had not made her hard and bitter, but mellow and self-reliant. It was hard to guess that she was just going on twenty.

Her father sat at the front of the house, beneath a guava tree. An unlit cigarette hung on his lips. He was staring at the whistling pine trees in the distance. There was a restrained sneer on his face.

'Morning, Papa. You are out early?'

'My daughter, good morning.' He looked over at her. She wore a smart skirt suit. It was a bright blue and looked well on her. She had combed her hair in Afro style. She had on black high-heeled shoes with a flowery design on the instep.

'You grow more beautiful every day. Who knows when they will come and take you from me?' He turned his gaze towards the whistling pine trees again. For a moment she thought he had forgotten her presence.

'Look at those trees,' he said, suddenly pointing in the distance. 'Each time I look at them they give me a funny feeling, it as if they are talking to me. The air is fresh this morning, did you know that, eh? Ah the mornings are spiritual, makes me feel alive . . .'

'But you are very alive, Papa . . .'

'And do you know what?' he asked as if he hadn't been interrupted. 'I feel your mother around. She is always here with me, singing those church songs she always liked . . . But beware . . .' he added suddenly, predictably. 'For man is wicked. Beware.'

'Not always . . .'

'Ah . . . your mother would have said that too. She learned too late.' He spoke sharply. 'Didn't I tell you your mother was killed by witchcraft? It's a pity you didn't see her body. Her blood was sucked dry and ugly marks were found all over her thin body . . . In this our country your best friend is yourself . . . Why did they kill your mother? Why? Tell me. Look at me now, eh? I was a whole supervisor, eh? They took me to jail for something I didn't do. And God is my witness. Man is wicked. Woe unto the poor man.'

As always when he talked like this, he got up from the chair and went back into the house. She saw tears on his cheeks. Somewhere in her throat was the sediment of the depressing feeling she had picked up from him.

The sun shone cheerfully through the branches and leaves of the guava tree. Overhead the carefree birds were chirping and flying from one tree to the other, wetting their beaks with the morning dew. They seemed happy. She looked at the whistling pine trees in the distance. They were like a fuzzy postcard picture. Through their branches snatches of the sky beyond could be glimpsed. The wind blew softly and the air smelt fine. A lizard scampered down the trunk of the guava tree and disappeared behind the clump of bushes.

The previous night's revelation came back into her. The lightness spread again within her. The warm glow of the promise of a new life danced in her heart.

She felt light-headed for a reason she could not analyse. Walking gaily, ignoring the taunts of the boys in the house next to theirs, she went back to the house to start cleaning up.

3

Leaving for work late on a Monday morning was always an ordeal. The bus-stop was usually full of people and the rush for buses was maddening and frustrating. Everywhere was a bedlam of cacophonic clashes: the endless hooting of impatient drivers, the conductors bellowing 'Eko, Tinubu, Eko, Tinubu!', the revving of cars that had faulty carburettors and had to be pushed, the blaring of records from the record shops, the screaming and shouting of passengers, the haggling and cursing of market women.

At the bus-stop the rush was so frenetic that some people resorted to climbing into the Kunbi buses through the boots.

Women with children on their backs were demanding easy entry. Men with thunderous looks flexed their muscles among each other as to who would get in the bus. Drivers watched with twisted glee. Some drivers would suddenly move while the rush was raging on, causing some people to fall and be injured. There was a girl wearing jeans and fashionable high-heeled shoes among them. She tried to imitate a smart man and jumped into a moving bus. She was flung off and left sprawling ungracefully on the muddy floor. People around laughed loudly. Cynthia shook her head.

An empty bus going her way came but before she could get there people had surged round it like insane bees swarming a honeycomb.

Just then she noticed a man who was pretending to be struggling to get on the bus, but was really fishing a wallet from another man's back pocket. In a moment he was off. The victim shouted after him. The shout gathered momentum, and soon the bus-stop was filled with wild cries of 'Oleh O, Oleh, O!' The next moment the pickpocket was caught and beaten to an unrecognisable pulp. It was crude justice. For many it was 'free cinema', a moment of diversion from the arduous business of catching a bus. But for Cynthia, who was waving a cab, it was a terrifying glimpse of the hunger within.

When she got to the office, she was told that her boss wanted to see her as soon as she came in.

'There's a policeman there with Baldhead,' Cecilia told her discreetly. She was surprised. The last time a policeman came to the clinic was when 'Baldhead' was being charged with siphoning drugs from the hospital (where he really worked) to nourish his clinic. Not to mention the uncountable times he had referred patients to his clinic for 'out of store' drugs. Not to mention also the expensive equipment and instruments he readily helped himself to.

'One of those frustrated, stagnating hospital doctors reported me,' he had told them later. But he had got out of the case. He knew his way through the labyrinthine but effective 'back doors'. Experience had proved them to be much more reliable doors.

She went straight to her boss's office, and knocked.

'Come in.'

She opened the door, and went into the office. It was fairly large. The walls were high and typically blue. A few gloomy paintings of human anatomy hung on the walls. There was a standing fan next to the doctor's table. It made a scraping sound each time it did a complete turn. On the right was a diagnosis bed. Hanging on the wall above the doctor were framed documents of dubious import and a pair of stethoscopes. Scattered on the floor were bottles of different shapes and sizes. And pervading the room was the combined smell of different medical odours.

The doctor sat behind his table. He almost seemed lost behind it. For it was covered with scattered pills, medical cards, ballpoints, injection tubes, business cards and files.

'It makes people think you are a busy man,' he used to tell them. He was a tall, stooping, fast-balding man. He was in his mid-forties. Behind his glasses his eyes had a know-all glint, but without his glasses he blinked constantly and lost confidence. His face had numerous scarifications, giving him an uneven, sandpapery complexion. People called him a businessman, and he ran his clinic as a strict business. He wore a stained suit, and his collar looked dirty. He had an expression on his face which, though it was grave, made one want to laugh. Those glasses did it. They hung on his nose, and hung on his ears. They seemed too big for him.

'Ah, good morning, Cynthia. Come in and meet Sergeant Okwadia of the police force. He's here in connection with a case of assault turned murder. Mr Okwadia, meet Cynthia, the nurse who brought the man in.'

Cynthia looked at him, then at the policeman who had turned round in his seat. She was momentarily confused. The policeman studied her closely. He was a black, burly man with a little goatee. His eyes were large, menacing, unblinking. He twirled his beard in a peculiar manner, as if it aided his thinking. But his lips had a stubborn set to them.

'Nice to meet you, Miss Cynthia. I'll come straight to the point. The man you brought in on Saturday night is dead. He died early this morning without regaining consciousness.

This is murder, you hear. Now what do you know about what happened on Saturday night, or Sunday morning if you like?'

All this time she sat stiff and silent with bewilderment. She looked at the doctor as if pleading him to help her out of the embarrassing situation. The doctor adjusted his glasses and smiled thinly the way he would to a patient whom he believed had little hope of recovery.

'Let me make it easier for you. You received a telephone call about an injured person being brought down here. A few hours later you wander off into the night and came back in some strange man's car carrying an injured man who died this morning. All I want is for you to tell me what you saw.'

She began narrating the event. The policeman whose face had been inscrutable, listened attentively, and took notes. He stopped her and asked her questions now and again.

'What about the man who helped bring him in?'

'He was just passing by. He wouldn't know anything about it. He even looked afraid when . . .'

'That's all right. We cannot afford to leave anything out.'

'I don't know anything about him . . . but he might be coming here today to check on the man.'

'I see . . .' He had barely said that when one of his 'boys' barged into the room breathlessly. He was holding something in his hands.

'Oga sa, Oga sa.' He stamped an awkward salute. 'I see this letter pick for near the place, sa,' he said excitedly, and handed the letter to the officer.

It was a squeezed and torn-up letter. It was addressed to a Sainu Shibi asking him to come for an interview as a driver. The address was at Ajegunle. The officer wrinkled his nose in contempt.

'And this too, sa.' It was the patch of a shirt pocket. The officer nodded his head. It was beginning to make sense.

'Smaila.'

'Sa!'

'Smaila, take two of the boys, rush down to this address and arrest this man. If he refuse to come, take him by force, you hear? Quick!!'

'Yes, sa!' The subordinate stamped another awkward salute which reverberated through the table and chairs. He looked more than anything like a parody of a policeman. He hurried out of the office.

The doctor, who had been silent, removed his glasses and cleaned them. He held them up to see how clean they were, then deciding they were clean enough put them back on.

Cynthia played with her fingers.

'Excuse me, let me go and give instructions to my remaining boys,' the policeman said standing up. 'And don't you go away. There are still some things I want to ask you,' he said to Cynthia. He went out.

'Goat! That man wants money,' the doctor said as soon as the door closed behind him. 'You can't miss the restlessness. Ah, these people, eh.'

Cynthia was silent.

'Why did you go out to the main road alone, on Saturday night?'

'Well, sir. That's a question I have been asking myself. I wanted to be alone, by myself, that's all.'

'Emmm. I see,' the doctor said. He removed his glasses again, and proceeded to polish them. He stared at her, smiling. But he appeared to be staring at a finger close to his face. He looked comic, but it didn't make her want to laugh.

'You are quite a remarkable girl.'

'How did the police get to know?'

'Oh, I came in this morning and found the man dead. There were numerous wounds over his body, the man could have died early this morning, I think. I asked Cecilia, she said she didn't know exactly what happened. So I rang the police. Me ke, I don't want an unaccountable dead man on my hands. Later Jane came in and told us you brought the man in somebody's car . . .'

'Where's Jane now?'

'Gone to the Ajegunle hospital.'

'What could all this mean? I don't know anything . . .'

'Don't worry. Just say what you know. That's all.'

They fell silent. The doctor scratched his pate. He reached over and increased the speed of the fan and put his head directly in front of it to get some cool air. The fan made its scraping noise from time to time.

'By the way, Cynthia, I wanted to invite you to a party we are . . .'

'No thank you, sir.'

The doctor removed his glasses, and began polishing them again.

'Why don't you wait and hear what I have got to say, eh?'

Cynthia was just about to reply when someone knocked on the door.

'Come in, please,' the doctor called in his most professional voice.

Jeffia stepped into the office. He wore a cream-coloured safari jacket.

Cynthia smiled when she saw him.

'Good morning, sir. Morning, Cynthia. A lady outside said you were in here. How is your dad?'

'Oh, he's all right. He's fine,' she replied a little hurriedly. 'Eh . . . meet my boss, Dr Kpele, he owns the clinic. Sir, meet the young man who brought in the injured man.'

The doctor looked from one to the other. Emotions struggled on his face.

'I see,' he said coldly. To his consternation Jeffia had pulled up a chair, muttered, 'May I sit down please,' and sat himself down, without awaiting consent.

'I didn't ask you to sit down, did I?' the doctor said suddenly, banging on the table. Both Jeffia and Cynthia were surprised. They looked at each other. Jeffia jumped up from the chair as though it had burned him.

'I'm sorry,' the doctor soon said. 'You young people have a way of getting on one's nerves sometimes.'

'It's all right,' Jeffia said, standing.

'You can sit down. Are you the young man the policeman wants to see? Just wait here, I'll be back in a moment,' he said quickly, and hurried outside. There was a tangible silence in the office when he left. Jeffia spoke first.

'What's that about a policeman?'

'The man we brought in the other night is dead. They say it's murder.'

Jeffia stared outside the window. Every day was bringing more and more bizarre experiences. Outside the window, in the courtyard, a few children were innocently playing 'catch me, catch me' around a clump of hibiscus flowers. What his mother had told him that morning came to his mind.

'I'm afraid for you, son. I've never felt like this before. Look at what happened to poor Ode. Look at what your father was saying in the night. I'm afraid for all of us.'

She looked at him, distantly, as though she were not going to see him again.

'Little flowers in the shadows: that's what we all are. Nobody knows what the larger shadows will do to the flowers: nobody knows what the flowers will become.'

All this was spoken with an oracular intensity, in a voice of unfamiliar hoarseness.

'The shadows, Jeff, the shadows. They are so many, and so strange.'

'Do you know the man?'

Cynthia's voice was a strand to the present. He turned to her. In her eyes he beheld a tenderness that he hadn't seen anywhere but in his mother's. And in the tenderness there seemed a glimmer of understanding.

'You'll keep it to yourself?'

'Yes, if you want me to.'

'He's somebody I know. He used to work for my father.'

'Do you feel distressed?'

'Not really. I'm only confused. I can't keep up with the way things are happening. Too fast. I don't understand.'

'Don't try to. Things will order themselves out with time. I was like that once, but in my case it was the worst that happened . . .'

'My mother was right. We are not just flowers in the shadows. We are flowers in the storm.'

'Your mother must be a poet.'

'She's sensitive,' he said, staring out of the window. Birds were flying around in the sky. The children still played their 'catch me, catch me'. He thought about Ode, whom he'd dreamt of last night. Then he thought about what his father said, and about the clanking of cowries at night. He remembered the nest of birds that somebody stoned down and the way the birds flew around wildly.

'Mum is right,' he said finally. Cynthia looked at him, frowned and said:

'Dad is wrong.'

4

The door opened abruptly, and the policeman walked in. There was a satisfied gleam in his eyes, like a child who had solved one part of a jigsaw puzzle.

'So you are the good Samaritan who helped carry the man here, eh?'

'I helped the nurse and a certain injured man here, yes.'

The policeman eyed him.

'Where were you coming from at that time?'

'A friend's party.'

'What friend?'

'A former classmate.'

'What's his name?'

'Simon Olaide.'

'Where does he live?'

'No 11 Tokobo Crescent.'

'And what time was it?'

'Was what?'

'The time you came across the nurse and a "certain injured man"?'

'I can't be too sure. Somewhere between eleven and twelve o'clock.'

'Look here, young man, I have dealt with people a hundred times tougher than your wretched self, you hear? And I have cracked them down. Now don't try and be smart with me, you get it! Don't try and bring that nonsense you read in novels to me, you get it?' The policeman stared hard at him.

'I don't know what you are talking about.'

The policeman made a conscious effort to be patient.

'Do you know the man?'

'What do you mean "the man"?'

'Have you had a look at the "certain injured man" you helped here?'

'No. Not properly. There wasn't enough light to see him with in the streets.'

'What about in the patient's room?'

'He was too injured, too wounded, to have a good look at. From the little I saw of him, however, I don't think I know him.'

'He doesn't remind you of anyone?'

'No.'

'You are not being very helpful. I can be hard on you if I have to, you know. It only pays in the long run to swing our way.'

'It's certainly not my fault if what I know can't help you.' *Besides,* Jeffia thought to himself, *it didn't pay me to swing your colleague's way yesterday. I paid him instead.*

'I see,' the policeman was saying, twirling his goatee in his peculiar fashion. 'I have no choice but to take you both to the police station where you will have to make a statement.'

'Would you mind if I make a phone call, first?'

'Who to?'

'To my father. At least to let him know where I am.'

'Okay, but don't be longer than two minutes.'

The policeman and Cynthia went out of the office. Jeffia dialled his father's office.

'Hello.'

'Is that Afioso Paints?'

'Yes, who do you want?'

'Mr Okwe, please – it's urgent.'

'Is that Jeffia?'

'Yes, Maria. Please put me through to Dad.'

'Oh Jeff dear, where are you calling from?'

'Look, Maria, please save this for later. Get me my father.'

'You sound worried.'

'Now you know. Get him, Maria!'

'Okay.' She put him through.

'Jeff?' his father said. 'I'm in the middle of an important discussion. Can't this wait?'

Just like Dad, Jeffia thought.

'No, it can't wait, Dad. I'm being taken to the police station.'
He heard his father catch his breath.

'Police station? What for?'

'I can't explain over the phone. It's about Gbenga.'

'Which Gbenga?'

'Daddy! The one that used to work for you. He's dead. I
was around at the time. I helped to take him to the clinic.
I'm being questioned . . .'

There was a silence over the phone. Then after what
seemed ages, his father spoke.

'Jeff, I hope you know what you are talking about. Why
didn't you tell me this at the time?'

'You shouted at me.'

There was another brief silence.

'Which police station are they taking you?'

'I don't know for sure. But I think it might be Funtu.'

'Okay, I'll find out and be there. Say nothing until your
lawyer comes. That's what you should say, right? "I will say
nothing until my lawyer comes." '

'All right, Dad,' he said, and dropped the phone. Just then
the policeman came back in.

'What the hell! Do you know you've been over five minutes
on that phone?'

'You know how these telephones are. Besides,' he added,
smiling, 'I'll say nothing until my lawyer comes.'

The expression that appeared on the policeman's face was
indescribable.

Jeffia smiled sweetly.

Chapter Twelve

Jonan was having problems of his own.

To say he was in the middle of a discussion was an understatement. He was in an unusual meeting with top members of staff and the board of directors. They were discussing the grave internal and external threats facing the company's existence.

The company's previously suppressed trade union had reorganised itself and was now calling for an immediate strike by the workers. They demanded an unconditional forty per cent wage increase. They accused the management of being unfair to them in not giving workers any substantial increment over the past three years. They pointed to their colleagues at Zaki Paints, where the workers had better wages and working conditions. Large numbers of skilled workers had resigned to join other paint companies.

This was just one aspect of Jonan's problems with the company. Profits were falling badly, a minority of the board of directors were calling for his resignation, and as if all this were not bad enough, a new paint company was attracting a great deal of attention, undermining Afioso's position.

These elements had not come to Jonan at once. They emerged bit by bit, imperceptibly. The factors had always been there but it was his absence that had given these elements the chance to surface.

Jonan was iron-handed with his workers and had kept a strict rein over annual increments. He believed that workers were only entitled to increments if profits had topped themselves, and those who didn't like it could well leave the company. There were always skilled people around who would take on their jobs at less than the original wages. Besides he had a way of keeping a hold over the union officials that made them reluctant to pursue their demands further. That was what Gbenga used to be there for. He would dig out something about them, or implicate them in some way. They would gratefully keep quiet afterwards.

But now things were different. All the elements were now manifest. The reshuffle that had taken place in his absence baffled him. He was not familiar with those in the new positions. He couldn't trust them. He always liked to deal with people he knew.

It appeared as if there was a deliberate attempt to confuse him from the inside.

There were also recent suggestions in the air that there should be a merger with either Geruger or Zaki. These two companies had been increasingly eating into Afioso's market. Besides, the public seemed to prefer their products to Afioso's.

After all, people said, Afioso is the only paint company with a black man as managing director.

'Wetin you expect? Black man too make economy!'

Jonan had felt the tension of these mounting pressures: the conflicts within, the changes of attitude from without.

'Enemies are at work!' he often muttered when confronted with yet another problem. He had thought about these things seriously. He had begun making arrangements. But more than anything else he wanted to find out what was at the bottom of the tremors.

It was becoming disturbingly clear to him that his power and hold over the company were waning. And even more troubling was the realisation that he had little control over the things that were happening in his personal life. The telephone call. His wife's behaviour. Jeffia's rebellion. His heart attack.

He had thought about all these things with a feeling of growing helplessness which he didn't want to admit. He needed more faith. He needed some kind of external help and guidance. He needed more power. In times like this it was only too natural for him to return to his juju corner. In his juju he hoped to find renewed vigour.

Before he left home that morning, he went through the rites.

'O manaka ko . . . manaka ko,' he chanted loudly.

'May the business flourish. May all paint buyers turn to Afioso, this is the paint of our land. My name shall be the greatest on Wilm Street, people shall see me and bow, the

Flowers and Shadows

sound of Okwe shall make people stand straight, my enemies shall quaver and collapse.'

He paused to take a solemn step forward, turned his neck round, made dramatic motions with his hands and continued.

'May my son find his feet in life and be strong like me. Let him not be weak and lazy and too full of books. My enemies shall not near him and his feet shall not walk the crooked or dark road. Let my wife produce more children for me, eh, ah . . . all those planning evil against me, all of them, let them perish the way this chicken will die. They will always crawl to me for food and I will always shit on the floor for them to eat . . . let only peace and health and good things come my way. All I have not said, add for me . . . O – manaka ko . . . O – manaka ko.'

He brought his hands down, and licked the smear of blood and herbs and white chalk that were pasted on the floor in front of him. He muttered some more incantations, shook his head, and spat towards the idol that stood before him. He bent and repeated the motions. Then he proceeded to behead the chicken. He poured its blood over the three carvings, muttering and chanting. When he had finished he poured some powdery, smelly substance over the blood. He took three solemn steps backwards, did a dramatic dance movement, closed his eyes and soon came back to where he had begun. He blew out the candle that stood on the images' heads.

'As I said so it will be. O – manaka ko!'

Just then his wife opened the door. Even her capacity for quickly adjusting did not prepare her for what she saw or what it implied.

On the table was a carved image holding a small cutlass in one hand and a ten-Naira note in the other. Its over-large foot rested on the carved image of a beaten man's head. On the wall beside it hung the heads of two chickens. Native drink, native chalk, and other potions had been spilled on them. Their eyeless sockets made them look ugly and strangely evil. Figures had been drawn on the floor with chalk. The combined smell of everything nearly made her vomit. Her husband was bent double, sweating, a white cloth round his waist, his upper part bare.

Her head throbbed. What she saw made her dizzy. There was something about the setting that reminded her of the past. Harrowingly she could not place it.

She opened her mouth for a moment, dumb, terrified. Then she released a high-pitched scream. He was startled. Then surprised. Then afraid. He caught her before she fell.

'Why all this, Jonan, eh? Why?' she cried.

'It's that urgent, dear. It is . . . But all will be well . . . all will be well,' was all he could say.

'Where is all this leading to, eh?' she whispered.

He didn't say anything. He simply stared at the blood flowing out from the chicken's neck.

2

As he went to the office, he thought about the phone call. It bothered him. His mind wandered to Juliet. Could she be the woman in the photograph? Or was it all just a bluff? How could anybody get to take a photograph like that anyway? But he wasn't sure.

Things happen strangely in this country nowadays, he thought. *In catching up with the Western world in such activities, we are becoming unpredictable.* He remembered the newspaper report of a bank manager who was killed in his bathroom. There had been no signs of forceful entry, yet the man had been murdered. Just like that. The police knew no more than they did when the investigations started. *Terrible*, he thought.

It had to be Juliet in the photograph, if anyone.

He knew how to get hold of her. Jeco, the manager of the Sky Blue Hotel, would know.

The driver was humming 'Sweet Mother' and shaking his head while driving. They soon came to a go-slow. There had been an accident in front. A Volkswagen owner had hit a Citroën. Furious exchanges took place. The road was jammed. Motorcyclists, taking extra delight at the jam, meandered through it all. Bicyclists waved, carried their bikes, waded through and continued.

'Sometimes, foot-ron better pass car sef,' a frustrated driver said.

It was hot. The sun had risen on the horizon. The land was drenched in its golden, scorching shimmer. Motorists looked frustrated. The furious exchange continued between the owners of the smashed cars. The Citroën owner shouted something about his car costing twenty times more than the Volkswagen.

' . . . specially imported . . .' the man said, taking off his coat and tie.

'Specially imported but see how e spoil when e jam small,' Jonan's driver was saying.

'Shut up. I'm trying to think. Put on the air-conditioner, and wind up the windows.'

'Yes, sa!'

Jonan thought about Sowho. *What does Sowho want to come and see me for anyway? What does the fool want?*

And then there was his wife. She had looked so shocked when she came into his room. *Why didn't she even knock before coming in, eh? Women sef!* She had been gloomy at the breakfast table. There had been silence throughout. *It must have been hard on her. All these years.*

Things would work out, they must!

He brought out his pipe and lit it.

A policeman had come to the scene of the accident. Soon, also, the soldiers arrived. They had whips. They looked fierce.

'Oya, you move!'

'Yes, now you . . . you, yes, I'm talking to you, this fool, you move . . .'

'Where are you going? Wait there before I cane you!'

They shouted at the motorists. The jam eased up slowly. They flogged the bonnets of cars and screamed at drivers as though they were partially deaf. One of them pounced on a motorcyclist who was without a crash helmet. The soldier lashed him three times on the back. The rider wobbled and tried to speed off. The soldier grabbed the brake and stopped the machine.

'Bloody fool!! Get down, you idiot! Bastard! You want to kill me, eh?'

Other soldiers had gathered there. The defaulting motor-cyclist was beaten and reduced to a whimpering mass of respectability. His face was soon swollen, his neck where the Koboko had landed was bleeding and rope-like.

'Get down, you goat!'

He got down, and was told to frog-jump. He was a man of about forty. He had on a black suit and a tie. He looked absurd frog-jumping at the corner of the road, beside his fallen motorcycle. Jonan shook his head.

'Oga sa, this people wicked – O!' his driver said.

Jonan said nothing. The go-slow, as if by magic, eased up, became a smooth flow. They drove past the frog-jumping man. He was crying. The soldiers shouted at him:

'Where your helmet, eh? Where am?'

'Fuckin' man. Where you licence?'

'Where your insure?'

A kick was aimed at his buttocks. He had stopped frog-jumping. The kick landed, and he fell flat on his face. Jonan's driver laughed. It was funny but wicked. The scene passed. They drove on hurriedly.

'Na only God fit punish those people. Only God who dey for up. Na only him fit punish them,' his driver said.

They were now descending the bridge. The sea was an expansive wave-laden surface of blue and grey shimmerings. There were ships sailing in the distance.

Jonan looked out of his window at some children playing football. They shouted and sang and called happily, unmindful of the sun. One side scored. They sang a famous football song. They jumped. They seemed so joyful in their game, so free from the problems and fears of life. They laughed and played, with sand all over their bodies.

He watched them nostalgically. He envied their ease. His own childhood had been rough. He had worked endlessly in the farms with his father. In the mornings he had to trek to the only school in the district that was three miles away. His whole life seemed to him like that. No sweetness anywhere.

They were caught up in another go-slow. Kunbi bus drivers rode along the pavements.

'Don't follow them – O,' he told his driver.

'Ah! No, sa.' The driver began whistling 'Sweet Mother' again.

'Look, why don't you stop whistling that stupid song, eh? I'm trying to think.'

'Yes, sa. Sorry, sa.'

Jonan puffed at his pipe. The car moved by inches. The sun was shining outside. A figure crossed his window, then came back. The shadow intruded on his thoughts. It was the figure of a beggar. Jonan looked at him with disgust.

The man was wiry. His face was the colour of sand, but mottled and patched with sores, scabs, pimples and freckles. He looked sick and ugly, and unkempt. He was a travesty of a man. It was as if all the woe of mankind had found expression in him. He looked like a thinly fleshed skeleton. His teeth gave the impression that a slight puff of the wind would blow them out. He carried a dirty plate and in the other hand was a piece of rag with which he began to clean Jonan's Mercedes.

'Amazu!' Jonan shrieked at his driver. 'That filthy beggar is staining my car with his diseased rag. Get him off!'

The beggar only shook his plate, in which a few coins jangled. On his face was a woebegone expression. It was as if he were accusing Jonan, saying with his face, 'Look what you done!'

'Oga sa. If I push am he could die – O!'

'Find ten kobo to give him. Let him not spread his disease on my car.'

'Yes, sa. But, sa, I no have ten kobo, only one kobo and one Naira.'

'Give him the one kobo.'

The driver tossed the one kobo coin to the beggar. It hit the plate, then fell on the floor. The beggar looked at it and made no attempt to pick it up. He went on cleaning Jonan's Mercedes with his rag. The woebegone expression had deepened. He looked as if he was quite prepared to die on Jonan's Mercedes.

'Okay, give him the one Naira. I will give it back to you in the office.'

'Yes, sa!'

Amazu let down the window nearest the beggar, put the money in the plate, and quickly withdrew his hands. The beggar looked at the note. The woebegone expression lifted a little from his face. He went to the next car and used the same method.

'Na them dey pray for this go-slow. Beggars get choice now, sa.'

'It's blackmail,' Jonan said more to himself than to the driver. 'The whole system sustains this senseless social blackmail.'

His face was screwed up. After another ten minutes, the go-slow eased up. The children were still playing their game. The clouds floated artistically in the bright sky. The wind blew sand about, rustled the leaves, and made the trees sway. The sea rocked. The ships sailed in the distance.

But all the way to the office, Jonan's face was still screwed up.

3

He walked down the corridors of Afioso. He passed a group of junior staff. They stood idle and silent. This was unusual. Whenever they saw him coming they would look smart and busy. They would greet him officiously. But now they didn't seem to see him. The receptionist said an unsmiling good morning.

He climbed up the stairs two at a time.

He reached his office, but decided to go in through the back door. He pressed the intercom for his secretary. She came in. She was slim and tall, always wore gowns, and had a flair for horn-rimmed glasses.

'Morning, sir.'

'Morning, Tola. Can I have a cup of coffee to start the day? And send in all my correspondence.'

She hesitated a bit.

'Yes, sir.'

'And by the way, have Chief Hans and Jeccaro come in yet?'

'I'm not sure, but I'll find out.'

'Do that and tell them there will be a meeting at two o'clock.'

'Yes, sir.' She went out, closing the door behind her as if it were made of eggshells.

There was a pile of documents on one side of his table. He picked up a piece of paper from the pile. It was a cash voucher for a senior staff member who had returned from a tour of Kano state. Angrily he flung all the documents on the floor. They scattered on the expensive carpet. There were other documents on the 'Urgent' tray. There were seven bill reminders, all of them months behind time. He frowned, then put them back in the tray. One of his rules was never to start a day with uncertainties.

He stared in front of him, thinking seriously. From time to time his eyes would stray to the portrait which hung on the wall beside a picture of the Head of State.

His table was neat and orderly. There were no unnecessary papers and documents. Everything was in its place. He picked up a ballpoint and made some notes in a notebook. He then opened his letters and read through them. They were the same old business letters. He didn't go through the pile that had been arranged there before he came in. He went on thinking, staring at his portrait. He got up, increased the air-conditioner, then came back to his seat.

The door opened. His secretary came in with a tray on which was a cup of coffee, milk, and sugar. She put them down on the table. She looked at Jonan from over the rims of her glasses and caught her breath when she saw the documents cluttering the floor.

'But sir, those are all expense sheets for senior staff. Many of them are outside waiting for you to sign them.'

She noticed the scowl on his face. 'Eh, sorry, sir.'

'Tola, they are not important. They can wait.'

'Yes, sir.'

When she had gone, he sipped his coffee, slowly. He always liked the smell of his morning coffee. It gingered him. While he drank, he picked up one of the vouchers.

Thieves, he thought. *These expenses are absurd!* He threw it back on the floor. *Thieves!*

The office had begun to cool. The windows, draped in velvet, gave the office a rich, comforting feel. The office was a calm centre. Outside, the world raged with all of its mania. He liked going to the window and looking down at Wilm Street. People walked the streets up and down like ants. In the distance he would see the long line of a go-slow. Or he would see an accident or people fighting. He would watch them briefly, shake his head, come back into his office, and continue whatever he was doing.

He thought about the bills he had seen in the 'Urgent' tray. He put it out of his mind. A time for everything.

He buzzed the Marketing Manager.

'Okporu.'

'Yes, speaking.'

'Jonan here . . .'

'Oh morning, Mr Okwe.'

'Morning, Okporu. Look, can I have those reports, surveys, expenses and the other things I asked you to compile for me last week? Please bring them along with the budget procedures.'

There was a brief silence.

'They will be up in a minute, sir.'

There was another silence.

'Okporu, are you in the coup too?'

'What? I don't know what you are talking about, sir.'

'Fine. Have you read the papers already?'

'Well . . .'

'Somebody's given a hint to the press that there might be a change of hands at Afioso. Anyway, forget it.'

He replaced the phone. He stared at the wall in front of him. But he wasn't seeing anything. His thoughts jumped across the open stage. The expansiveness of his office, which usually filled him with a certain relaxed feeling, now only seemed to depress him. The space seemed too big for him, it seemed to elude and confound him.

For the first time he was beginning to sense he had lost touch with that basic feel and pulse of his organisation.

He got up and made for the drinks cupboard he had at the back of the office. Midway, he changed his mind.

'O – manaka ko . . . O – manaka ko!' he muttered to himself. He soon felt uplifted.

A few minutes later the messenger came in with a bundle of documents. He was a short, fair Ibo man, eczema spreading on his face, his khaki uniform dangling on him as though he had lost weight working for the company.

'Morning, sa. Oga manager say I should bring this to you, sa.'

Jonan indicated that he should put them on the table.

'All right, sa.' The messenger turned to go. The office, its expansiveness, its richness, frightened him.

'Wait!'

'Yes sa?'

'What's happening, eh, Chukwa?'

The messenger's face became dull. He was a man aged about fifty-five. He looked embarrassed. He fiddled with his fingers.

'Them dey on strike, sa.'

'Eh heh. All of you?'

'No, sa. Only them, sa. Me I no dey, sa.'

'When did it start?'

'Them never start complete yet. They say them want to talk first. But they call am half-strike.'

'Okay, you can go. No, wait. How much do you earn now?'

'Sixty-nine Naira, sa.'

'How big is your family?'

'I get two wife and three pickin, sa.'

'How do you feed your family with that?'

'Overtime, sa. And my wife them they work small, small work, and my pickin them dey sell some things, sa.'

'Can you feed your family till you get to pay day?'

'No, sa! No, sa!' the messenger burst out suddenly. 'I beg sa no sack me – O! I no dey for the strike!' He begged, prostrating.

'It's all right,' Jonan said, smiling thinly. 'All I want is this: I want you to tell me everything your union is planning, eh? Keep me informed, you hear?'

'Yes, sa. I go tell you everything, sa.' The messenger rubbed his hands together.

Jonan brought out his wallet. It was thick and heavy with rolls of money. He peeled out two one-Naira notes. The messenger's eyes shone. Jonan gave him the two new notes.

'Thank you, sa, thank you, sa. Na God go bless you, sa.' He left the office. Jonan smiled to himself. The secretary soon buzzed to say that Chief Hans and Jeccaro were in their office but that they were busy.

'Good. Tell them there will be an important meeting this afternoon.'

'All right, sir.'

Jonan looked through the sales summary and the other documents. He couldn't believe his eyes. The figures were fantastic.

Sales figures for last year were 2 126 000 gallons of paint as against 2 820 000 in two years previously. Two depots were burnt down. Eleven per cent decrease in estimated sales of gloss. Thirteen per cent in emulsion. A staff shortage on the technical side. Too few workers doing too many jobs. Result: poor quality, poor production, and less output.

My God, he muttered to himself. He looked furtively through the rest.

Factory machines broken down eight weeks throughout the year. Over 100 000 gallons lost. Shipments of parts not yet arrived. Alloprene and synthetic rubber still delayed at sea. Port congestion. Calcium carbide, perklone and sulphuric acid. No news of them yet. Demurrage costs skyrocketing. Production momentarily held up in five plants.

Sweat suddenly broke out on his forehead. He mopped his face with a handkerchief.

Profit margin: 26½ per cent short of the estimated 2.32 million Naira. Major customers: Carealla 10 000, Frenco 26 000, Okeozi 18 000. He stopped. What about Jael, Capro and Afgian? He jerked up the phone.

'Get me Mr Okporu.'

'Yes, sir.' There was a pause.

'Mr Okwe?'

'Look, no time for formalities. Can you come up here for a minute?'

'Okay.'

Jonan looked at the phone in his hands and slowly put it down. He stared at his portrait. It stared back at him with a blankness he was beginning to notice. It's in the mind, he said to himself.

There was a knock on the door. Mr Okporu walked in. He was bulky and tall, looked every step a boxer and walked with a left-sided stoop. He had a very distinctive Oxford accent that sounded a little odd when one realised it was an African speaking. He selected himself a chair.

'Look, Pete, what's happened to Jael, Capro, Afgian and the latest deal we clinched with CSS before I travelled?'

Jonan flung the sheets towards him.

'Mr Okwe, we lost them to our competitors . . .'

'Lost what? To which competitors?'

'Geruger got Jael and Capro, Muxor got Afgian and CSS. It all happened very fast . . .'

'Things seem to happen fast when I am away . . .'

'When I telephoned them they simply told me that they had changed their minds, they said they got the sales for much less.'

'How much less?'

'Ten per cent.'

'Ten! But we had a cut last year by three per cent, and then we were two and a half per cent lower than all of them?'

'But the sales were not big deal, they were all retail. Their ten per cent is on the first 30 000 gallons and increasing with one and a half per cent for every other 5 000 gallons to a limit of twenty per cent.'

Jonan didn't say anything. He scanned through the other documents.

Expenses. Staff travels: 37 000 Naira. Personal expenses: 12 453 Naira. Overtime: 11 354 Naira.

Mr Okporu coughed. Jonan ignored him, and asked for Mr Ofioseku, the office controller (so called when there was no other title to give him during his upgrading) over the phone. He soon came up. He knocked and came into the office. He was a tall, pot-bellied man with a pear-shaped head, and a rather blunt nose. He spoke clumsily, as if his tongue were too heavy for him, but he was a diligent and strict worker. He was one of the few managerial supervisors who had not been reshuffled.

'Now Keme,' Jonan said to him as soon as he came in, 'I'm going to be brief with you. I want all receipts, all overtime sheets, all registers for signing in and out, everything related to these group of papers. I want them by next tomorrow. I'm sure you know what to do.'

'All right, Mr Okwe.'

'Speak to the accountant about them. The figures for overtime and so on can't be true. Some of the workers are collecting what they don't work for. The accountant, yourself, and a few accounts supervisors should work on them. All doors for that kind of free money-making are going to be closed.'

'That's all right, Mr Okwe.'

'Good. Make a photocopy of these documents and send them back to me. And when you are going downstairs please tell the administration manager I want to see him now. Thanks, eh.'

The office controller went out of the office.

'Can I go now, Mr Okwe?' Mr Okporu asked. He was beginning to feel uneasy.

'Not just yet, Mr Okporu. Not just yet.'

The admin manager knocked and came into the office.

'Sit down, Tony,' Jonan said. There was a dynamic glint in his eyes. Things were moving. People would be made to quiver, made to go up and down the stairs. He would sit and give them orders, make them move. He felt a confidence in the motion of things now. He sat back in his swivelling chair, looking relaxed and quietly calculating. There was an expression of mild contempt on his face.

'What's the position of things at your end, Tony?'

'The union are . . .'

'I know,' Jonan said, cutting into his speech. Tony was a new reshuffle. He needed a bit of shaking up.

'I know all that, Tony. I'll tell you what I want: Let me know how much increment has been granted to what grade of workers, and when last. What percentage are they agitating for? How many people have resigned this year, how many have we taken on, and how many have we sacked? Speak to leaders of the trade union and let me know their grievances. Send it all in by next tomorrow morning. Thanks, Tony.'

'All right, sir.' Tony got up and went out. Jonan watched his stocky frame, his shuffling walk, till the door closed behind him. Jonan sighed. He suddenly felt tired. His heart seemed to be pounding a bit too fast. He thought he could hear it. He could feel slight pains and constrictions inside his chest. He made for his heart tablets and took two from the remaining four. He drank some water, and downed them. When he came back to his table, he eyed Mr Okporu.

'Now, Mr Okporu, whose ship are you on?'

'I still don't know what you are talking about.'

'Apparently not,' Jonan said as though he were talking to a child that had told a transparent lie. He picked up his Parker ball-pen and made meaningless notations on a piece of paper.

'There are certain things about your activities I know. You shouldn't fool around with me you know, really you shouldn't. I know you go around the junior staff and buy many gallons of paint in their names and sell them outside at a lower price than even our agents. I know many other things about you, you know. Really you surprise me. You really do.' Jonan looked up at him. It was as if he were talking to a student he had caught eating at the back of the class.

'Tell your newspaper friends to think before they publish next time. They could get themselves a libel suit they have no chance of fighting. Anyway be at the meeting this afternoon. My secretary will inform you of the time. That's all I have to say.'

Chapter Thirteen

The documents in the 'Urgent' tray were explosive. Two of them were reminders from the bank for loan repayments. The other two were bills for three air-conditioners and office furniture. He couldn't remember authorising any Local Purchase Orders for them. And the loans. What had stopped the reminders coming up to him?

Once more he called up the administrative manager, and the office controller. Before long the whole grim affair was exposed.

They had belatedly detected an L.P.O. stealing racket in the company. A group of people had been pinching blank L.P.O.s, typing requisitions on them, forging quite successfully the signatures of one of the company's three signatories, and then collecting the goods.

There was simply no telling how long this had been going on. The goods collected were never delivered to the company, and the company had been saddled with debts it hadn't incurred.

For the first time in years Jonan was in a tantrum. He shouted and screamed at the senior staff he found sleeping on duty, and who were supposed to offer an explanation for the costly oversight. He vented his anger on all those who had delayed the bank reminders from reaching him. The whole place vibrated with his rage. His eyes became red hot specks, flickering fury as never before. His subordinates stood around him, looking stupid and embarrassed.

By the time he had finished, he had worn himself out nervously. He shook all over with uncontrollable spasms. He was later taken upstairs to his office.

In his anger he had lost himself. He thought of how furious he had been, the way he had suddenly burst out shouting and banging tables. He was angry with himself. He had behaved like a demented child. He had given himself away. He had told them that his hands were not so steady on the controls.

His enemies would be delighted.

He banged the table with his fists.

After a few moments of reasoning his anger dissipated. The office oppressed him. The spaces receded from him, and yet seemed to close up on him. A feeling of emptiness replaced his anger. He tried not to think, tried not to be angry again, he just tried to relax and coolly take stock of the situation.

Then he felt something clutch at his heart. Something like a claw. Cold and inexorable. Fear ran through him. Heart attack! He had ignored his doctor's advice not to indulge in anything that would wear him out physically or emotionally. A sharp, fleeting pain went through his chest and ended somewhere in his brain. He coughed, held his chest, and reached desperately for his heart tablets. He swallowed the last two. After a moment the pain cooled off. But the empty fear hung like a wicked memory at the back of his mind.

He looked once more through the bank reminders.

That meant in a few days' time if he didn't do something about it, the bank had the right to ... *Oh, I see*, he said to himself. *It's all arranged. Chief Hans and Jeccaro! Sit pretty through the tremors and when the crumbling begins they will step in and utter the magic words!*

When Gbenga had told him long ago that Chief Hans and Jeccaro had some kind of relationship with Sowho, he didn't take it very seriously. He dismissed it. *Could it be true? What does it matter, anyway?*

About a week ago a friend of his, another top business man on Wilm Street, had told him about the new paint company that was coming out in brilliant style.

'Ah, they are bringing in expatriates from Britain ... their machines, eh, are some of the most expensive ... and just look at their adverts filling the whole place, eh?'

Jonan had laughed and waved it away as a mushroom company.

'It's all Nigerian noise-making! No action. There have been many like that. They just die away like mushrooms.'

But the talk that had since reached him had it that the company was undeniably serious competition. Their prices of paints and other chemicals were eight per cent lower than

110

any other paint company's in the business. Jonan had seen their relentless advertisements in the papers, he had seen newspaper features about them, he had heard about their grand launching. In one brilliant, sustained action they seemed to have made the existing paint companies virtually obsolete. They had the latest in paint manufacturing technology. If it carried on the way it was coming out, it would certainly be a threat to Afioso. Certainly.

Was it age that was making him take things for granted? Was it conceit? Or was it simply that he had capacity for adapting to new demands?

He dismissed the questions from his mind. Instead he thought about the new strategies he might use to get his company back on its feet. Again, he looked up at his portrait. Then his father's dying face, crushed and wasted, came to his mind. He was a young man then. His father was dying a strange death. The disease had eaten into his life, there was no money to get him treated, and they were shunned in the village. He was terribly alone in his plight. It was a lonely battle with an inexorable death. His father's last words came back to him. 'My son . . . poverty is a curse . . .' Then he died. Jonan had felt unbearably helpless.

The memory filled him with melancholy. He was not used to thinking about it. But it had always been a driving part of his life. It gave him his energy.

He thought about Chief Hans and Jeccaro.

'Heh,' he said to himself, 'they don't know anything. Heh!'

After a moment he chanted silently, 'O – manaka ko . . . O – manaka ko.'

He felt stronger.

Now he remembered Juliet. Another problem.

'Maria, could you get me Sky Blue Hotel and ask for Mr Jeco please.'

A moment later the call went through.

'Mr Jeco here.'

'Mr Jeco. This is Jonan Okwe speaking. Remember me?'

A voice laughed over the phone.

'Who could forget you? Yes, I remember you, How is it going, sir?'

'Fine, thanks. Now there is something I want you to do for me. You remember Julie? The lady I lodged with you for a month?'

'Yes, sir. She left later.'

'I know. Can you find out where she is now? She has left her Surulere residence. And please can you find out before three o'clock?'

'Well, sir . . . you know these things take money . . .'

'I'll take care of that aspect. Just get me the address, right?'

'Done, sir.'

'Good. I know what to do for you.'

'All right, sir.'

Jonan dropped the phone and wondered what it would be like meeting Juliet again. There were so many things. So many.

How many battles did he have to win? How many people did he have to fight to keep his own? Why did they have to keep coming back stronger? And there was himself . . . his background in the boiling, disease-infested slums . . . the horrors of mass death and deprivation that drove him frenziedly, hook or crook, up the ladders of endless strife to success . . . it suddenly was too much for him. He was a man who seldom looked over his shoulder at the trails he had left behind. Now the accumulated weight of his past seemed to force itself on him. The things he had suffered, the enemies he had destroyed and shoved out of the race . . .

And the strain stole into him, into his brain, his heart. Sleep came along with it and eased him from the dark shadows of himself that stared back at him from the world.

He slept there in his extra-large office. He slept the deep and troubled sleep of the hunted.

2

The ringing of the phone brought him back into the world of activities that he had always known. He felt refreshed. His secretary told him that those he wanted to have a meeting with were now waiting. He looked quickly round his office. Everything was in order. The office was cool and fresh.

112

Everything showed quiet action.

'Send them in now,' he said finally.

Jeccaro walked in first. He was tall, bamboo-like, loose-toothed. About fifty. His hair was greying. His cunning eyes darted everywhere. If one hadn't met him previously, one could mistake him for a shrewd insurance salesman. He had a straightness about him which belied his capacity to shift grounds and switch tents. He was unpredictable. He had fifteen per cent of the company's shares. He walked into the office with the air of a man who knew exactly what he wanted. He selected a chair and, without saying anything, sat down.

Jonan watched him coolly. He was someone to be watched. Someone to be won over. If he was crushed, like Samson he would bring the whole edifice down with him. He was a strong voice anywhere along Wilm Street. He was a co-director with Jonan. This was one of the things Jonan hated. Once when the company was about to fold up it was Chief Hans and Jeccaro who set the company back on its feet. In return they were to be co-directors. It was a thing he regretted doing. It meant the company was no longer entirely his, though he was still the managing director. But he had been able to manipulate them in the past and make them do what he wanted. In recent times, however, they behaved differently. Suspiciously.

Jonan wanted to draw them out, wanted to make them reveal their hidden motives and plans.

One is never safe when a partner's hands are in his pockets, he often said to himself.

Then came Chief Hans. He was with Okporu. He had a big mouth. He talked and shouted a lot. He was a very short man, with a bird-like head, a long nose, and sharp eyes that had earned him the nickname 'Piccolo' for the two years he was at secondary school. He wore an *agbada* which covered him like a large blanket. He had on rubber shoes. His hair was combed backwards and he had a parting in the centre. He liked throwing around the fact that he was a chief. But it was reputed that he was a brutal man. He both respected and disliked Jonan.

113

Both of them sat down and said an almost grudging 'good afternoon'.

Jonan eyed him casually. Chief Hans was not an intelligent fellow. The only thing he had was money. 'He sense small as he money plenty,' people used to say about him. But he always had a half-foolish, half-cunning smile.

There was a general silence that could almost be felt. But it was not for long. Just long enough for each to know that though impromptu, it was an important meeting. This was something Jonan often did. Let the silence tell them.

'There is no need for formalities, gentlemen,' Jonan said pushing himself back in the chair, swivelling from side to side in a relaxed manner.

'Formalities never help tight situations. The company is losing strength, its popularity is waning. Our sales figure has fallen far below estimated sales increases. Three of our major customers have been snatched from us.' He spoke slowly, deliberately. Then he sat straight, his hands placed authoritatively on the table before him. 'The fault comes more from within the company than from outside it. And it is from the top, down to the roots.'

He surveyed them to gauge their reactions. Chief Hans adjusted his *agbada*. Jeccaro picked his teeth with his finger-nails. Okporu wiped his face with his white handkerchief.

Jonan got up and walked slowly round the table. For effect. He had learnt it from Mr Longhose, the English expatriate who had started Afioso on its way. He stopped in front of his portrait.

'I have no intention of blaming anybody. The blames that stick are the ones we pin on ourselves. I was ill for six weeks. That was my fault. I overworked.' He stopped. Then suddenly faced them. All for effect. 'But I don't have shares in competing companies under the names of brothers and unborn children as one of you here has.'

The silence that followed was palpable.

Chief Hans made a show of adjusting his *agbada*. Jeccaro rubbed his clean-shaven jaw. Okporu blew his nose.

'Who saw the bank reminders first?'

114

'I did. It came when you were away. You signed for the loan so none of us could act on your behalf on that matter.' Chief Hans spoke loudly as though he had a personal grudge.

'Look, let's not shout like village chiefs. This is a business meeting. We are mature men.'

'I wonder even,' Okporu put in.

'Look, gentlemen, this is not the way to approach the situation. Let's be realistic,' Jeccaro said.

'Yes, go on, Jeccaro.'

'The trade union has called for a strike. They want a forty per cent wage increase and other allowances. The sale of shares in the last two years was made only to staff. The administration has been lax because tribal groups have divided themselves into different tents and fighting factions . . .'

'Eh, go on before you blow grammar, ah,' Chief Hans said flinging his *agbada* up his arms. Jeccaro looked at him, his eyes shone.

'The senior staff come and go because we feel it's only graduates who can do the best jobs, when in fact they are always on the look-out for better jobs and more money. And a large number of our skilled workers have been sucked up by other competing companies because of better working conditions. The problems were there long before you were ill. We need some kind of thorough overhauling.'

'Good talk. Good talk,' Chief Hans said. Jonan eyed him coolly.

'How do we go about this overhauling that you propose?'

'Well, we could start by settling the workers reasonably, then giving fire to the chemical aspects of the company. We are too dependent on our paint products. Step up the quality, and advertise more . . . it's all obvious . . .'

Silence crept over them. Nobody said anything for a moment. Jonan had returned to his seat.

'Well, Chief Hans, what do you have to say?'

'The company is in crisis. We need stronger direction.'

'Meaning?'

'Stronger direction.'

Jonan nodded. It was quite clear to him. Quite clear. He stared hard at Jeccaro.

'I think somebody is stirring up the union,' Jonan said suddenly. Chief Hans looked up, then looked at Jeccaro. Jeccaro avoided Jonan's eyes.

'I think somebody is inciting them. A form of sabotage. Why are they agitating all of a sudden? Why is one of the directors all of a sudden sympathetic to them?'

Jonan sat forward and put his hands palm up on the table. He had learnt that too from Mr Longhose.

Chief Hans was going to say something, when the phone rang. Jonan picked it up. It was Jeffia. His eyes misted. He looked worried.

'Which Gbenga?'

'Which police station are they taking you?'

While he spoke, Chief Hans and Jeccaro looked meaningfully at one another.

He soon finished and put the phone down. He sat silent for a minute, thinking.

'Hope it's nothing serious?' Okporu asked.

'No. Nothing serious. Just a mistake,' he replied. He suddenly looked old and tired. He got up and poured himself a drink. After a moment he seemed to regain himself.

'Where was I? Yes. Somebody . . . somebody wants me to fall. That's why the bank reminders by some official magic didn't reach me on time. Anyway, I am making definite arrangements for the re-allocation of controlling shares of the company. I have made propositions to the shareholders, and already have a majority. We are going to throw the company's shares open to the public. I have the voice. It's up to both of you whether you want to come along or go with your secret associations and shareholdings in competing companies. The shareholders' meeting will be next Monday . . . there are some games about secrecy I too know how to play, and I play ruthlessly. Tomorrow, myself, Chief Hans and Okporu will begin negotiations with the union. Jeccaro, I leave it to you to find out who is stealing and forging L.P.O.s in the company . . . Has anybody anything more to say?'

They said nothing. Jonan nodded. It all seemed so easy.

'Good. Many changes are soon going to take place. Be ready for them.'

Nothing more followed. They went out of the office. There was a heavy silence about their exit.

Jonan seemed to have beaten them again.

Okporu went downstairs to his office. Before Chief Hans turned into his office he paused.

'If one doesn't talk doesn't mean one is foolish, abi.'

'Some people don't notice when the rain is falling.'

'Eh, until they are soaked and shivering like rabbits.'

Jeccaro smiled at the chief.

'Time would take care of that, eh.'

They shook hands.

'Eh, true.'

Alone in his office, Jonan stared intently at his portrait.

Chapter Fourteen

Before Jonan left for the day he received a phone call from Sky Blue Hotel. Jeco had Juliet's address ready for him.

'Thanks, Jeco. My boys will bring the money to you. You know, it never fails to amaze me how you get your information.'

'Ah, contacts, sir. Wherever the he-goat goes it leaves its smell behind. That's what our elders say.'

'You are right, Jeco, and thanks again.' He hung up, took a quick drink, and hurried down to the car.

'Drive me to Kuntu police station.'

'Yes, sa.'

'Hurry up, Amazu. My son might be in trouble.'

'All right, sa. Hope nothing, sa.'

'Nothing. Now move.' He settled back in the soft velvety cushions of his Mercedes. The car drove slowly through the company's grounds. Workers went up and down the place listlessly. The buildings were freshly painted a bright yellow. Supervisors and managers gave orders, sweating. There were large metal drums and cylinders of chemicals along the asphalt road that led to the gate. The car slowed down at the gateman's blue shack.

'Afternoon, sa,' the gateman called, sitting up straight. Jonan nodded slightly. They drove into the streets. There was the usual go-slow at Wilm Street. The usual heat. The usual swarms of human beings.

'Put on the air conditioner.'

'Yes, sa.'

He shut his eyes. He could hear the din and noises of life outside the car. He tried to think.

What could Jeffia have been doing there at that time? Did Saiou and Joe slip up anywhere? The questions were accompanied by fears. *I didn't want Gbenga killed, only roughed up a bit. To be taught a lesson that he could not walk out on the person who made him what he was.* Besides, Gbenga knew too many secrets for Jonan's safety. The last person who had threatened Jonan's security went straight to jail. He had seen to it that all the magistrates and lawyers involved bent his way ... *Who was that again?* Jonan tried to remember. The man's name eluded him.

Jeffia. Each time he thought of his son a feeling of guilt stirred within him. They seemed worlds apart. He saw in his son reflections of his own guilt, his own unintentional indifference. He couldn't help being the person he was. Could he?

As he pondered, he caught a glimpse of someone looking at him in the mirror. Someone he didn't recognise. *Who is that man staring at me?* It was a wrinkled, care-laden face, capped with greying hair. It frightened him to realise that he was staring at himself. He was getting old! *Maybe it's the strain, or the heart attack.* As if to aggravate his disturbance, his wife's nightmare, which he had dismissed, crept into his mind. The vision unfolded as she had described it, as if it were some sort of incubus trying to take possession of his mind. He quickly reached for the newspaper lying on the cushion beside him and tried to read it.

A grey desolation crawled over him.

When they got to the police station, he went straight to the assistant commissioner's office. The commissionaire at first didn't want to announce Jonan. He was busy eating the bread and beans he had bought for his lunch. Jonan inspected his stained uniform, his unwashed face, and decided a non-person like that could not make him stand around unnecessarily.

'Oga dey busy,' the man said, stuffing a chunk of bread and beans into his mouth. In the corridor other people sat quietly. Some were wounded. Some were crying. Others looked sunkenly resigned. There was a crushed air about them. There was also a depressing air about the corridor. The walls were a dirty white, the floors unswept. The windows had become concentrated with dust. At the corners of the walls and ceilings were huge groups of cobwebs, defying justice.

A woman behind Jonan sobbed. A man at another extreme of the long bench muttered, 'Well, God dey.' A baby began crying, and its mother spanked it. The commissionaire had cut himself another piece of bread, cleaned the edge of the plate and, looking around at the horde of people watching him, stuffed it into his mouth.

'Go sit down now, Oga. When my Oga ready he go see you. First come, first served, abi.'

Jonan pulled up his trousers and, without another word, walked into the assistant commissioner's office. He didn't knock. The commissionaire, the plate of bread and beans in his hands, his mouth full, trailed behind him.

'Mr police officer,' Jonan boomed. 'Is that how this place is managed? So that a citizen cannot see a police officer because an idiot standing at the door – who is not even fit to be my houseboy – is eating?'

The assistant commissioner had been asleep at his desk. He was a smallish, black Yoruba man with impressive face marks. He looked more like an underworld character than a law-enforcing officer. He had the quick-moving, red, sharp eyes of a man who was long used to handling criminals. He yawned quickly, rubbed his eyes, and flashed them at the commissionaire.

'I thought I said nobody should disturb me, eh?'

'But Oga . . .'

'I came in by myself.'

The assistant commissioner looked at his commissionaire, and then at Jonan.

'So it's because you are sleeping . . .'

The assistant commissioner stood up.

'Get out of the office, you lazy fool,' he bawled at his commissionaire, who stumbled out of the room, bread, beans, and all.

The assistant commissioner apologised to Jonan.

'Sorry for the inconvenience. What can I do for you, Mr Okwe?'

Apparently he knew who he was dealing with. If he didn't he wouldn't be in that chair for long. Nevertheless, there was a coldness about the question which was necessary when dealing with the high-horsed behaviour of the wealthy who came to him to bend justice.

'I am Jonan Okwe,' he boomed again, not quite satisfied with the manner in which the officer had addressed him. He

120

dragged up a chair and sat down. 'And I am here on behalf of my son, who was brought here for no just reason.'

The assistant commissioner looked at Jonan, then looked away.

'I am not aware that your son has committed any crime, or has he?'

'My son Jeffia Okwe was brought to this station in connection with an assault case along the . . .'

'Oh, I think I know now. Jeffia. So that chap is your son? He kept saying "I won't say anything till my lawyer comes" and got on our nerves.'

'I told him to say that. Now where is he? I demand to see him. That is how you people hang on to the innocent while the real criminals laugh behind your backs. How can a young boy like that do such a thing, eh? I demand to see him. You are all taking advantage of him because he is a boy and does not know his rights.'

The assistant commissioner regarded him. He decided that it was a lot safer, in terms of keeping his job, to play it gently rather than attract unfavourable attention to himself. He had got into that mess before. That was why he had been transferred to this hot seat. Before he knew it he received warnings from upstairs. The wealthy had a lot of influence in the city. It was better to be on their side. It was a kind of insurance. *People never forget small favours like this.* He smiled thinly at Jonan, who looked swollen and business-like. *That's the way to get what you want from these people. Be tough.*

The assistant commissioner pressed a button on his table. The commissionaire came in. He was gulping down some of his bread. He wiped his mouth with the back of his hand.

'Yes, sa!' he stamped.

'Get me Sergeant Okwadia and tell him to bring along the young people with him.'

'Yes, sa!'

'What are you eating, eh?'

'Nothing, sa.'

'What is in your mouth then, eh?'

'Kola, sa,' he lied.

'Kola? Who give you Kola?'

'Not that Kola, sa. Kola nut, sa.'

'Oya go. Get out and do what I asked you, fool.'

'Okay, sa.'

After a length of time Sergeant Okwadia came into the office. Behind him were Jeffia and Cynthia, but they stayed outside.

'Sir, you wanted me?'

'Yes, I did. I want you to release both of them since we have got what we want. In the meantime till other developments come up get their addresses and let them go.'

There was a moment's pause.

'Yes, sir.' Sergeant Okwadia stamped a salute and went out.

The assistant commissioner smiled at Jonan.

'There's your son, Mr Okwe.'

'Thank you, Mr Commissioner. I won't forget this.'

They shook hands. Jonan went out. He smiled at Jeffia.

'Hello, Dad.'

'Hello, son.'

The horde of people on the various benches looked at them. Some sobbed. Some looked crushed. Others looked infinitely resigned. One said, 'God dey.' Another said, 'God no dey for us.' The baby was still crying, and the mother who was sorely impatient spanked it. The commissionaire who had finished eating and was now drinking water, looked contemptuously down the row of people and then at Jonan, Jeffia, and Cynthia going downstairs.

'It's good to be a big man. It's good.' He chuckled.

In the car Jeffia briefly narrated to his father the events of the day.

'Hope they didn't treat you badly?'

'No. They didn't, but they tried to intimidate me. I saw prisoners and criminals. It was frightful in there.'

His father turned to Cynthia.

'Is this your friend, Jeff?'

'Well . . . eh . . . yes, Dad.'

Jeffia was remembering what had transpired between them on their way to the station. In the police van they had sat opposite each other. Her dress was a little tight. When she sat down her dress caught on her knees and Jeffia caught a glimpse of her panties. He looked away. She smiled.

'You could have been blinded.'

They stared at each other. She had rearranged the dress. Then she bent her legs sideways as an extra precaution.

'That's better,' he said.

She looked out of the window, then came over and sat beside him. The policeman who was with them turned and looked out of the window.

'I can smell your perfume,' he whispered. She didn't say anything. Her eyes held a gentle flame. He continued,

'I felt close to you the first day I met you.'

'No, you were afraid. You were surprised when I spoke to you.'

'But when we drove to the clinic we talked as if we had always known one another.'

'I felt the same way too.' Her voice was low and sweet. The policeman shifted uneasily. The van bumped over potholes, jolting them against one another.

'When I saw you carry your father in, I felt something, an emotion I can't analyse. You are a strong and soft person.'

She merely regarded him. Her eyes had become dreamy. The van had stopped. They had come to a go-slow.

'Aren't you going to say anything?'

'What is there to say? I can't analyse my emotion either.'

Silence fell over them. But it was a kind silence. They stared into each other's eyes. The policeman who kept looking at them didn't exist. The stuffy heat that filled the van didn't bother them. The occasional jolting of the van only brought them closer and made them bump into each other.

'I think you are wonderful.'

'I think you are too.'

Their lips met in a gentle kiss. The van bumped. It became a big one. The policeman stared. Between them the fire had started.

Jeffia turned to his father.

'She is the nurse with whom I helped to carry Gbenga to the clinic. Her name is Cynthia . . .'

'Cynthia Oduko,' she said.

Jonan looked across to his son, then to her.

'Oduko . . . Oduko . . . emmm . . .' Jonan stared absent-mindedly in front of him as he repeated the name.

'You know the name, Dad?'

'Yes . . . the name is familiar.' In his mind were fast-moving scenes of a court room. 'Indeed it is familiar. Where do we drop her off, eh?' His voice had become distant.

'Near Marine Beach. Are you going home, Dad?' Jeffia was puzzled at his father's change of attitude.

'No. Not yet.'

'Uncle Sowho is coming today.'

'I know.' It was said sharply, bitten off short like a trap. Behind that response came across to Jeffia an intense irritation. He remembered what his father said about Sowho the other night. Jeffia glanced at his father. He was deep in thought, his forehead was creased in furrows of flesh. Suddenly, briefly, he looked like an utter stranger.

They drove on. Outside, Lagos life was as wild, as fascinating, and as frustrating as ever. People trudged down the streets as though they had lost their souls. Occasionally some cows would dominate the road. The cow drivers would lead them along leisurely, then they would branch them off down another road. At bus-stops people furiously struggled among themselves to get onto the buses, while the drivers laughed. Near a petrol station two men were fighting. One had been flung in the mud, had got up, and picked up a bottle. Somewhere in front a dog had been run over by a car. The animal's bloody innards spread out on the road like a testament of man's cruelty.

'Jeff,' his father said suddenly. 'No son is ever free from a father's shadows. We all have intangible influences of those who have gone before. Nobody is alone. Beside you, before you, behind you are a thousand and one shadows you are heir to. It is always like that.' He stopped speaking. He put his hands round Jeffia's neck. For a moment he couldn't speak. Jeffia could see the emotions struggling on his face.

'My son. We are never alone. And it will be a hard life.' His voice was barely a whisper.

'Jeff, I'm tired.' It seemed more a tiredness of soul than of body. Jeffia was silent. What his father had said had surprised him. His father seldom said things like that. And never in the presence of an outsider.

His mother had lately become silent and withdrawn. His father was wrapped up in his thoughts. He had been left alone to find some kind of meaning for the experiences he was going through. All the meaning he could extract was that life was rather purposeless, events somewhat random. His perplexity had grown and intensified.

While Jeffia rapidly reviewed the past days, his father tiredly previewed the future. Side by side, they sat in the car pondering different aspects of confused lives.

Cynthia put her hand surreptitiously on Jeffia's. It was warm and soft. Jeffia thought about Cynthia. *In a sense we're alike: two young people who have to come to terms with life as we see it, even if we don't understand what it's all about or where it's taking us. Strange how people come into your life. We only met yesterday. A time comes when you don't try to understand these things. It's enough that they just happen.*

'Jeff, what if I drop both of you? I'm going in the other direction,' his father said.

The crossroads! Jeffia thought.

'All right.'

'And when you get home tell the doctor to give your mother a check-up. She was a bit ill when I left her this morning.'

'Hope it's nothing serious?'

'No, nothing serious.'

'Goodbye, sir. Thanks for the ride,' Cynthia was saying as they got down from the car. Jonan nodded stiffly. He stared straight ahead.

'Bye, Dad,' Jeffia said. *Dad's behaving strangely*, he thought. His father waved almost impatiently. The car sped off, took a side road, and came out again in the opposite direction.

'What was that about your mother?' asked Cynthia.

'She's not too well.'

'You love her very much.'

'Yes. When I was younger she used to read poems to me before I slept and would wake me up with music. One can't grow old with a mother like that.'

'You are lucky. My mother and I never got on well at all. But I love my father very much. Maybe it's because I'm a girl.'

They were walking down the hot street. Jeffia waved a taxi to take them to Marine Beach.

'Enter. Na four Naira – O!' the taxi driver said.

'We will use the meter.'

'Which meter? You dey go, abi you no dey go?'

'Okay, we'll pay you two Naira.'

'I no agree.' The driver drove on. Then he stopped in front and beckoned them to come in.

'Unnecessary bluff,' Jeffia muttered. When they had got in she asked, 'What do you think about being involved in a murder case?'

'What is there to think? It makes one feel that being helpful is sometimes foolish, doesn't it?'

'Well, yes. Who do you think might have done it?'

'It's hard to guess . . . you know, life sometimes has its injustices . . .'

'Why do you say that?'

'Because it's true. A man suffers for the sins of his father, which he knows nothing about. The hard-working man suffers while the lazy lounge in an abundance they never truly earned. The weak are oppressed while the strong go on in their oppression, evil rages in spite of good . . . it's endless. I don't pretend to understand the contradictions any more.'

'My father says the same things.'

'Tell me about your father.'

She looked at him. A veil dropped over her eyes. She deliberately shut out her pain to the outside world.

'It began with his hard work and . . .' she went on telling him, in snatches, softening when she could the pangs of injustice, of how he was jailed and the other things that happened to her family. It was the first time she had talked to anybody about them. When she finished she was sobbing gently. Jeffia was indignant, he was angry.

'I read his diary yesterday evening. He must have given it to Mummy after the sentence had been passed. Until recently I never knew he was innocent. I cried. A Mr Okwe . . . or something like that, framed him . . . That's what Daddy wrote in . . . '

For Jeffia that was enough. His father's strange reaction when Cynthia mentioned her name . . . *Where do we drop her off ?* . . . made it all clear. His thoughts, running wild, became distorted, phantasmagoric. *A son lives out the sins of a father* . . .

What trick of life had thrown them together?

'Driver, stop!' he shouted suddenly. He turned to the surprised Cynthia.

'You must forgive me for stopping like this. But you wouldn't understand. You couldn't.'

He got out of the taxi, paid, waved sadly to her, and ran off in the opposite direction. He'd had enough of these shocks . . . it was all too much. As he ran wildly, looking for another taxi to take him straight home, he heard voices in his head. Relentless voices.

A son lives in the sins of the father . . . the father sows, the son reaps . . . the son becomes the father . . the cycle continues.

He was sure that he was going mad. But the voices went on.

Chapter Fifteen

He walked past the gate into the compound. For once he didn't stop to chat with the watchday, who looked at him expectantly. Jeffia stumbled past, staring at the ground before him, engrossed in his thoughts.

He didn't even go into the house, but walked to the backyard. He stood under the mango tree. The garden was nothing special to look at. But it was tended by his mother with loving care. The soil, parched with the intensity of the sun's heat, always needed watering. The roses that looked so promising when they were first bought by his mother had turned pale. Their petals had curved inwards and were covered in speckles of black and brown. Only the hibiscus did well. They were tall, proud, red. It looked strange to see the two flowers side by side, one set dying, the other thriving. Spaced some distance from them were exotic plants of many exciting colours, that smelt like wild grass.

Beyond the garden was the close-cut lawn. Jonan used to entertain his visitors there under the shade of a table umbrella. But these days, with the heat increasing as the months approached the dry season, it was a lot less comfortable.

Some of the family washing still hung on the lines. They flapped with every breeze. The tennis court on the other side was already falling to ruins. The cracks in the cemented floor had begun to sprout defiant grass.

An army of ants marched across its outer perimeter. They were laden with impossible loads of bread-crumbs, sugar, and other useful booty that had spilled over from the dustbin. A baby beetle unknowingly broke the cavalcade, causing chaos to the troops of ants. In no time the baby beetle found itself swarmed by the mobilised ants. The beetle gave off shrill, almost inaudible noises. Meanwhile at the edge of the lawn, the bigger beetles were having quite a time rolling in the grass and unravelling the new experience that was a plastic bag.

Jeffia stood under the mango tree. He stared into the distance, trying to sort out the jumble of his thoughts.

He had always thought he was self-reliant. He had always looked upon himself as being able to think his way out of a problem as through complex details of advanced level physics. But recent events confounded him.

How could his father have done the things he had? What kind of person was his father anyway? Did his mother know about these things?

He remembered Cynthia's face as she told him her father's story. It was quite sad. But she still held herself strong. Her resilience and courage were unmistakable. She had character. The more Jeffia thought about her the more he felt responsible for her family's plight. She was unlike any other girl he had come across in his life. Most of them had pretensions about values they didn't possess.

He remembered the way she had looked at him. Surprise had quickly disappeared from her features and an accusingly understanding expression had taken its place. That was when he had jumped down from the taxi. It was as if she was on the verge of tears, yet very collected. The fleeting look she had given him served all the more to increase his feeling of guilt.

As he stood there racking his nineteen-year-old brain a mosquito flew past his ear and settled on his nose. Jeffia slapped his nose but missed the mosquito. He was enraged. The buzzing continued in his ear. He strode back angrily into the house.

The intensity of the sun had lessened. The army of ants, having tormented the baby beetle, resumed their march and went their mysterious way through the grass, dragging their supplies of food into their holes. The baby beetle, smarting from their attack, rolled over on its back, while the bigger ones that were playing with the plastic bag had gone in search of food.

The hibiscus stood proud and red, while its distant relative, the rose, bent over pale and weak. The mango tree towered above them both, casting its shade over them, and taking a large share of their nourishment. The flowers swayed in the dry wind.

Inside, Jeffia found that Doctor Sam was just leaving. He was tall and ugly. But his ugliness was somewhat benign. His eyes, which stared perpetually over his glasses, were crossed. Doctor Sam was a benevolent old man. He'd had a failed career as an independent medical practitioner.

'Come in, son,' he said gently. He put his dry and veined hands on Jeffia's shoulders and steered him towards the sitting-room.

'Your mother is in a troubled state of mind. This morning she telephoned me saying she was feeling ill so she came back from school. She is worried about something. I gave her some sedatives . . . but she was afraid to sleep . . . seemed afraid of something inside her . . .' Doctor Sam scratched his face and looked down at Jeffia. 'Seems afraid of herself . . . but she will be all right . . . just try and be with her a bit more, eh?'

'But is she all right?'

'Medically, yes. You see, pills can't cure a mental state . . . but she'll be all right . . . You are becoming a man, you know. Almost as tall as myself. Eh, that's how it is. I must be going. You know, I think your mother is afraid of something in the past . . .'

'Or in the future?'

The doctor looked at him as a teacher would look at a child who had given an unexpectedly bright answer.

'But then I'm not a psychiatrist.' With that he opened the sitting-room door, ran down the small flight of stairs, and walked briskly, stooping, to his car. Jeffia watched till the car vanished from sight.

He ran upstairs, opened his mother's bedroom door, and tiptoed into the room. She had on a nightdress. She lay sleeping with her arms stretched out straight beside her. The expression on her face was relaxed, except that her eyes were too tightly closed and her lips were pressed together. The position of her hands strangely resembled the way dead people's arms were placed in coffins. The room was neatly furnished, reflecting her quiet good taste. From her well-stocked wardrobe, which stood beside a television and a record-player, to her dressing table, which held all sorts of expensive cosmetics, there was nothing overdone. On the marine blue walls were huge elegant landscape paintings and photographs of Jeffia. There were also photographs of herself and Jonan which they had had taken many years ago. One painting stood out from the rest. It was a predominantly black and red painting depicting tortured souls. It was supposed to be hell as visualised by a Nigerian painter. There were images of masochism, suffering, bliss. Jeffia, and even Jonan, never ceased to wonder what it was doing there, why she liked it so much.

She turned over on the bed and mumbled a few incoherent words. Then she settled back into sleep.

As Jeffia watched her, he remembered how she had shouted the other day. He had the vaguest notion that she was possessed by something both indefinite and terrifying. He let the thought pass. He sat down in the comfortable chair.

He wanted to ask her some important questions. But she was asleep. Thoughts of Ode returned. He had been thinking of him all along.

Why did Ode have to die?

It didn't make sense.

Was Ode's existence justified? Had he fulfilled himself?

He remembered one of the arguments they had in class before their examinations.

One of the boys in the class had said that God had endowed the white man with more intelligence and creativity than the black man. Many other boys agreed. Ode and Jeffia were violently against.

'Show me one great invention a black man has made,' said the boy.

'It doesn't make sense. Even if I point out some to you it would not answer the question,' Ode had replied.

'You are talking about two different cultures. You can't measure the greatness of one with the yardstick of the other,' Jeffia said.

'Besides, why should skin colour difference, a purely earthly thing, mean superiority of endowment? After all,

131

true civilisation is believed to have begun in Egypt, not so?'

The argument raged on in class. They came to some conclusions. Either God was a racist, which was inconceivable, or the white people had endowed their God with their own racism, or white people had wiped out the achievements of black civilisations from the history books, or the black man, though equally gifted, had applied himself in different directions from the white man. 'We have to reclaim our history,' one of the boys said.

'Ah, but Africa man go want to kill his brother who is doing well, you know,' another student, known for his dullness, had put in. The argument turned into a national schools debate. It didn't settle anything. Injustice is being perpetrated, whether around us or inside us, Ode used to say.

Jeffia drew the same conclusion now that he looked back.

What lies beyond death?

What happens when people die?

Why do people die anyway?

Suppose his mother were to die? No! It was unthinkable.

He shrugged the thought away. The weight lifted. But he felt a metaphysical loneliness, as if he were alone right down to his soul.

He also felt a sense of conspiracy. People, events, society, seemed to be conspiring against him. And there was nobody for him to talk to about these things.

He had been sitting in the room, thinking, for quite a long time. His head throbbed. He needed some rest. He got up from the chair and rearranged the cushion that had sunk in between the springs.

He went towards his mother and bent to give her a kiss. Her face was wet. Jeffia straightened up.

What makes people cry in their sleep?

On the window-sill he noticed an exotic vase. It was a Chinese vase. Multi-coloured and skilfully ornamented, it had the images of round-faced Chinese peasants on its sides. There was some water in it, and a freshly-cut rose. He walked out of the room, quicker this time. He paused at the sitting room to see if his father had returned. Seeing that he hadn't, Jeffia went to his bedroom.

Lying on his bed he thought about the flower in the vase, for no other reason than that it freed his mind momentarily from the dark thoughts that had been plaguing him. How soft and fresh the flower had felt in his hands when he touched it; how finely it tingled his nostrils and opened his senses to a whole new dimension of love when he breathed in its fragrances.

Chinese vases and flowers are beautiful things, he thought as he fell asleep. *But crying in your sleep isn't.*

Jeffia was dreaming of Cynthia when, for the first time in many months, his father came into the room and woke him up.

'Jeffia!' he called, standing at the door. 'What are you doing with that tramp girl, eh? Don't you know her father is an ex-convict? You must not mix with people like that, you hear? You must be with people of your own level!'

Jeffia glared at his father, who had by now come into the room. His surprise gave way to indignation. His eyes flashed. He opened his mouth to speak, but the words didn't come out. He was choked with anger. His father, in the same rough tone, continued:

'Don't let me hear that you are going about with her again, you hear! I will not take any nonsense. You must be careful about the kind of people you know . . .'

In the only way he could express his anger, Jeffia got up, stamped out of the room, and slammed the door behind him.

Chapter Sixteen

Sowho didn't show up as expected.

Jonan had returned home late that afternoon to take a short nap and to prepare for the ordeal of meeting Sowho again. Jonan knew it was not going to be easy. He wanted to be fresh for the encounter. When he came in he had gone straight to Jeffia's room. He had wanted to be hard in his warning. But Jeffia's reaction had unnerved Jonan. His own son had walked out on him. Jonan had laughed quietly to himself.

Children, eh. He will learn. He will learn. Then he will realise the truth of what I was trying to tell him.

He dismissed the incident from his mind. He went upstairs and changed into a wrapper.

On his way to the toilet he stuck his head into his wife's room. It was hot and airless. She sweated in her sleep. Jonan moved silently into the room and put on the fan that stood near the head of her bed. She turned over on her side and revealed a bit of her back. She was all sweaty under the nightgown. Jonan contemplated her. He felt himself getting warm. He decided whether to join her in bed. The sweat which made the nightie stick to her skin aroused desire in him. His eyes travelled down from her upper back to her buttocks and rested there for a moment. When she was like that she always aroused him. What he remembered best about their early days was his fascination for the mould of her buttocks. He preferred a shapely pair of buttocks to a beautiful face.

('Ah, the size and shape of our women's behinds is fast becoming a tourist attraction – O!' one of his friends used to like saying.)

But his wife combined the qualities he liked. Those days! Then her buttocks were not quite so bouncy, but they shook just right. He liked her fresh face and her decent behaviour. One doesn't find her type easily these days he thought. And she hadn't changed much. Good living had filled her out just right.

He suddenly remembered Juliet. That beautiful mistress of his who used to entertain his weary hours after work. She had suddenly stopped seeing him. He could never understand why. She had even moved from where she used to live at Surulere. He often wondered if his wife had anything to do with it. But he doubted it. She wasn't the type to get into a frenzy. He was sure that she had been informed by all those busybodies who had seen them at various hotels. But he could trust the discretion of his wife. She never asked him about it, never quarrelled over it. Despite the occasional diversion that a few other women offered him from time to time, Jonan loved his wife. He felt in his bones that she had brought him good luck. With her the twenty years they had been married had passed by without too many uncomfortable jolts. It seemed to have drifted by imperceptibly. She didn't show many signs of the passing of the years. She still looked youthful, while he had aged visibly. He remembered the stranger that had looked back at him in the car mirror.

He reached out and gently caressed his wife's buttocks. He decided to let her rest. He would wait till night. It was always better then, he thought. As he moved out of the room he too noticed the Chinese vase and the flower. He paused long enough to establish in his mind that it was a vase, and wondered why people were so sentimental and sometimes pretentious about flowers.

He didn't particularly like flowers. They never did a thing for you, never solved one of your problems. It was the same with religion, he reasoned, a thing people did because they were stupid creatures of fancy, of fear. They were even more foolish to think that a god that was supposed to be out there in the reaches of space cared about the problems, sufferings, and deaths of people here on earth. He remembered what one of his workers who had defrauded the company had said when he was sent to prison. 'Na only God go get you back.' *Foolish people.*

He would much prefer a nice pair of buttocks or a platter of roast chicken to a bunch of flowers. Flowers were for women and lazy-minded fools.

The toilet was clean and white. While he was in there he thought about how he would behave when Sowho came. He needed to draw out of Sowho his secret intentions.

After all, Sowho too was just another fool. A dispensable passport to fortune. A failure. He considered it degrading to think about Sowho at such length.

'Water must find its own level,' he said to himself.

The family gathered round the table for dinner, taken early because Jeffia's mother had suggested that they all spend the evening at Ikoyi Hotel if Sowho didn't turn up. Jonan had agreed. Left to himself, he had no wish to meet Sowho, except to satisfy his curiosity.

The table was full of assorted dishes: rice and dodo, chips and chicken, salads and pounded yam. It was always like that when the family ate together, which wasn't often enough for Jeffia's mother. She had arranged this dinner. It was one of her constant devices to get the family together as often as possible. Jeffia's remark about not seeing much of his parents along with the tensions in the house, had nagged at her.

Apart from the clinking of cutlery and the movement of plates, they ate in silence. From time to time Jeffia would look at his mother. She looked refreshed, but not relaxed. He watched his father from the corner of his eyes. His father picked his teeth. Occasionally he would sit back and rub his stomach, miming that he had over-eaten. Once in a while their eyes would meet and quickly drop. Jeffia was still in a sulk. His mother ate slowly, throwing worried glances at both of them. She tried to fathom why the uncomfortable silence hung over the dining table.

'Jeff, did you see my new vase?'

'Ah yes, Mum.' His mouth was full. After he had swallowed the spoonful of dodo and rice, he continued, 'It looks lovely. It's a Chinese vase, isn't it?'

'Yes. A friend of mine bought it for me when she travelled to China recently.'

'Which friend is that?' asked Jonan, speaking for the first time.

'Oh, that newspaper columnist, Emeye. You know her.'

'Her? What did she go to China for?'

'She went on tour. On holiday.'

'Huh, these chaps in the journalism business must have quite some money.'

She looked at him. What did he say that for? Jonan never talked for the sake of it.

'Why do you say that?'

'Oh yes they do. Rubbish!' His face had darkened into a frown. She gave it up. Maybe he was in one of those moods when anything he cast his mind on seemed horrible.

'Did you get the flower from the garden, Mum?'

'Yes! I wanted to see how they would survive in water. Looks beautiful in the vase, doesn't it? The colours all blend into one another. I cut them from that group of flowers me and Chema planted under the mango tree.'

'That was a good job, Mum. They might do better that way. The mango tree protects them from the sun . . .'

'But may rob them of their nourishment.'

Jonan looked from one to the other with vague contempt. Especially Jeffia. He had long concluded Jeffia would grow up soft and lazy like a woman. He was too close to his mother and too soft in his values. What did Jeffia see in flowers?

When he was Jeffia's age he used to work in the farms with his parents. Now times had made things easier for the young. He wondered if the sons of today could be as tough as the sons of yesterday. *There is too much 'book' now, too many petty and unrealistic values. They are too weak, and too short-sighted. Poor fools. If only they would listen!*

'Mum, for some time now you've stopped painting. Why?'

'Ah, the demands at school are getting too much. I am taking two classes now . . . and I've not been feeling very well.'

'Well, what are you thinking of painting next?'

'I've been thinking about that for some time. I think I'll do a painting of a group of flowers in the shade.'

'That would be nice.'

His mother smiled at him. He looked down, and forked a piece of fish into his mouth.

'Look, the time is almost seven. If you all hurry up we could start to get ready.' Jonan's voice betrayed his lack of

137

interest in such discussions. It also betrayed his irritation at being excluded. In a way he was jealous of the relationship between Jeffia and his mother. It only served to illustrate his poor relationship with his own son.

2

They went to Ikoyi Hotel.

The place was busy with guests. It was also busy with those who went there merely to be seen, who identified being there as a sign of their arrival. Waiters bustled with trays of food and fascinating arrangements of drinks. They kept saying 'excuse – O' to the people that thronged the corridors.

White men could be seen free of most of the constraints their own societies imposed on them. Some of them laughed with almost demented delight. Some danced oddly to the traditional music in a way that was always an amusement to those watching.

The Okwe family made their way to the hotel bar. This was where they usually came to relax when they had the time. Jonan came alone or with his wife. It was a rich man's setting, a place for those who had money to spend. It was the kind of place that tickled the Nigerian ego, the closest approximation to visiting Europe in an armchair.

A waiter came along. Jonan ordered two brandies and a Chapman for Jeffia. Occasionally a few people would stop by the table and say hello to them. There was an exclusiveness about the place. The lights were a romantic violet-blue. At a corner of the bar, not far from the Okwe table, sat a couple who were being more intimate than decorum usually allowed.

The Okwes had their drinks in silence. Classical music filled the place. They talked now and then, in brief spurts, dispirited, and lapsed back into silence.

Later they went to the cinema. The hall was full, but a surreptitious tip got them a front seat. It was an American spy film. Jonan, as was his habit, slept throughout the film, snoring gently.

The evening passed. Their silence deepened, and it was clear that though they had all come out as a family they had not really enjoyed themselves. They all remained locked up in their private worlds.

When they made to go home later, Jeffia's mother suggested to Jonan that they go and visit the Doyes.

'She telephoned a few days ago . . .'

'I remember, you told me. About their anniversary, not so?'

She nodded. Jonan agreed that they should go.

'Quite some time I've seen Kpanku,' he said, referring to Mr Doye.

'Jeff, what about you and Adama, are you still good friends? Do you still see each other?'

Jeffia spoke grudgingly.

'Not quite, Mum. I am just a family friend now.'

Jeffia saw his father's face crease into a smile.

They drove down in silence. The driver had finished for the day, so Jonan did the driving. His face was set and intense. Jeffia's mother, who sat in the front, watched him. The cast of his face, its intense aspects, reminded her of the nightmare. She quickly dismissed the thought from her mind.

Ikoyi was always a lovely place to drive through. The streets were well tarred and well inter-connected. Tall pine trees with branches that swished in the night air lined the streets. The air was fresh and smelt of distant seas. The houses were decently spaced, dignified. Some people cynically called Ikoyi 'the Europe of Lagos'. For it was here that most of the rich and powerful relaxed away from the turmoil of Lagos mainland life. It seemed to look down its nose at other parts of Lagos. It stood proudly as one of the most enduring stamps the colonialists had made on the structure of the city.

The Doyes' house stood on a boulevard, its front view adorned with whistling pine trees and a large garden of flowers. The drive leading to the house from the gate was freshly tarred.

Jonan rang the bell, and Adama opened the door. She was the only child of the Doyes. She was about nineteen years old, of average height, fair-complexioned, and sharp-nosed. Her hair was braided. She wore a lounging gown. Her over-developed breasts strained the brassière which showed under the slightly transparent gown. She smiled sweetly when she opened the door for them.

'Hello, Adama. Are your parents in?' Jonan asked.

'Yes. We've been expecting you. They are in the sitting room.'

Jeffia's mother was fond of her. At one time she had marital hopes for Adama and Jeffia. They went out together for a while, didn't get closer, then they fell into casual friendship.

'It's part of growing up,' Jeffia's mother had said to him. 'People grow away from their friends.'

They all climbed up the stairs. They were well carpeted and steep.

'I will never understand why your father likes his sitting room upstairs. It's like the hanging gardens,' Jonan was saying. Adama laughed politely.

'Adama, you are becoming a woman now. Why haven't you been to visit us? Since all this time, eh?'

'It's because of my exams, ma. But I'll try and come some time in the week.'

'That's good. How did your exams go?'

'Fine. We are just waiting and hoping.'

'I'm sure you'll pass. Jeffia, aren't you going to say hello to . . .'

Jeffia, who was behind them, grunted, 'We've said hello already.'

'Oh, have you? You children are fast.'

Adama laughed politely again.

The Doyes welcomed them warmly and entertained them lavishly with drinks that were supposed to be banned from the country.

The sitting room was large and elaborately furnished. The armchairs bulged with rich cushioning, the sofas and settees were soft and colourful. The walls were decorated with paintings and carvings and framed pictures of Mr Doye with the former Head of State. Mr Doye had been a commissioner. Now he was a businessman. He had been thrown out of office for malpractices and corruption. But it was decently called 'resigned'. His wife was a manager in one of his companies. They looked like brother and sister. He was an immensely bulky man. His paunch was a caricature come alive, a six-month pregnancy. He even had difficulty getting into his car. His face oozed flesh, bulging here and there with excessive good living. His voice seemed to come a long way from inside himself. It was said the luxuries of his former position were now choking him. People said he was as dry as stock fish when he took up office, and now he was as fat as butter. His wife was just like him.

They chatted, joked, and laughed. The Doyes had been family friends for a long time.

'I saw the newspaper article about your company. You say it's not true? These boys can be so malicious, eh?'

'That's why they get thrown in prison sometimes, you know.'

While their parents talked on, Jeffia found himself alone with Adama. They had been good friends at one time, but the relationship had slackened. She was now involved with an undergraduate.

Jeffia didn't quite feel at ease with her. He had been disappointed when she left him for the other man. Jeffia had heard that she had become pregnant by him, but that she had sorted out the problem. Since then Jeffia had never felt the same about her.

They didn't have much to talk about. They chatted dispiritedly, lapsed into silence, and watched their parents seemingly enjoy themselves.

Time passed. Darkness fell. Jonan said they had to go. After the usual promises of seeing each other at the club, Mr Doye saw them downstairs. The Doyes stood at the door like two formidable guardians of secret palaces. They waved as the Okwes drove away.

They drove home silently. When they got home they fell into their beds.

Jonan forgot the promise to himself that he would sleep with his wife that night.

His wife didn't have her headaches for a change.

And Jeffia slept easily. For the time being, he was unperplexed.

Chapter Seventeen

The next few days were uneventful. It was as if a normal pace had found its way into the home.

It was Thursday. Jeffia's mother had finished her day's teaching and was sitting in the rest room waiting for the principal. She was tired, though the children had been well behaved. But she missed Debekema. He was one of the most intelligent boys in Form Two. He was always reading books ahead of his class and had a fascination for literature. He had come to her one day and asked her, 'Teacher, what should I do if I want to write books too?' Mrs Okwe had looked at him with a mixture of respect and surprise. He couldn't have been more than thirteen.

'Well, begin with your homework. Do all your homework, then when you've finished that, you can write stories for your school magazine. When you are a bit older you will know how to write books. That is one thing I cannot teach you, Debekema.'

'Thank you, teacher,' he had said, and ran away towards the field. He hadn't come to class throughout the week. When she inquired why, she found out that his mother had died. Poor boy, she thought.

In the corridor outside she could see a couple of boys being punished. They were kneeling down under the sun. She could hear their classmates howling in the classroom next door.

She turned her mind from the things about her back to her own problems.

The days had passed. There had been no sign of Sowho. His not showing up represented something sinister to her. Jonan had told her that some of his friends said they had seen him about town.

Then there had been those strange telephone calls. The phone would ring and she would pick it up.

'Hello, Mrs Okwe here,' she would say.

'Can I speak to Jonan, please?' a muffled, airy voice would reply.

'He's not in. May I know who's speaking?'

'Don't worry about that.'

'Any messages?'

'Tell him "tables turn". He'll understand.'

'Who's that speaking?'

A sinister laugh would come over the line, frightening in its disembodied quality. Then the phone would be dead in her hands. She had received two calls like that. Whenever she told Jonan about them, he would dismiss it with an irritating wave of his hands.

'Don't mind the crazy poor people. When you get calls like that simply drop the phone. The jealous poor people are crazy. Mad.' Then he would slip into his silence.

She saw less of him. The little she saw disturbed her. He had almost become a stranger in his moodiness. He seemed to have grown lean, to have visibly reduced presence. She couldn't explain it. It might have been the heart attack. It could even be the present crisis he was going through.

But more than anything she felt an impending evil brooding over the house. She had tried to suppress her fear. She had tried not to alarm the family. Every waking morning brought the feeling closer, made it more intense. Her greatest worry was that thinking about it would somehow bring about its materialisation.

Then there was Jeffia. He stayed locked up in his room. When he went out he told nobody. He had become silent too. It was as though there were some kind of unspoken hostility between father and son. She had tried to get Jeffia to talk but he wouldn't.

The other day when he was going out she asked him where he was going.

'I'm going to post a letter,' he said, pausing.

That sounded a bit strange to her. If he were going to post a letter he wouldn't normally announce it to her like that.

'Who are you writing to?' she asked, casually.

He looked at her, then stared at the distance. Then he looked at the violet envelope in his hands.

'It's just a letter, Mum. Just a letter.' With that he walked away.

He had announced to her that he was going to post a letter, but he didn't want to say who it was to. *That was odd*, she thought. But many things in the home were becoming odd. The silent tensions. The anticipations. The threats. Her headaches.

She sighed.

'Hello, Mrs Okwe.'

She looked up. It was the new tutor who took Form Five students in Literature. He was a tall, bearded man. But the beard was a camouflage. Anybody could see that he wasn't more than thirty.

'Hello.'

'How was the class today?'

She looked at him and said tiredly, 'Fine, thank you.' But he refused to take the hint.

'May I sit next to you?'

She stared suspiciously at him.

'Oh, no . . . you see . . . there are no other chairs in the room . . .'

He sat down self-consciously. She had a high reputation in the school. She was very well respected. A word from her and his job might be threatened.

She carried on with her thoughts.

The young teacher's intrusion made her think of her first son, Jobo. He had died when he was a year old. The following year she had Jeffia. Memories. She remembered the doctor telling her that she would never be able to bear children again. The intense unhappiness she had experienced flooded her now, but less so. Her immediate thoughts had been of Jonan. As a man he would need more children. That meant he would have to marry another wife. That had been her deep fear. But Jonan didn't. They had gone on like that, had seen each other through the years. She was grateful to Jonan in a way he would never know. That meant he loved her and was content with her. The knowledge of this, coupled with the growth of Jeffia into an intelligent and loving child had filled her days with a joy that crowded out most of the

144

doubts and fears she had.

'My father used to say to me "a good wife means happiness" and the man knew what he was talking about,' Jonan used to say to her at night. Then she would feel happiness suffuse her.

But now things were different. Silently different. Like things hidden in the dark. In the heart.

The principal came into the room. He was a short, thickset man with large eyes. The school children called him 'Okpolor' behind his back. And he spoke fast, as if he had hot pepper in his mouth.

'Ah good afternoon, Mrs Okwe. How was the teaching today?'

'Fine, thank you.'

'Good.'

'I just wanted to ask you about those teaching positions in the junior school.'

'Yes.'

'Are they vacant now? You see, my son who has just finished his H.S.C. wants a job, if there are any vacancies.'

'Oh yes. You mentioned it. The training college teachers are leaving next week. Now what grade did he have in his School Certificate?'

'Grade One.'

'Oh, that's good. Well, when the training school teachers leave we will discuss it further, all right? I think we can find something for a brilliant chap like that.'

'Thanks, Mr Jose.'

'You are welcome.'

The principal went into his office. She resumed her seat. The new tutor who had been sitting next to her smiled. He wanted to speak to her but checked himself.

The office messenger brought her a cup of tea.

She turned her mind to the painting she had already begun. She could almost see the finished work in her mind's eye. She wondered if she should use florid and tawny colours. But she was not sure if she was prepared to risk the experiment.

Other teachers came into the room. They said their greetings and made the usual after-teaching remarks. There

145

was a dusty smell in the air, which came from the teachers clapping their hands together to rid them of chalk.

One of the teachers tried to begin a conversation with her. He was an upstart of a young man. She ignored him as politely as she could and sipped her cup of tea.

Flowers in the shades, she thought balefully. *Sounds better as a tragic poem.*

2

He was in his room reading Achebe's *Arrow of God* when the telephone rang.

For a moment he hoped it was her. But he knew she wouldn't phone. He wondered if she had got his letter. How would she react? It had been a brief letter.

> *Dear Cynthia,*
>
> *I'm sorry the way I ran out on you that day in the taxi. Even in this letter I don't know how to say it. But somehow I feel guilty for everything. I feel ashamed. I wish we had met under different circumstances, I wish I were another person. I don't know if you will understand but that's all I can say.*
>
> *Jeffia.*

He had debated for a whole day whether he should post the letter or not. In the end he posted it.

The phone was still ringing. He went into the sitting room and picked it up.

The high-flown, exaggerated voice was unmistakable. It was his principal, and he announced with gusto Jeffia's result to him. At first Jeffia couldn't believe his ears. A in Biology, B in Physics and B in Chemistry. It was an excellent result, the best in the school, his principal told him.

'I am proud of you, Jeffia Okwe. You are a good example of how a student succeeds by conscientious study and singular sincerity of purpose. This is the attitude to hold through life.'

Jeffia was short of words. He was excited. But his joy froze when he heard the principal's next words.

146

'Those whom the gods love die young, the Greeks say. It is true. Your friend, Ode, also did very well. He had the same result you had. He had A in Literature, the best grade for many years. Ah no, ah no. It's such a pity. May his soul rest in peace. Let me telephone his parents. Goodbye, son. God bless your efforts,' and the phone died in Jeffia's hands.

Slowly he replaced the receiver. Mist formed in his eyes and condensed into tears. He felt the same way when he went to Ode's parents' place. When Ode's mother saw him, she burst into tears. Ode's brothers also burst out crying. He too had cried. It all seemed so unreal.

He remembered how Ode's father had looked at him. The man struggled with the pain within, but lost the struggle. Tears rolled down his face.

Jeffia fell into his father's favourite reclining chair, and let his own tears come again.

His joy was no longer complete. As always there was something missing. He had arrived at the ante-chamber of their childhood dreams alone. His dear friend had left him behind.

The joy couldn't be complete when there was no one to share it with.

3

For Jonan too it was a rather turbulent day. He, Chief Hans, and Okporu had tough negotiations with the workers' union. They were unbending in their demands. By now most production had come to a standstill. Only two of the five factories were partially working. On the walls of the company buildings were caricatures of Jonan, depicting him as miserly and hawk-nosed. There were also slogans of their demands:

'Forty per cent or nothing . . . Afioso is stingy . . . pay the workers well . . . More money to the workers . . . Workers must live . . . We are being exploited . . .'

The workers hung around the premises looking for trouble. It was the first time that the union had gone on strike on such a scale. They were determined.

Jonan had been locked, horn to horn, with the union officials. He threatened, intimidated, and swelled. But it didn't get the talks anywhere. He blamed the workers for the company's poor profits of the past year. He blamed the union for exploiting the company's good relations with its workers by being unconcerned when they oversigned for their overtime and signed for days when they did none at all and generally made fantastic claims on the company. By the time he had finished piling accusations upon the workers, he was exhausted.

Then the negotiations began.

They talked away for most of the morning without reaching anything near a solution. They had a short break during which the management took the union officials to a nearby restaurant for an expensive lunch. This was a subtle ploy that the management used to loosen them up a bit. Jonan didn't go with them.

During the second half, the union pointed out that many of the workers had resigned, and that the company was understaffed. And many more would soon leave. They pointed out that the new paints company was attracting Afioso's staff because they offered about forty-seven per cent more than Afioso in terms of basic salaries. Not to mention fringe benefits.

Was it fair that some of the oldest workers in the company still received less than seventy Naira a month?

Had the workers not been patient enough?

All they asked for was a forty per cent increase with housing and transport allowances, increased leave allowances, and meal subsidies.

Jonan had been as adamant as the union. He refused to budge. It reached such a state that communications almost broke down between them. The management soon persuaded Jonan to call off the negotiations for the time being while they worked out their side of the offer.

For Jonan, a hard-core conservative who couldn't see the merit of an action when it undermined his person, the company's industrial crisis was another challenge to his authority. He intended to make his decisions paramount.

After all, he was the managing director of the company. Out of the sweat of his brain and muscles the company had come to life. No stupid union was going to bend his will if he could help it. No union.

Throughout the negotiations Chief Hans was watchful and not very talkative. Okporu and Jonan did most of the negotiating. The three union leaders had their facts and knew what they wanted. For now they had the muscle.

Throughout the day a suitable compromise could not be reached. Jonan would not hear of anything more than a fifteen per cent salary increase with an annual increment of three per cent for three years. He wouldn't even consider any other allowances except transport.

He stamped his personality on the second half of the day's negotiations. But he knew. It was winning a skirmish. The real battles still lay ahead.

On reaching home later in the evening he was greeted by an overjoyed wife. But the joy didn't reach him, he was all wrapped up in himself and his worries.

'Jonan, Jeff did very well in his H.S.C. exams. His result was simply marvellous!' she told him excitedly.

Jonan nodded his head. 'I knew he would do well,' was all he replied, pulling off his coat, and making his way to the stairs. She stopped beside him and held his hands.

'Is that all you are going to say?'

Jonan was almost angry.

'What more is there to say? My son did well, that's all right, ah. He's a brilliant boy. Now has there been any word from Sowho or has he shown up yet?'

She shook her head, and quietly went down the stairs, leaving him looking down at her.

He felt tired. He could sense a certain constriction inside his chest. *I mustn't overwork*, he thought furiously, *it wouldn't be worth it*.

He was still thinking, in his cushion chair, when sleep chose to close upon him. His legs were spread wide apart, his arms flung carelessly in different directions, and his mouth flopped open. He was an ugly sight.

A little line of spittle rolled down his shrunken, unshaven

cheek.

When his wife came in to see him about some small matter she could not help laughing. He looked like a clumsy actor doing the part of a drunk.

She wondered that sleep made such a fool of people, made them do things that would positively horrify them if they knew.

For a moment she was tempted with the thought that he looked a good subject for a painting. But as she closed the door after her, having decided to leave him as he was, she could not help asking herself what Jonan had on his mind that made him so indifferent to his son's result.

She went to her room and prepared for sleep. Though she'd had many things bothering her, it had been a calm enough day. At first she tossed and fretted on the bed, plagued with questions. After a while sleep crept over her.

The house was strangely quiet.

Darkness

Chapter Eighteen

Juliet walked into the sitting room feeling refreshed from her herbal bath. She had just put Joey down to sleep and wanted to listen to some music. She selected a Sunny Okosun record from the rack that stood on the burnished cabinet.

Then came the knocking on the door. It was uncertain at first. It grew in intensity.

'Coming,' she called, wondering who it could be. She had no appointments with anybody.

She dropped the LP. As she made for the door, she swept her eyes round the place to make sure that everything was in order. She paused to rearrange the position of a chair and then shifted the centre table.

Satisfied, she went to open the door. The key turned in the keyhole. The cold evening air rushed into her face.

'Good evening, Juliet. May I come in?'

She could have walked right into a punch.

She caught her breath, her face crumpling into a mask of bewilderment.

'I didn't know you'd be so surprised to see me. I'm flattered,' he said, moving uninvited into the room.

'Nice place you've got here. Emm. Nice place indeed.' He sat down on the double sofa. And as if to register the fact that he was not a stranger he raised his feet and put them on the table.

She closed the door slowly. Her mind reeled in confusion. She couldn't have been more dumbfounded if a ghost had kissed her. What did they say about shadowy vampires of the past ever sucking one's life-blood? Nausea spread through her.

'How . . . how did you find my place?' she stammered, finding her voice.

He looked at her. For a moment a flame lit up in his eyes.

'Wherever the he-goat goes it leaves its smell behind. The only thing is you are not a goat. You're perfume.'

She studied him. The bewilderment no longer showed on her face. She had momentarily mastered her emotions.

He had aged visibly in under a year. His hatchet-shaped face with its jutting jaws was as she last remembered, but the wrinkles had deepened. His forehead had creased further into ridges of flesh. His cheeks had a slackness which wasn't there before. His eyes, tired and red, had a strange depth to them. He had puffs under his eyes.

Here was a man who was no longer possessed of certainty: here was a crumbling man at odds with the very weapons of his success.

She too knew about the state of his affairs. News had been filtering through to her that Jonan was having problems. When news started circulating like that down Wilm Street there had to be something in it. Feeling more confident, she sat down on the chair nearest the door.

'What do you want with me, eh? What do you want?'

Jonan laughed breezily, much too breezily. His eyes flashed on her.

'Are you trying to be an actress with me?' he laughed again. 'You know what I want, don't you?' He stopped laughing. His face became very serious.

'If it's me you want I'm not in for all that game of hide-and-seek and secret bookings of hotels and all the rest of it. I have other things to do.'

'Don't make me lose my patience, Juliet. Just tell me about it. Tell me all about the pictures you took with me.'

At first she nearly burst out laughing. But seeing that he was very serious she asked, 'What pictures? What are you talking about?'

He got up, quick as a blur, and slapped her. It landed on her cheek. It sounded like the lash of a whip.

'Juliet, don't let me start being violent with you, you hear.' He dragged the centre table forward, sat on it and pulled her head towards him. The mark of his fingers showed on her cheeks. But her eyes were calm. His face was the mask of cruelty she knew so well.

'Juliet, tell me all you know about the nasty pictures of us in bed. Aren't you ashamed? Why did you have to do it to me? Why? Is that how you repay me for all I have done for you?'

She pulled her head back, and looked away from him. She wanted to cry, but couldn't. She stared at the shadowy patterns on the carpeted floor.

She thought she had come a long way from the shadows of her past.

Jonan watched her, allowing her time to think, time to confess. *She'll talk, she'll talk by force.*

The room was silent except for the fans which blew hot air back into the room. The aimless patterns on the carpet in a way reminded her of the chaotic events of her life.

Her father was an unthinking, confirmed, and greatly avoided religious fanatic. That summed up what he was.

When she became pregnant while still at school, he promptly turned her out of the house, and drove her into the streets, telling her to go and find the man responsible.

He was a young university undergraduate.

She could remember particularly well what happened that night.

'I'm responsible for the pregnancy?' he had asked, smiling, when she told him.

'Who else?' she had shouted back.

'Well, I don't want it! Can't you see I'm still a student?'

'You don't, eh? I thought you said you would take care that nothing happened?'

'Did I? Well, I seem to have said a lot of things then. But I certainly can't help your stupidity in choosing the wrong time to have sex, can I?'

'Was it I who wanted sex, or you? Anyway you don't want to do anything about it, eh? Not so?'

'How much would it cost you to get rid of it?'

'About fifty pounds. My father has turned me out of the house.'

He thought for a moment, then snapped his fingers, his face lighting up.

'Tell you what. We'll go and ask my father. He's a perfectly reasonable man and besides I don't take decisions till he ratifies them. A kind of family parliament, see?'

A perfectly reasonable man: his father exploded, shouting at the top of his voice, calling out shocking names that would make a dictionary of obscenities. He maintained the unimpeachable character of his son, and intimated that she was carrying the child of some other person.

'You brought it here because you see he has a promising future and because you know I am a prosperous man, eh, I know your type . . .' he stormed. Then he flung her a couple of fivers and screamed at her to get out of the house.

'You want to ruin my son. Don't let me see you near him again or I'll bring all hell on you . . .' and he slammed the door behind her.

Her father still wouldn't hear of her, wouldn't take her back in. Her mother had long left her father. She was married to another man and lived in England. Juliet had not heard from her for a long time. So she travelled to Lagos to live with her aunt in Ajegunle. After helping her to get rid of the pregnancy, her aunt attempted to convert her into prostitution. That's the best way to survive in the city, her aunt had told her, and even made arrangements for some men to come and inspect her. Juliet couldn't stand it. She ran away from her aunt and rented a room of her own.

But things were so difficult that to get a job she had to pay the price. She made one suicide attempt but abandoned it at the last minute. She was a survivor.

Through the years of turbulence she managed to keep her personality intact. She developed a detached philosophy towards men and their sexual demands.

It was at a cocktail party, which she attended with the manager of the bank where she used to work, that she first met Jonan. He had thrown the party to celebrate the opening of a new factory. After their first encounter, he arranged subsequent meetings. She became his mistress. He rented a flat for her in Surulere, took care of her financially, and carried on their surreptitious affair.

Then suddenly she stopped seeing him. He didn't really appeal to her and she got fed up with the whole arrangement.

'Why did you do it, Juliet, why?' he said, shaking her.

She looked deeply into his eyes before she spoke.

'There are no pictures, Jonan. You should know better.'

It was now his turn to look baffled.

'What do you mean, no pictures?'

'That's precisely what it means. You are being made a double fool of.'

He released his grip on her and sat up straight.

'I'm being made a fool of? All those phone calls ...' He paused for a moment, and stared at her. 'He's been using you against me, not so? Sowho has been using you ...'

Her eyes seemed to twinkle.

'He was here a couple of hours ago. Said he would touch a few places before coming to you. What a shame you missed each other ...'

'Why didn't you tell me this before?'

Her eyes were cold.

'Because I hate you. You are a wicked and selfish man. I have heard many of the things you have done to people. I regret knowing you at all. You, Sowho, and the rest like you are scum in society, walking all over people's lives ... Your Waterloo is just somewhere around the corner,' she said, bitterly.

'Thank God your son is nothing like you,' she added.

'My son ... ? When did you meet my son? Have you started ... ?'

'I have started nothing.'

Suddenly he pounced on her and began hitting her.

She screamed. The dog came into the room, and began barking, jumping around Jonan.

He breathed heavily. Her clothes were torn. She cried freely. Anger rose in him like a thermometer on a hot day.

155

The dog barked at his feet, pulled at his trousers, and bit him on the ankle. Jonan turned round and kicked it savagely. The dog howled, landing near the door. It gave a short sad whimper. Then fell still.

Without a moment's thought, he stamped out of the room, into the cold and dark night.

He heard Juliet wailing about her puppy. The sounds faded into the distance.

He drove home madly to confront his enemy. He drove in a kind of white-heat, his heart beating erratically. Not for one moment did he question the destination of all his rage.

Chapter Nineteen

Earlier in the day mother and son had gone to the school to see the result for themselves.

When they arrived a surprise welcome awaited them. His mother had cried with joy.

It took place in the staff office. The teachers had arranged themselves behind three classroom tables joined together. They sat like judges. The principal, a fat, round-faced man, sat in their middle with a delighted expression on his sweaty face. There were many others of Jeffia's classmates. Juniors watched the proceedings with unusual interest. Downstairs, two teachers were poised at the notice board to 'capture' all the students who came to check their results. They sent them to the staff office.

The awarding of prizes began after the office was crowded. The principal coughed noisily for attention. There were many conflicting noises and talks going on. The moment he coughed the noises quietened suddenly as if a noisy radio set had been turned down.

The students recognised that cough very well. And they pinched each other after he had done it. Ordinarily, that cough meant he was straining his patience. The cane would come immediately after. But it was now a habit, and he often gave the cough at home with his wife.

The noise died down, and he smiled. He looked round the crowd. He saw notorious students, good ones, and non-descript ones. Some parents looked anxious, others looked pleased.

'Every parent's prayer for their children is that they should be successful in life,' the principal began his speech. 'And every child's prayer is that they should do better than their parents and those that have gone before.' He paused to gauge the response. A murmur passed through the crowd. Some parents nodded, some students smiled. The teachers clapped without making a sound.

'Success in life often starts from success at school and it is always a product of hard work, determination, and a simple love of work. Those who have passed these H.S.C. exams are those who we have noted for their sincerity. There is no such thing as luck in exams. It is only a freaky figment by which the dull and lazy aspire to chance success. This college has produced generations of men who have become successes in their different fields of endeavour. They carried the seeds within themselves, which we helped them nurture, into the larger life. More than ever before we need geniuses and brilliant people. In many ways today's society has failed us in our most important needs, and my message to those who have done well in their exams is that they should go on reaching out, go on applying themselves, to go out and become original thinkers and achievers and scientists and writers and what have you . . .'

The crowd clapped at length for him. Parents were happy, teachers were proud, and the boys cheered and called out his nicknames. They knew he could afford to be tolerant on this occasion.

'To those who attained that condition society calls "fail" my message is this: if you are re-admitted to this or any other college, study harder and be sincere in what you want to achieve. Our attainments are limited only by our sincerity. And to parents who have come here today the onus rests on you to help make your children the greats of tomorrow.' The wave of clapping began again and rose in crescendo. The principal sweated, beaming. One of the teachers had opened a bottle of whisky. The principal was on the point of sitting down when he decided that his speech was not quite complete. He added: 'And if that happens tell them to remember us.'

Then they called the names of those who had won prizes, and gave brief histories of the student's career. The prizes were for those who had done best both overall and in individual subjects.

They called out Jeffia's name first. When he went out his classmates hailed and cheered him. His nicknames were hurled at him.

'Roundhead!'

'Mr Biology!'

'Rich man pickin!'

His housemaster gave him his prize of a tape-recorder and had nothing but praise for him. He ended up by saying that Jeffia was one of the school's most promising students and that they were going to keep an eye on his future.

When they left the school premises, his mother decided that they should go and have a quiet little celebration in a restaurant in Tinubu Square. They drove down Broad Street. It was noisy and thronged with all sorts of people. There was the usual go-slow, and the heat was unbearable. In the restaurant they ate quietly. Jeffia had settled for a chicken salad while his mother chose to eat an egg sandwich and tomato soup.

'Your principal made some interesting points, you know, Jeff,' she said, trying to break the silence between them.

Jeffia nodded.

'Yes, I think so too.'

'That sincerity is important to success . . .'

'Yes. As I heard him talking, and as I looked round the people in the room, a sudden unhappiness swept over me.'

'Why, Jeff?'

Jeffia didn't say anything for a moment.

'I suddenly realised I wouldn't ever be at school again. When I was there I couldn't wait to finish. Now I've finished I suddenly want to go back.'

'Don't worry, you'll have many more exciting days when you are at university.'

'You know, it's funny, Mum, that one thinks one hates a thing, but one is only too sorry when it's over.'

'Somebody has said "there is a love in hate". That might sometimes be true. I feel the same way when I'm leaving one school for another school, or when a class I have become used to moves one step upwards. Change is one of the facts of life.'

They lapsed again into silence.

Jeffia looked around the restaurant. It was a Phoenician restaurant. On the walls were a number of exotic paintings, etchings and carvings of what he supposed was from Phoenician mythology.

The place had the peculiar fragrance of some outlandish incense. In the background calypso music played, filling the room without being obtrusive. A number of people were in the restaurant. Some of them stuffed the food down their mouths in such a hurry. People always seem to be in a hurry, he thought. It was as if visible hurrying had become an outward symbol of progress and action. Some of them had briefcases. Jeffia smiled. Briefcases had become a business cliché already. They had become another status symbol for the petty businessmen. The bigger the briefcase, the less the person carrying it had. He had seen these dubious business-men in lots of places. They mostly came under the vague categories of importers and exporters, general contractors, suppliers, wholesalers. He had seen one such man trip over while crossing the road the other day. His briefcase had burst open. Blank sheets of paper and empty files had scattered about the street.

Jeffia soon noticed that the waitress was watching him. He smiled. Then he winked at her. She smiled self-consciously. A man who stood near the counter waved her to go round and attend to the various people. His mother had seen him wink. She looked back and, seeing the waitress, turned back to her sandwich as if nothing had happened.

Jeffia regarded his mother. She looked tired but still youthful. He remembered how often friends used to say that she looked as if she were still in her mid-thirties.

His thoughts passed away from her and turned to Ode, his father, and Cynthia. The mood of past days came back to him. The things he had wanted to say rose in his mind, began repeating themselves, enlarging themselves, in his thoughts. He felt anger, resentment, sorrow surface inside him. And when it did, the joy of his result faded somewhat. He could feel moodiness creep over him. He sank deeper into the silence that he had carried about him at home.

Some of the clientele who ate in a hurry shuffled out of the restaurant. One of them, having soiled his white shirt, was buttoning his coat to hide it. The waitress, standing at the other end of the restaurant, watched him. He didn't feel in the mood to smile or wink. He let his eyes dwell on hers for a moment. When she dropped hers, he dropped his. The volume of the music had been raised so that it lost its serene quality and intruded on his thoughts. The smell of the exotic incense grew stronger and lost its subtlety.

His mood deepened. The silence within him widened. He could contain it no longer.

'Mum!'

'Yes, Jeff?'

Jeffia, playing with his glass of water, avoided looking at her.

'What's on your mind, Jeff, eh?'

'I'm angry with Dad.'

The words didn't spill out. They had come out easily. But there was a controlled bitterness about the way he had spoken.

His mother looked at him. She was surprised.

'You mustn't talk like that . . . you mustn't. Your father's been so good to you.'

Jeffia looked sharply at his mother.

'When you talk like that I get angrier with him. So much has been going wrong under this guise of being "good" to me.' These words had spilled out. There was a stubborn expression on his face.

'Jeffia, we are celebrating your . . .'

'Mum, I heard what Dad said to you last night. I heard it. There's no use pretending it didn't happen.'

'Jeff, he was tired, that's all. He's a very busy man and has more important things to think about.'

'Yes, Mum. Like telephone calls and newspaper articles about his company. Like people he's done wrong to and his business problems. Yes I know, I am never given a chance to forget that he has more important things to think about.'

'Jeffia, you are trying to be a bad boy. If that's the way you want to talk in public let's be going home.'

'Look, Mum, I'm no longer a child. Things are not right at home. Why is Dad suddenly going back to his . . .'

'Jeffia! We are in public!'

She gave him a long disapproving stare. Then she signalled for the bill. The waitress came up smiling and revealed her browned teeth. Jeffia's mother paid. They got up and went out without another word.

When they got to the car she said, 'I don't think I can drive. I've got a splitting headache. I think I'm going to be ill.'

Jeffia drove them home. They were both quiet throughout the journey. His mother sat in the front seat and stared blankly ahead.

They hadn't said a word since they left the restaurant.

She sat with her chair facing the window. She had already done the outline for the painting and was mixing the colours. She had always loved painting. Her husband disapproved of it because it stole her attention from him. But she kept it up nevertheless. It gave her something to concentrate her mind on. Besides, she loved the feeling of realising her interpretation of a subject, infusing the blank canvas with symbolic life.

Jeffia put down the novel he was reading and went to the window. The sun was going down. The sky was a splash of yellowy-red and blue. It looked beautiful: it made him think of death. The sun was a fading orb sinking on the horizon. The trees were touched with the radiance of yellow and red. The leaves looked strangely rusted.

He gazed at the branch where the birds had been building their nests before they were stoned down. He thought he could see remnants of the nest. There were no birds about, not even in the melancholy expanse of the sky.

All nature seemed to him at that moment to hold its breath at the coming of night, the slow turn of another day; just as humans with the fall of death, the imperceptible turn of another life.

In that moment of contemplation Jeffia experienced inexplicable and quite profound serenity.

He spoke for the first time since they had come in.

'The sunset looks beautiful, but sad, Mum.'

At first she didn't say anything. Then she raised her head, and looked towards the sunset.

'Yes, it's beautiful, son. It's a pity not many of us notice.'

The brief moment of serenity passed. And in its place rose the silences of bygone days.

'I'm going downstairs, Mum.'

'All right,' she said, without raising her head. 'I'll have a rest.'

He looked at his mother. She was deeply involved in her painting. The rays of the dying sun flushed her face and revealed little wrinkles of tiredness and age.

Quietly, he went out into the corridor and shut the door behind him. Disjointed thoughts floated through his mind.

As he went downstairs the tense silence of the house weighed upon him.

Chapter Twenty

Someone knocked on the door.

Jeffia was reluctant to get up from the settee where he sat watching television.

He threw a look at the large oak door. The burnished brown surface reflected the blue light in the room in scattered, muted rays.

Who could be knocking at this time of night?

One of the prices of living in Ikoyi was continual fear. Doors were not always opened when they were knocked upon. Too many costly mistakes had been made this way.

The knocks sounded again. This time they were more insistent, as if querying why there was no answer.

Jeffia slowly got up from the settee, he turned down the volume of the television, and made for the door. He detested this intrusion on his privacy.

'Who is it?' he called.

Silence.

'Who is it?' he raised his voice. The silence bothered him slightly.

'It's me, your uncle.'

The voice sounded familiar. Jeffia eased open the door a little, and peeped through the crack.

'You don't have to be afraid, Jeff. It's me.'

Jeffia threw open the door, a smile splitting his face.

'Look who's here.'

Standing in the doorway, a faint smile on his thick lips, was his uncle Sowho. He stood there tall and spare. He had a pipe sticking out of his mouth and a black walking-stick in his left hand. He had on a baggy pair of brown striped trousers. He wore a sleeveless shirt which wasn't tucked in, and which detoured the protrusion of his stomach. He kept twirling his moustache with a bemused expression. The smile on his face spread from his puckered cheeks to his rumpled forehead. He was about the same age as Jeffia's father, and

164

looking at him closer brought out resemblances that age had made less apparent.

'And see who's opened the door for me,' he replied airily.

He embraced Jeffia lightly.

Jeffia led the way into the sitting room.

'It's been a long time, Uncle. How's everything?'

'Oh fine. Fine.'

Sowho sat down on the settee where Jeffia had been sitting.

'Ah, Jeffia, look how you have grown so big. You're a man already.' Only his mouth seemed to speak, his face was sombre, and his eyes were bleak. 'I won't be surprised if you have got a wife already.'

Jeffia laughed.

'Ah, no, Uncle.' It was a joke he was used to, his father's friends never stopped saying it.

'Is your father in?' Sowho asked at length. The warmth in his voice had dropped. It wouldn't have been noticeable if the afterglow of his smile hadn't completely vanished.

'No. Daddy is not home yet. But he'll be back any time now.'

'That's all right. I will wait for him.'

He seemed to have spoken to himself, in a voice of determined patience.

'Would you like a drink, Uncle?'

Sowho looked at Jeffia, then looked away.

'No, son. I am all right like this.'

'Won't you have anything at all?'

'No, thanks.'

Jeffia sat back in his father's reclining chair. Why was he refusing a drink, he asked himself, then dismissed the thought. He went on watching television. But he found he couldn't concentrate. He kept glancing at Sowho from time to time.

Sowho allowed his eyes to roam the room. It was some time since he had last visited Jonan. He took in the rich decor of the sitting room: the chandeliers hanging from the ceiling, assortment of sofas and settees, the lavish hi-fi equipment, the air-conditioner that purred gently, the rich-looking draperies, the fluffy carpet, the set of glass tables next to every chair, the sculptures and carvings and paintings that were arranged

165

about the room . . . and his eyes came to rest on a large picture of Jonan with the Head of State. He looked at that picture for a long time.

Jeffia watched him. He remembered what his father had said about Sowho the other night.

Sowho's lips seemed to have pressed harder on themselves and a sneer had crept into his expression, unnoticed.

Jeffia followed Sowho's intense gaze to the picture of his father. Then he looked back at his uncle.

Sowho's face was by now moulded into an impenetrable mask. There was an abstract expression that hadn't been there when he first entered the room. His throat moved as though he had difficulty swallowing and his hands were clenched.

In order to do something to relieve the silence and stillness in the room, Jeffia got up and tried other stations on the television. There seemed nothing interesting. Finally he switched the set off and came back to his chair.

His uncle hadn't moved. His face was still a sombre mask, his eyes bleak. He seemed to be suppressing an implacable emotion. A nameless fear passed through Jeffia.

When Jeffia looked up again, his uncle was twirling his moustache. It was as though nothing had happened. There was a satisfied, earthly expression on his face. He was almost smiling again.

'How is your mother? Is she in sef?' His voice was hollow.

'She's upstairs sleeping. She's not feeling too well. Shall I call her for you?'

'No, don't worry. Don't worry.'

Time passed quietly.

Soon, as if unable to contain whatever was within him, Sowho got up and began pacing the floor. He would walk up the room, walking-stick in hand, and would walk back again. There was nothing dramatic about the motion. But there was something sinister in its restraint.

He watched his uncle, who had stopped pacing, and who studied the sculpted bust of an African child that stood on the television.

After a moment Sowho went back to his seat and sat down. He stared at Jeffia.

166

Jeffia felt the silence and the melancholy character of the room weigh down upon him again.

'Come and sit here beside me, Jeff . . . come on,' his uncle said, suddenly. Jeffia stared at him. The blue light gave his eyes a strange glimmer.

'Do you want anything, Uncle?'

'No, just come and sit down here. I want to talk to you.'

Jeffia said nothing. He could feel the unnameable fear climb within him.

'Are you afraid of me?'

'Eh, no . . . Uncle . . . But I would prefer to sit down here.'

His uncle let out a breezy laugh. Jeffia had the curious impression that the laughter was coming from somewhere else in the room, somewhere in the dark corners.

There was a brooding silence. Jeffia felt it bristle the roots of his hair and slide down his spine.

It felt strange, but Jeffia had the sensation that the silence seemed to emanate from his uncle like an aura, reaching out and engulfing him with invisible ectoplasmic hands.

'Jeff, do you know that your father is a wicked man?'

Lurid silhouettes crossed Jeffia's mind. He felt rooted to the chair, mesmerised.

His uncle spoke again.

'The sins of the father are visited on the children . . . have you heard that quote, eh?'

Jeffia swallowed hard. The blue lights in the room had become a shade darker. His uncle's voice seemed farther and farther away. Too many alien and fleeting images crossed his mind.

His uncle went on speaking. Coolly. Calmly.

'Your father is going to suffer. The wickedness he has done will bounce back at him.'

Why was his uncle saying all this? Jeffia wanted to shout, to scream, to explode . . . but he couldn't. Something seemed to be holding him down, as if he were in a dream. He couldn't understand. His limbs went numb.

Naked horror blanketed into his mind.

167

2

The controlled hatred Sowho felt towards Jonan was a burning part of his memory. Since the day he had been released from prison he had lived for nothing else save the small idea, paranoid and terrible, which grew in his mind the way letters etched on a young tree grow with the tree.

It was he the white men had come to meet, wasn't it?

It was he who applied to them that he would like to be their agent and partner in Nigeria. He had read their advertisements in the papers and had written to them. At the time the possibilities of a paint industry were promising and its market unexploited.

He had been studying for his G.C.E. for the fourth time. He lived with Jonan, who was a salesman for a company importing soaps.

The white men had written to Sowho that they were coming to Nigeria to survey the potential of the market. When they came he didn't have the money they wanted as a deposit.

He didn't know that Jonan had been reading his diary. And before he knew what was happening Jonan had edged himself into the deal.

Jonan knew a lot of people: bankers, lawyers, business-men, and politicians. He was able to raise the deposit.

Sowho was angry when he found out but Jonan told him not to be foolish. What one of them owned was for both of them, wasn't it?

Finally the company was established. Gradually Jonan gained a lot of power and knowledge. Jonan studied Mr Longhose carefully. He watched the way he handled the workers and controlled the business. Then eventually, with Sowho's help, Jonan broke away from the company and used propaganda to destroy it. In disgust Mr Longhose sold off the company and went back to England.

Jonan formed his own company and called it Afioso Paints. At first they imported paints. As the profits grew and they could get loans, they built a factory and began manufacturing locally. Then a quarrel broke out between the half-brothers.

Sowho wanted to be a director, not just a marketing manager. Jonan refused.

Sowho accused Jonan of stealing the company from him. He said Jonan now wanted to ditch him because the company was becoming successful and because Jonan had met other wealthy people who were interested in the company. At first Jonan ignored him.

Then Sowho seized vital documents of the company. He even ordered that the plant be closed down. There was confusion.

Jonan got angry. When there is a thorn in the flesh, he used to say, just remove it. Jonan knew a couple of police officers. It was easy. He framed Sowho for theft and got the judge, who belonged to the same secret society, to bend a bit. The fool should be taught a lesson.

Sowho got six months.

In court Sowho swore that brother or no brother he would get his own back one day. He swore he would exact revenge, even if it was the last thing he did.

All that was a long time ago, and many things had happened since. After a few weeks, when he came out, Sowho left town and set himself up in Port Harcourt as an importer, contractor, and general businessman. But he never forgot. He only waited for time to cover up the tracks. He had been scheming and planning silently. He had even taken pains to give Jonan the impression that the past was forgotten and forgiven. But he knew what he was doing.

He wanted to make the revenge complete and terrible.

He had been seeing Chief Hans and Jeccaro and had reached a conclusion with them. They had told him about Gbenga's death. Sowho recognised Jonan's touch. Juliet had been telling him things too. He had met the assistant commissioner. Nice chap. He was very helpful. Sowho couldn't have wished for better.

Now his plans were almost completed. Now that he had got Jonan where he wanted him without his knowing it, he could afford to come out from the shadows where he had been operating.

Jonan could now make a choice between business suicide or business murder. The choice would be his, Sowho thought, the one was as completely devastating as the other.

Sowho relished the thought of how Jonan might react . . . It would be like watching him drink the hemlock of his own success. No other vengeance could give Sowho greater satisfaction.

Chapter Twenty-one

The door burst open, and Jonan strode into the sitting room. He switched on the bright lights. He looked around. Sowho stared at him coolly. Jonan remained where he was. He regarded his half-brother for a moment.

'It's been a long time, Jonan.'

'Dad!'

Jonan turned to Jeffia.

'It's all right, Jeff. Go to your room. This is a matter for men.'

Jeffia got up slowly. He felt dizzy. He stood there looking at both of them. Then suddenly he shouted: 'All of you are evil . . .'

'Jeffia!!' His father stamped his foot, slamming the door.

'Behave yourself, you hear. Behave . . . Now go to your room. This is a matter for men . . . not for rats.' He pulled Jeffia roughly out of the room. He opened Jeffia's room door and shoved him in. Then he shut the door behind him.

When he came back he went to the sideboard, took off his coat, and poured himself a drink.

'It has been a long time, Jonan . . . aren't you going to say something?' Jonan didn't say anything. He tried desperately to control himself. As he stood there, thinking, the many odd things that had happened in the past days began to fall into place. They began to assume clarity. All that Juliet had implied had told him more than he needed to know. Sowho wouldn't dare come to his house with a weak hand.

The whisky simultaneously hit his stomach and exploded in his brain.

All these years Sowho had clearly been fooling him. All the time they had buried their truce with traditional ceremonies had been a ruse, a clever strategy of making the enemy believe what you want them to believe.

Jonan's hands began to tremble.

That was why he had sent the telegram . . . and instigated the phone calls . . . and perhaps he had even been a catalyst of his business crisis.

Was he, Jonan, a bigger fool than he thought, taking people and things for granted?

Jonan remembered his past. The memories flicked through his mind.

He remembered how his father had died young, consumed by an unfathomable disease, whitish streaks covering his whole body. They had burnt his remains. He remembered how the people of his village began to isolate him, how they disposed of his father's property, how he had escaped to Lagos. The most important thing for him became to make something of his life. To make money, and be rich. It didn't take him long to realise that only money and power had any real meaning, and only money and power could make him survive without fear of the past.

The whole of society seemed to him then like one big plot to keep him in the depths he had emerged from. He had been conned and duped and framed. He learnt to stay above it all by mastering the rules that cavemen must have mastered, but in a different way.

Living a tough, unbending existence became a part of him. He became a perpetual business warrior, an obsessive, sometimes fighting against himself and often losing touch with realities about him.

His head throbbed. He could feel the veins in his head swell and subside with too much reckoning.

He remembered vividly the year Sowho was thrown into jail. It had seemed such a triumphant act of power flexing. All Sowho's witnesses had refused to testify in court.

Jonan had laughed. It had been so exhilarating.

But soon afterwards some friends and a few village elders began to put pressure upon him. People from the same village are all of a family, they told him, and what more of a half-brother. He relented and withdrew his charges. When Sowho came out a ceremony was held. Both of them promised to forgive even if they couldn't forget. Sowho said he had already forgotten, and he left town for Port Harcourt.

Since then Jonan had closed the chapter, though he left a figurative slip of paper to remind him of it sometimes.

As he stood there, a snatch of his wife's nightmare flitted through his mind. The nightmare of his father's death played havoc with his thoughts. His father's death had become a symbol of everything he dreaded. He feared that he might plunge back to the depths he had sprung from. He had come a long way.

Then there was Jeffia. There was his wife. They too had come a long way into the sunlight. The night would be too dark for them, the earth too cold, the past too shocking. They were flowers that had to be caressed and sunkissed. The storms and valleys had to be spared them.

He alone must go forward . . . forward.

In that moment he suddenly felt stripped of all the confidence and energy that had seen him through the years. He felt naked. Yet at the same time he felt a terrible rage rise slowly from the primeval turbulence within. The rage expanded and filled his being. His hands and legs trembled.

All the grim contemplation had taken no more than a fraction of time, all the time it took for him to toss the drink down his throat and for it to swim around his system alerting all emergency stations.

'I know what you are here for, you coward!' he shouted suddenly.

Sowho turned round on the settee and then stood up. He looked mildly surprised.

'Is this how you greet a brother, eh, Jonan?' The distilled mockery struck home. Jonan felt even more enraged. He staggered towards Sowho.

'How do you greet a brother, eh? By making stupid phone calls, eh?' Sowho looked him straight in the eye.

'Look at who is calling someone a coward. This dead fowl, eh?'

'Who's a dead fowl? Who's a dead fowl?'

Sowho laughed out loud. Jonan slapped him.

'A bastard like you . . . you come to my house to talk nonsense, to call me a dead fowl, eh . . . you think I don't know all your stupid plans, eh . . . fool . . .'

Sowho was deadly cool. His eyes were narrow openings of hatred. His fists were clenched. He struggled to control himself.

'You bloody fool . . . you are finished . . . don't you know it? You are going to be deader than your father ever was . . .'

Jonan spat into his face.

'You blind fool . . .' Sowho went on, calmly cleaning the spittle from his face. 'I am not going to fight with a skeleton that doesn't know its flesh is gone . . . I will only show you a mirror . . . murderer . . . murderer . . . that's what you are . . . just wait till the inspector comes . . . you will know how sweet it is to go to jail, and we will distribute your company the way your father's property was . . .'

Jonan shouted. His vision hazed and a spasm of insanity gripped him. He pounced on Sowho and flung out a punch. Sowho jumped back, more out of surprise than anything else. The momentum of the punch carried Jonan and he tripped over the centre table. Sowho dived for him. They scuffled. Sowho hit him anywhere his hands could reach. Jonan reached for his penis and gripped it. Sowho screamed and gouged at his eyes. Then they both let go. They stood breathing heavily, like two enraged wrestlers.

In another insane moment Jonan turned round and rushed for the Hausa sword which hung on the wall, and which his wife had bought as a decoration. He unsheathed it, shouting and foaming like a man possessed by demons.

Jeffia, who had been listening to the frightening exchange, ran into the room.

'I am going to kill you here now . . . I will fling off your neck . . .'

'Daddy!' Jeffia shouted.

'Get out of here, you young fool,' his father spat out. He picked up a glass ash tray and flung it in Jeffia's direction. It broke on the wall. Jeffia scurried out of the sitting room, and watched the whole grim event from under the stairs. Jonan had made a furious swing with the sword at Sowho's neck. Sowho jumped back again and stumbled over the settee that was behind him. Jonan burst out laughing raucously. He kicked away the table that stood in his path. He stalked Sowho like a deranged hunter.

'What is happening here . . . ?' called a voice from upstairs. Then there was a short scream, followed by the heavy sounds of falling and tumbling down the stairs.

Jeffia screamed and rushed out.

His mother who had been woken by the commotion was running down the stairs to see what was happening when she tripped.

Jonan paused, then froze when he heard the scream. He turned towards the staircase.

Sowho saw his chance and ran to the door. Pushing tables and chairs over in his desperation, he fled into the night.

Jonan saw him escape and gave chase. In the darkness a car started and drove off. That didn't stop Jonan. He ran back into the room, took his keys from his coat pocket and jumped into the car which he had parked outside in his anticipation to meet Sowho.

Sowho swerved off the street. He didn't know the roads well. They branched off a lot. In his hurry he had taken the wrong direction. Nevertheless, he sighed at the narrow escape. He rubbed his head where he had hit the ground when he fell. *The police station is the next place to go*, he thought.

Jonan gained on him. He knew the roads better. His mind was bent on one thing: destruction.

Then it happened.

Suddenly Jonan slumped in the seat and lost control.

His heart had, in a final spasm, outdone itself. The heart-attack had come full circle.

The world through the windscreen turned a cruel red. His muscles slackened. The steering wheel turned, as if finalising the climactic swing on destruction. At ninety m.p.h. the car careered through some wooden sheds and crashed into Sowho's car which was just negotiating a corner.

There was a clanging din of crashing metal and the two cars tumbled on their sides.

The next moment they burst into flames.

A crowd gathered like materialised shadows. It was two hours before the fire brigade could rouse themselves to come.

Sowho had died instantly.

Jonan had survived long enough after the crash, with blood and piercing shadows of death and hatred all around, to utter, the names of his wife and son. The last word he said was: 'forward.'

His tormented spirit struggled out of the reluctant wreck of his body and soared away from the ruins it left behind.

Two souls joined in one and blood burned on metal.

Back in the house Jeffia, who had just witnessed a horrifying dimension of hatred, stood over his unconscious mother.

His brain was a cesspool of confusion. There were no thoughts in his mind. Only shadows.

As he looked about the disordered sitting room his eyes fell on the sword and then on the black walking stick.

Unable to control his confusion he ran outside, raised his hands up in utter distress, and cried:

'God, please take this nightmare away from me . . .'

His anguished cry was carried by the gentle winds, through the trees, up to the clouds, and out into the indifferent night.

Flowers

Chapter Twenty-two

For two weeks I lived in small confines of hell, with pain and sorrow numbing my brain.

I would wake up in the cold mornings and remain on the bed staring at the ceiling, seeing nothing, feeling nothing, except an icy inner emptiness; as if my very soul had slipped out of my body.

My mother's image would flash into my mind. I would shut my eyes but it would still be there. Then I would reach out for the sleeping tablets to knock myself back into unconsciousness, when, appearing to protest, the image would quietly fade from my mind.

Then memories would inundate me.

The doctor came that night. One look at the bruises and bumps on my mother's body made him shake his head.

He looked around the sitting room. It was in complete chaos, as if beasts had fought there. Then he looked at me. I said nothing.

'It is serious,' he muttered at length, his eyes returning to my mother's pale face, which seemed to me to have the shadow of death.

'What happened?' he asked, indicating my mother.

At first I didn't want to speak. My lips were heavy and energy seemed to have drained out of me.

'She fell down the stairs,' was all I could say. My voice didn't sound like mine, it was hoarse and hollow.

'We have to get her to the hospital fast.'

It was all a dream. It was a waking nightmare. *What was all this about? What was happening?*

My brain was confounded and no answers came. Only dream-like shadows that moved slowly as though under water.

I helped carry my mother's limp body to the waiting car.

'You don't have to bother to come, son. It's all right. You stay behind and take care of the home. I'll ring you up tomorrow.'

I remember standing there and looking at him, saying nothing. He patted me on the shoulder and smiled at me.

'Courage, son, courage.'

I looked at the back seat where my mother lay, her hands by her sides, reminding me of the day I went to her room when she was asleep.

'All right, son.'

The car drove away into the bleak night.

I stood there at the roadside peering into the darkness.

An awesome loneliness came over me. I shivered. It was as if ghosts had walked through me.

The clouds had never looked so miserable. They were like tatters of cotton wool soaked in ink. The moon was hidden by a mass of clouds and the sky looked generally distressing.

A profound silence seemed to have crept upon the land and I couldn't hear the incessant drill of crickets or grasshoppers. I could only hear silence. An uncanny silence. It was as though all nature held its breath, waiting for something to manifest.

I couldn't sleep. It had never been like that with me before. When I shut my eyes and tried to relax myself to sleep, images would jump into my mind. My father, brandishing a sword; Uncle Sowho struggling under the settee.

Why was father like that? Why did he want to kill Uncle Sowho?

Who really is this Sowho?

Where have they gone? What's going to happen?

Mum had fallen down the stairs. I could hear her scream, hear the rumble as she rolled down and finally hit the ground. By the time I reached her she was unconscious. Uncle and Dad suddenly ran out of the house. Mum was dying on my hands. I was alone, as I always seemed to have been in the past few days.

I felt helpless. Things were happening to my life, in my family, confusing my mind, and I could do nothing about them.

Nothing made sense any more.

First there was Ode. *Dear friend, where are you?* I remembered our days at school together. I remembered how the family had burst out crying when I went there. Even his father, that tall, friendly man, had broken down and cried.

Then there was Cynthia. A horrible glimpse into the shadows my father had left behind. A dark past stretched forward through time. How could I possibly confront her again?

The sins of the father . . .

That was the last uncomfortable thought that slipped into my mind, arousing distorted shapes and images before I finally drifted off into sleep.

I could hear the thumping sounds of drums from far away . . . it became louder and seemed to be coming closer till it became clear that my head was the drum . . .

Why were they beating so hard on my head? I told them to stop but they wouldn't listen. I grew angry.

And I woke up. Someone was banging on the door.

What time was it? A few minutes past twelve.

I had barely been asleep for two hours.

What do they want? Can't they leave me alone? Haven't I gone through enough already?

I walked unsteadily to the door of my room.

Then I noticed that my prick was sticking out from the flap of my pyjamas. I wondered how it came to be sticking out so obscenely. I tucked it back where it was supposed to be but it was stiff and unyielding. *This thing can be stubborn sometimes*, I thought to myself. *Why is it choosing to misbehave now?*

I changed into a pair of underpants and jeans and made the stubborn thing face upwards. And then I went to see who was at the door.

My brain was still drugged with sleep and I walked lazily.

The cold air hit my face and cleared my mind.

'Yes?'

'Hello, young man.'

'Yes, what can I do for you?'

'Everything. But let us come in first. It's cold outside.'

It was the sergeant I had met at the clinic where Cynthia worked. Sergeant Okwadia. There were two other policemen with him. I opened the door for them to come in. They filed into the room silently.

I rubbed my eyes and looked at them.

They stood there in the disorganised sitting room. They looked round the mess which I had been too stunned to try and clear up. Okwadia removed his cap from his head and twirled his moustache pensively. The other two policemen stood, arms akimbo, their eyes roving round the room.

There was a silence about the place that I had come to recognise. It was an airy, charged silence. I felt uneasy.

'Sergeant, I'm sorry if I am going to be rude but this is a terribly odd time to come visiting . . . there's nobody at home . . . your standing there is not helping things at all . . .'

I moved towards the door.

'Young man,' I heard the sergeant say softly. 'I have not come to harass you or anything. I have come to tell you something . . . but where is your mother?'

'She's been taken to the hospital.'

He looked around the sitting room again, then his eyes came to rest on me sympathetically.

There was another silence. A spooky sensation crawled up my back. What had they come to tell me?

'You will have to take this like a man,' he continued at length. 'It can't be worse.' He paused and fiddled with his police cap and then looked up. There was a drop in his voice. His eyes shone unnaturally.

'Your father is dead. He had an accident. Your uncle died with him . . . I'm sorry.'

I don't know what happened inside me, I can't remember. Just shadows and more shadows getting darker and redder.

'Did you know he was responsible for Gbenga's death?'

'Let's leave him, Oga. Let's leave him alone.'

The door opened . . . Somebody said, 'God give you the courage to bear your loss with fortitude.'

The door closed behind them. A car started and drove off into the night. I sank onto a sofa and cried myself miserable.

My brain was like wood. My body seemed lifeless. My senses dulled. Shadows from within filled me with the spell of the heaviest gloom. My soul weighed me down.

It was impossible to think. Too many things hung about my mind.

The sins of the . . .

I got up and rushed to where my father kept his sleeping tablets. I swallowed five. And died.

It was on the seventh day that my father's relatives did a temporary burial of my father's body. Before then there had been much ceremony. They said after a time his body would be exhumed and transferred to his village and buried alongside his forefathers.

There was a short church funeral. Not many people came. I wore a black suit that day.

In the past few days the papers had been full of my father's death but I wasn't allowed to read any of them. I didn't want to.

What surprised me most was that my father was buried side by side with Sowho. They were brothers, people said. They were brothers, no matter what had happened. I didn't understand any of these things.

Mother was still very ill and hadn't even been told that Dad was dead. My father's relatives refused to let her be told and, besides, the doctors felt it wouldn't help her recovery.

They buried my father at the Ikoyi cemetery. As they hoisted the big ornamented coffin into the grave, a deep, grim emptiness crept from my stomach into my heart and stole into my soul.

It was then for the first time that the full realisation of his death hit me. I had tried to be tough and hard-eyed but it was all too much for me.

It happened when the congregation started singing some dismal funeral dirges about the gaps death left amongst the living. Then they started pouring dust over the coffin.

I slumped to the earth. They said I lost consciousness. Later I was told that I very nearly rolled into the grave.

I lived the life of a recluse in the days that followed. I stayed the whole time in my bedroom listening to music and thinking. Sometimes I would wake up in the middle of the night, sweating. Then I would realise that I had been dreaming. I always dreamed, strange and horrible dreams that I was never able to remember when I woke up.

What surprised me was that after my father's burial I thought little about him. I could still feel the emptiness inside me but it wasn't as if it was my father that had died. It was like thinking of someone else. At first this horrified me, and made me think of myself as a wicked son who never cared sincerely for his father. It was as strange as it was disturbing.

Whenever I tried to think of him I discovered that my memory of him was vague, hazy. I couldn't place his face in my mind. It was like the picture of a man I had seen many years ago.

I could only keep telling myself that he was my father . . . but no definite picture or image would appear. Besides when as an alternative I tried to conjure up moments we'd spent together only the ones I didn't want to remember would surface. It was as if my mind had dropped all positive visions of him, as if something had plugged out memories of him.

This caused me great distress and nearly drove me mad.

My father . . . hard as adamant. Sometimes he reminded me of what I had read about Mafia bosses. He had brazened out the likes of hurricanes and monsoons . . . he had left broken structures on the roads over which he had passed . . . he had broken fragile stalks of flowers that grew in the fields adjacent to his interests.

He had left me and Mum behind to live for the rest of our lives in the ripples he had spread.

I could not think of him kindly. But still I felt his loss.

He had been a dutiful father to me. He took great care over my education. He was sometimes lavish towards me and as much as he could he filled my wants. He was like a great human institution.

182

But on a deeper level he neglected and distrusted me. I never had his company, I never really knew him for he always seemed to be closed up inside himself. I sometimes had the impression that I irritated him and that he didn't really like me.

As far as he was concerned his business came first. I have never seen a man more obsessed with business and success than my father. That was generally unfair to us but he didn't seem to mind.

He was different with Mum, though. I'm sure he loved her in his own peculiar way. I used to hear them laugh happily together in the nights and they used to go out together quite a lot.

In a way I felt out of the family. Sometimes it looked as if we were competing for Mum's attention.

And I knew one thing for sure: that my father considered me a foolish weakling who would never be as tough as he was. He didn't like me much because I had made it clear that I didn't want to be like him.

We often seemed like two people who had known each other for a long time and simply had to put up with one another. Like two people miming to each other and frequently getting the meanings wrong. Like two people trying to converse on different sides of a glass pane. But he was my father. I don't understand these things.

I would also never know what it was between him and Sowho. Maybe Mum would tell me some time. But I don't think I'll understand it. All I did know was that their hatred had followed them to their graves, and a part of it would live with us for ever.

I thought of my mother. She was still in a state of shock. The doctor had said it was concussion. They didn't allow me to go in and see her.

'What are her chances?' I had asked.

'She will be all right. It's just a question of time,' the doctor had told me.

I could see the pity in his eyes as he spoke to me. I didn't wait much longer. I couldn't bear people looking at me like that. My grief was a private thing, a private tragedy. That was the only way it could be without it turning into a public sham.

I didn't understand my mother either. I know her and yet I don't know her. Her eyes seemed to hold a certain secret, a certain pathos each time I spoke to her about Dad.

I remembered that day in the restaurant, the angry way she had looked at me in the car.

I also remember the day she came to our school many years ago, when I was in Form Two. She was distraught and haggard. She told me that someone had seen a vision that I would die either from electric shock or from drowning in a well.

With tears in her eyes she implored me not to go near any of them. She even went to the senior prefect and begged him to take care of me. I remember that she had hardly gone when two seniors sent me to go and fetch water from the well for them, and the following morning I had to press my school uniform or I couldn't go to school.

Deep inside me I prayed that she would get better.

The days passed wearily. When I wasn't at home sleeping or thinking or reading a novel, I would go to the hospital and be with Mum for a few minutes. Or I would take short walks down our street.

Ode's father telephoned me one day and told me that they had already had Ode's funeral. I was surprised, almost angry.

'I didn't want to add to your grief,' he said slowly. 'You need more courage than any of us. Ode wouldn't have wanted it harder on you. I'm sorry about your father's death.'

Then he went on to say that I could come down there and be with them any time I liked. I had said 'Okay,' but I knew I would not be able to go there for a long time.

A few days later I got a parcel. It contained books that I had lent to Ode. My novels, textbooks, and even some notebooks that I had forgotten about.

In the letter that accompanied it, his father had told me that the heart was deepened by sorrow and that no matter what happened I should never forget the magic of laughter and the promises of tomorrow.

That night I tried to laugh, but it fell flat. It was as if I was mocking myself.

I knew that in consoling me the man was trying to console himself.

One morning, in the second week of my confinement, Chema, our cook, who had all along been very helpful, woke me up from my dark reminiscences.

'Oga, one person find you come.'

I looked up at his smiling face.

'Who?' I began.

'One girl so.'

'One girl?' I repeated.

I could not think of any girl who would be so stupid as to come and see me at this time. Besides, I had given firm orders that I wanted to see no one. But I felt a sudden desire for human company, I felt a certain loneliness.

'Bring her . . .'

Before I could complete the sentence he opened the door and, of all people in the world, Cynthia walked into the room, looking more than anything like a picture of my mother taken years ago.

'What are you . . . I mean how . . . ?' I couldn't even find the right words, I was so surprised to see her. She wore a slim-fitting blue trouser suit, her hair, combed out Afro-style, made her look gorgeous. A black handbag hung from her shoulder. She smiled gently and sat down on the lone chair in my room. There was an awkward silence as I thought of what to say.

'Don't bother to say anything,' she said softly. 'I know.'

I looked down at the floor. For a moment thoughts were a haze in my mind.

'I got your letter . . . and I understood . . .'

What is she doing here then? I asked myself. Questions like that came and went, and I knew that I was just trying to be hard on myself. I wanted to say something. I didn't want to present a picture of mourning. I wanted to act natural. But the right words wouldn't come to mind. I looked up at her.

'Must have been hard on you,' she said shortly. I knew she didn't expect any answers from me. Her eyes travelled round the room, which was in a mess.

I looked at her. That was almost therapeutic in itself. Her face was pretty, fresh, and kind. Her hair gleamed. I liked the way she held herself, artlessly, attractively. She seemed at ease with her spirit. Then her eyes turned on me, and the next thing she said surprised me.

'It's all happened already, Jeff. Nothing you can do will change things. You can't go on like this for ever. Regardless of what has happened you must go on living, you must face life for what it is, man. Reality is outside the door, you must stretch out and reach for it and adjust to it.' She said, calmly. There was nothing pedantic about the way she had said it. She paused and stared at me.

I had heard it all before. But I didn't look into her eyes. For some reason I couldn't. Maybe it was the knowledge that she meant what she was saying and that she had gone through just as much. Maybe it was because I knew that she was speaking from experience. But I just couldn't look at her in return.

'Now you are going to have yourself a bath because the whole place stinks. I will help you clear up the place. You are a man and should set an example.'

She got up, removed the blanket from over my body, opened the window.

'Why don't you leave me alone, Cynthia, eh?' I protested.

She stopped and turned to me. 'Because I want you to wake up and face life. Because I remember what you said that night you took me home. About being ourselves no matter what happens . . . Do you really want me to go?'

I looked at her face. Her twinkling eyes held a sorrowful expression. The full meaning of her gesture dawned on me. And all of a sudden I felt a strength fill my mind. I felt a glow engulf me. I smiled for the first time in three weeks.

'No. Please stay,' I said finally.

I took up my towel and wrapped it round me and made for the bathroom. I stopped at the door and turned to her.

'But why do you have to sound so much like my mother?' I asked. Without waiting for a reply, I went to bath.

By the time I came out, feeling much fresher and lightened in mind, she had completely cleared up the room.

'Now you can live here,' she said as I came into the room.

Had I just been *dwelling* there?

I went to the wardrobe and took out a pair of flannel trousers. While I got dressed my mind went to the past, as if telling me I had no right to look happy. I felt depression again creeping into my soul.

'Why don't you go out and open the other windows of your soul?' she asked, intruding into my thoughts. I said nothing for a moment.

'Where is there to go?'

'I have a place in mind that would do you some good. Let's go. It won't take long.'

I gave her a long stare. Then I nodded.

I wondered why she was doing all this. Wasn't she the one who . . . I didn't want to think about it. I had plenty on my mind. It was enough that it was happening. It was enough that someone cared. It was enough that a little sunshine had found its way into my bereaved soul. I didn't want to spoil it all by trying to dissect the reasons for her action. I would find out soon enough.

We went out through the sitting room. The pictures on the wall smiled down at me. Just Mum's and mine. Our relatives had taken down all the pictures of my father. That day they had also carried away my father's juju in a metal container. I heard one of them saying they should burn it but when they turned round and saw me they all stopped talking.

'Later I will have to go to the hospital,' I told Cynthia.

'What for?'

'My mother is ill.'

'Oh. Hope it isn't serious?'

'It is rather,' I said blankly. She didn't say anything more.

It was cold outside. The winds were strong and sand was blown into our eyes.

I stopped to look at the mango tree, remembering when a nest had been stoned down and a bird killed. I remembered it so intensely that the same wave of sadness I felt that day swept over me.

When I wanted to stop a taxi, she made us go by bus. I was irritated by the struggle to get in, the endless bickering of the passengers, the crowdedness, and the stench. We took another bus to Ijora. At the back of the Kunbi bus were some foul-smelling he-goats. I was even more irritated.

'Are you taking me to your house?'

'No,' she replied, smiling and then lapsed into a mysterious silence.

We got off at Ijora bus-stop and started walking again.

There was a terrible stench in the air. The roads were bad, filled with ugly potholes, dirty. People who looked sickly and exhausted milled past us and I couldn't help being revolted by some of the sights I saw. There was a man under the Ijora bridge who had no legs. He was sleeping beside the spot people had habitually used as a urinal. There was a boy no more than fourteen lying on the side of the road with flies dancing all over his swollen body. He was dead. There was another group of children all crying round their beggar mother. Her breasts, I could see, were dry. We crossed the road to the other side and had to pass the bus-stop. A bus had come and people rushed to get on. They crowded, swamped, and pushed us. Some caught the bus, some didn't. A man who had shoved me in the rush, cursed. His breath smelt foul, his face was scored with suffering and misery.

'Fuckin' bus get only one free seat.' But he wasn't bitter. He went and rushed for another bus.

We walked down a series of side roads and soon entered a bleak yellow-painted building. As we got in I could hear the sound of crying and saw nurses going up and down. It was a hospital.

We went through the corridors and entered a ward. Cynthia stopped to have a word with one of the nurses.

'You know them?' I asked when she returned. She nodded. 'I work here now.'

The wards were stacked with sick people. There appeared to be no room left for them except the corridors.

Where was Cynthia taking me?

I saw a man with an amputated arm wailing blood-curdlingly and another with a heavy bandage round his face.

188

'That one was stabbed in the eyes by robbers,' she told me.

Then we came to a large cot. In it two babies were sleeping. She stopped and gave them a long look.

'They were born a week ago.' She paused and looked up at me. 'They are alone in the world. Their parents died yesterday in an accident. It's a miracle they were saved.'

She pointed to another fellow who had bandages all over his body. One of his plaster-cast legs hung up in a sling.

'Fell into a fire,' she said casually.

Then with the force of tragedy it all struck me.

At last I knew what she was getting at. Why she had made sure I struggled in the bus, to see those beggars, the dead, the starving, the deeply suffering and the hopelessly alone. Why she took me through the bus-stop and put us in the mainstream of rushing and struggling. She wanted me to see that suffering was universal; to make me for a moment look outside my own bereavement into a world teeming with pain, loss, and hopelessness; to shock me into identifying myself with the unacceptable continuum of the unfortunate. It was a great and poetic way to do it, but in my state of mind it was too forceful a message. Instead of helping me submerge my sorrow in the universality of its existence, it only served in some way to emphasise my loss. I ran out of the hospital and, without waiting for her, went home in the first taxi I could get.

Chapter Twenty-three

That evening I went to see my mother at the hospital.

The doctor told me she was getting better. I asked him if I could go in and see her. He smiled down at me and told me that she was sleeping.

'It's better that nothing should disturb her at this time.'

I was walking away when he called me back.

'We will be discharging her soon. I don't know how you will disclose what you have to without deeply troubling her again. She is in a very sensitive state of mind. Did you know that your mother had fainting fits?'

I looked at him. 'Yes. But that was a long time ago. She was treated then and the doctor said she was all right.'

He nodded, his eyes distant.

'When is she being discharged, doctor?'

'The day after tomorrow.'

'Will she be all right? I mean will she be . . .'

'Yes, she'll be all right. But you will have a difficult task on hand. She'll be fine but not as good as new. Only God can do that.'

If only God can make her as good as new, I thought as I walked away from Ikoyi hospital, then God better had. Nothing will be the same if she isn't good as new. Nothing will be the same if my mother turns out to be a different person from the one I have always known and loved.

When I got home there was a phone call from Jefu, the assistant sales manager of Afioso Paints. He was a personal friend. It was the first call I had received from the company since Daddy's death.

'Hello, Jeffia,' he said. 'How are you doing?'

'I'm all right. How's the company?'

'I have been sacked, Jeff. I've been sacked.'

I caught my breath.

'What do you mean, sacked?'

'The new administration does not like my face.'

190

'What new administration?'

'Jeff, you mean you don't know what's been going on since . . . ? Well, before your dad died, the union had already engineered a strike action. Your dad ignored it and refused to give in to the demands of the union, so they resorted to violence. They spoilt a lot of equipment and broke windows and threatened the management. So the company's co-directors made agreements with the union behind your father's back. The next day we learnt of your father's death. The company has since been taken over by Jeccaro and Chief Hans. They are weeding out elements they don't like. I'm one of them.'

For a moment I didn't say anything, there wasn't anything for me to say. I knew so little about my father's company. I felt completely cut off from his personal influences. In a strange way I didn't feel any sense of loss at the news. I only felt a wicked and strange relief. His company had fallen into the hands of the enemy, and the circle seemed complete. That company into which my father had put all of his energy was responsible for so many evils. It had raised him from the gutter and had been responsible for his death. It had made him a power merchant, a steam-roller, crushing the lives of many. It had forced a wedge into the family. It had made him an intolerable egoist. Now it had fallen into the hands of the philistines.

'Jefu, you called me purposely to tell me this, didn't you?'

'Yes, Jeffia. I felt you should know.'

After a little more talk I thanked him and hung up. I looked outside the window. A few cars drove past. Some children were playing football down the street. I dropped the curtain.

I didn't know what to think. My mind was in a muddle, in a whirlpool of mixed feelings. Gloom, fear, and anger, like an old blanket, settled on me simultaneously. I slumped into a sofa. I let the emotions come over me.

I had the urge to see Cynthia. I needed her comforting presence. I wanted to tell her how sorry I was for running out on her twice.

I drove to her place. She was in the parlour with her father watching television.

Her father did not look like the staggering drunk I nearly ran into that other night. He looked alive. I wondered what was responsible for such a marvellous transformation.

Cynthia was pleased to see me.

'Dad, this is Jeffia Okwe. He was the young man who brought me home that night. Jeffia, this is my father.'

'Nice to meet you, sir.'

'Thank you, my son.' He gave me a scrutinising look. 'Tell me, are you the late Jonan Okwe's son?'

'Dad!' I heard Cynthia say. She had stood up.

'Yes, sir,' I replied as politely as I could.

He looked deeply at me and his face shadowed, crumpling. His vitality disappeared. He suddenly seemed old. For a moment I thought he was going to have a heart attack.

I remembered what Cynthia had told me in the taxi. But that day I had been determined to face the past for what it was. It was a stupid kind of determination that presumed the avoidance of responsibilities. But I had to do it all the same. I had not been sure how Cynthia's father would react, I was even afraid. But I believed it was worth the attempt.

'Dad, what's the matter, eh?'

'His . . . father . . . his father . . .'

Cynthia covered his mouth with her hands. 'Don't, Dad. I know all about it. But Jeffia is different from his father. And you said you would forget, didn't you?'

I was embarrassed. Those incubi of the past. Those shadows of another life, crossing and re-crossing.

She got up and held my hands.

'Jeffia, let's go for a walk. Dad's not in a good mood.'

I got up and followed her. I was only too glad to leave the room. As we went out I caught a last glimpse of his face: it had the strangest mixture of bitterness and gentleness that I had ever seen.

Outside, the wind blew hard. We were alone in the street. The trees, like guardians, stood magnificent and proud. The sky, with its aesthetic splashes of colours, was a dream of harmony. We were alone. What had just happened seemed quite remote. She was close to me and our hands were locked as if they belonged together. I could smell her hair and her womanhood.

When she spoke her voice had a cooling clarity.

'Jeff, I am sorry about what happened. I suppose meeting you awakened those memories of what your father did to him. He is a very emotional and sensitive man.'

'What has happened to him since that night? He looks so . . .'

'He got a job in Zaki Paints as a production supervisor. One of his former co-workers at Afioso arranged it for him. Since then a great change has come over him . . .'

We said nothing for some time. We walked down the street.

'In a way you were right, you know.'

'About what?'

'About attitudes and experiences.'

'No, Cynthia, you were right.'

'Okay, then both of us were right.'

We stopped walking. I liked the silence that came over us. It was harmonious: the silence of the world outside us, the silences of the worlds inside us, and the silence between us. Maybe that doesn't make sense, but that was how I felt.

'How is your mother?'

'She is being discharged tomorrow.'

'I'd like to come and meet her some time.'

'You will.'

We began to walk on.

'Look, I'm sorry about the way I have been running out on you.'

'I understand.'

'You must think I am a coward.'

'You are not a coward, Jeff. If you were you wouldn't be here.'

I felt warm and free. Cynthia had that power of making me feel whole again. Just standing there with her made me joyful. As the pleasure of her presence glowed in me, the inner world where I had been hiding seemed to recede far into the background. And all I knew then was that I could be happy again.

'How is it that you came around when you did yesterday?'

'I looked up your address in the phone book.'

'Not that, I mean why did you come?'

She was silent for a moment.

'Why did you write to me?'

'A sense of guilt.'

'Jeff, it couldn't only have been a sense of guilt.'

'And, well, other emotions I can't analyse.'

'Well, that was why I came too. Emotions I can't analyse.'

'Cynthia.'

'Yes, Jeff.'

'Cynthia, I think you are unique.'

'And you too.'

There was a tree nearby. I steered her under it. We leaned on the trunk, in each other's arms. As I stood there feeling the warmth from her, I wondered how powerful was that state they call love. For I could hear its sweet music and feel its human personification.

We had not said anything about love. But it was there, in her eyes, in her half-smiles, in her presence, in the things she did. It was in me too. She had brought me out of myself and filled me with the possibility of happiness. I held her closer. Her body was warm and soft.

'I love you, Cynthia.'

'I love you too, Jeff.'

I liked the way she called me Jeff.

I kissed her. And we remained like that, kissing. There was nothing wild about it, but it was natural and sweet. It was one of those moments of sublimity which the mind strives to retain but never quite manages. We disengaged and began walking again. I began to think about her. I drew her closer.

Something made me look back. Standing at their doorway, casting a long shadow in front of him, was her father. He watched us. I would have given anything to know what he was thinking.

'Come on, Jeff,' she said, urging me on.

'Where are we going this time?'

We both laughed.

'To Jane's place.'

'Whose place?' I said stopping.

'Jane's place.'

The moonlight twinkled mischievously in her eyes.

'Jane knows. She knew all along. Every time she sees me she keeps asking about you.' Cynthia laughed. I looked at her and I laughed as well.

I went with her. I was sure she was about to spring another surprise on me.

Jane's place was not very far away. As we walked, we talked. We often fell into silences, which I liked. When we got there Jane didn't seem surprised to see me. She only smiled broadly when she opened the door. I think I must have formed the wrong impression about her, for I found that she was really a pleasant person. But she kept looking at me and Cynthia with a rather meaningful smile. After a while she said we must excuse her and she vanished. It took me some time to realise that she had left the place for us, two lovers who wanted to be alone. I looked at Cynthia, and she looked at me. We fell into each other's arms. The night wasn't long enough.

Chapter Twenty-four

I was sitting alone, on a bench, in the shade of a palm-frond tent. The usually crowded beach was deserted except for some couples and families taking photographs. They struck me as people who were trying desperately to cling onto the last snatches of a fine day, who didn't want to admit that the day was dying.

I came here a lot these days, especially since things began to change. I found the presence of the sea comforting. The sounds of wind and surf gave more power to my reminiscences. At first the great ocean, the great spaces, the engulfing sky, seemed to crowd on my senses, filling me with an intense loneliness and smallness. But I got used to it. Here I had learnt that everything had its time and place, strange as they might be. I had learned too that I was an infinitesimal part of nature and that I could not possibly understand all the strange ways of life. Such moments alone enabled my soul to soar and experience a joy that rose above the torments that I had suffered. I needed such moments. I needed anything that would bring some sanity and meaning to my battered spirit.

The wind from the ocean blew hard, sending sprays of salt water to the shore. The sun yielded to the slow passing of another day, its fading rays threw long shadows beside the tents on the beach. The waves raged from their distant journeys, from untold seas and oceans, and flung their tired waters on the glittering shores.

One of the men among the couples jumped into the incoming surf. He was covered with the foam-flecked waves and then carried on its crest. After a while he swam back to the shore where a woman who had been watching him and calling to him to be careful took his picture. They laughed again. Their laughter was carried away by the winds.

Soon the beach was deserted and I was really alone. That was the way I always wanted it. Just me and the elements. Then

196

I could be alone with myself and hold child-like conversation with the wind and the open sky.

I got up, left fifty kobo for the man in charge of renting the benches, and I leisurely walked down the shoreline.

I was in no hurry. I had come to find peace with myself and my memories. I had long ago discovered there was no such thing as finding peace outside oneself in the heat of a life's journey or in the hustle for material acquisition.

I had found it within me, in that calm centre where nothing could shake or disturb me like they used to. In finding it, I began to find myself. I breathed deeply.

In the harmony of sounds all around me I thought I could discern echoes of an elusive symphony. Love flowed out from me. The ocean was calm except for slight rufflings when gentle waves gathered and spread out with an extended hiss on the shore near my feet.

I looked as far as I could into the horizon but I could only see as far as where sky joined ocean in a smooth, masterly blending of colours. I bent and grabbed a handful of sand and threw it at the wind. I felt released from the cramps and tensions of daily existence. I let the memories flood my mind as they do each time I came here. It was a year since we had moved out of the house where we used to live at Ikoyi. Things had been difficult but what was worse was that the change I had feared had taken place.

It began the afternoon I went to bring Mum home from the hospital when she was discharged. She looked so thin and the pathos she always had in her eyes had grown deeper. I noticed a few wrinkles on her face and under her eyes that were not there before.

She smiled when she saw me. I ran up to her, joy welled up in my heart. I hugged her and kissed her cheek. People were watching us. The doctor stood near a pillar and shook his head.

I knew what that meant.

She commented on how tall I had seemingly grown since she last saw me. She was happy to see me. There were tears in her eyes, there were some in mine too. But for different reasons.

Then she asked me why my father hadn't come with me. I froze. I said nothing but led her to the car and in silence drove her home. When we got home I couldn't hide it from her a minute longer. I even felt sure she must have realised it. The whole atmosphere had a different weight, the gaps in the photographs on the walls and many other little things were enough to show something was missing.

But she didn't seem to notice. She was just silent.

I told her to sit down, that I wanted to tell her something.

I think it was then she sensed things. A bewildered expression crossed her face and she looked around the sitting room and then she looked back at me. She stared at me intensely as if wanting to divine my thoughts. I was terribly uncomfortable.

'What is it, Jeff?'

I couldn't speak.

'Jeff, something has happened, eh, something has happened?'

I nodded slowly. 'Daddy is dead.'

For a brief moment she looked at me with supreme incredulity. Then an immensely bleak expression followed. She craned her neck towards me. Her voice was tiny with disbelief.

'You said what, Jeffia?'

Taking my eyes off her, I repeated it slowly. She gripped me and shrieked, 'Dead? Jonan dead?'

The next moment she went into hysterics. She screamed and shouted and gripped my shoulders till her fingernails dug into my flesh and drew blood. I screamed and shouted with her.

She went mad with uncontrollable hysteria and flung herself on the floor. I rushed and called the doctor over the phone. By the time I turned back to her she had lost consciousness again. She had wounded herself in falling against a chair or something and blood oozed out through a cut on her face.

I gently lifted her on the sofa, and waited for the doctor to come. My heart bled for her and I felt the sorrow she felt. Unwilling tears filled my eyes. Both my arms were bleeding where her nails had dug into me.

Life has not been the same for us since then. But it was far worse for my mother.

A few days later words filtered to our ears that some of Dad's relatives had accused mother of being a witch. They said in their various ways that my mother had tied my father down in such a way that he didn't want to associate with his own people.

Worst of all, they said she was the evil behind the deaths of my father and Sowho. That she killed them because she wanted to inherit my father's wealth.

They even questioned why she had never borne any other children for my father, and said that possibly it was because she ate her children in her womb.

My mother sometimes met these relatives in the street but on seeing her they would turn back and walk away in the opposite direction.

My mother was never the same person again. She grew sullen, haggard, wiry, and pale. She resigned from her teaching appointment and dwelled constantly in dismal silence. She never went out and always wore black. She slept little and cried a lot at night. She seldom ate.

My mother, who used to have so much life and vigour, had in a matter of weeks become lifeless and almost frightful to look at. There was even a time when I could not help thinking that she was beginning to look a bit like a witch. The pathos in her eyes deepened and spilled over to any person she directed her gaze at. I feared she was going mad.

I had missed that year's opportunity to gain a place in the university. I had to find a job because Mother was not prepared, after what had been said about her, to fight for her rightful share in the company. She was a walking tragedy.

I never knew she could sink so low, become so deformed beyond recognition, become so engrossed in the terrible dimension of her despair. I could not say anything that would in any way relate to it for fear that she might sink into another uncontrollable hysteria. And so the days dragged by leaden-footed with no horizon for either of us in sight.

One night something happened which momentarily snapped us out of our dark cocoons. Thieves broke into our compound and stole the two cars remaining in the garage. It must have been an easy enough job; we had long ago asked Chema and the watchman to go; we were alone and vulnerable.

One morning, not long afterwards, Mother told me we were moving away from the house. It was too full of memories and nightmares for her. If there was going to be any hope for us, she told me, we would have to leave.

Our new place is in Amukoko. We live in two rooms. The compound is a dirty one, and the people are quite peculiar. The house is a storey building which we share with five other tenants and their huge families. For us it has been a big drop down, but it was necessary.

Mother didn't sell Daddy's house. It was in care of some housing agents. She told me that it was for me when I was old enough to own it.

The last time I went there the grass had grown all round the house. The mango tree had borne fruit and birds had started coming there again. Some of the flowers in the garden had withered and died but others had survived. The shack where the watchday used to be had been nailed shut and the lawn had grown wild. And there was a big hole in one of the windows where somebody had thrown a stone.

So now we live in Amukoko, a slum that gets swampy during the rainy season and dusty during the dry.

Mum is getting back to normal. But she is still thin and older-looking and her face has a perpetual stamp of misery.

Time has worn away the edges of her bereavement and carried away the outermost pangs of the loss that we both felt. But the deeper feelings of it remains like sediment in our hearts.

My mother and I have almost become strangers to one another. We see little of each other. She has recently started working in the Ministry of Education. I come home late from work and have to leave early. I even have to go to work on Saturdays because I need the overtime money. We only see each other fully on Sundays, when there is little to talk about. When we talk at all it is usually on the surface. We both keep our inner feelings to ourselves.

Life was never the same for me. Yet it was not entirely different, as Cynthia would say. I had grown up. In my own way I had become strong.

The tough voice of my father was heard no more. I never saw his name in the papers again except in the family's obituary.

Nobody asks my name twice these days. Only on a few occasions, in the office or sometimes in the bank, will someone turn to me and ask the same old question. What they usually do is turn and give me a long stare and then get on with what they were doing as though I never existed. Nobody wants my favours any more.

I had grown out from the shadows into the light. The past was far away and though its ectoplasmic arms reached me from time to time, what mattered to me was the future.

Not long ago I was at Leventis bus-stop waiting for a bus. The sun was beating down and I was sweating and felt miserable. Few buses came and there was a long go-slow. Then I saw someone I recognised. At first I could not place where I had seen the woman. Then as I stared at her I suddenly remembered. It was Juliet, the woman whose puppy I had returned. She looked older than I remembered. I had the urge to run up to her and say hello and ask about her dog, but she looked at me coolly, with a hint of hostility, and without a single sign of recognition. Then she turned her eyes away.

I was not even sure it was Juliet. But they looked very much alike. The go-slow moved and her car drove away. Whoever she was, she didn't look back.

I have saved enough money to sponsor myself for two years in the university if the government doesn't award me a scholarship. Mum has insisted that I must complete my education.

Cynthia comes round to our house quite a lot. The first time she met my mother was slightly tricky. I didn't want to mention anything about her father. But it worked out well. They took so easily to each other that sometimes I get jealous when she comes and has long laughing chats with Mother about things I am naturally excluded from.

Cynthia told me the other day that her father wanted to apologise for the way he behaved the night I went there. Cynthia asked me to come round and meet him. He's a nice man but his bitterness still creeps out sometimes. Often he stops in the middle of a conversation and lapses into dismal thought, other times he bursts out laughing for no good reason.

One of the things that has really made me happy is the knowledge that, despite what has happened to us, our social and financial drop, Cynthia has come down the long lonely road with me and has given me her love all the way.

Recently we celebrated my twenty-first birthday. Cynthia was there with a few other friends. Mum smiled a lot and seemed proud. She bought me a suit and gave me a card which read: 'I'm proud of the man you are turning into.'

I knew then that things were going to improve. It was just a matter of time, will, and luck.

I took some more deep breaths. I felt revitalised. The sky had darkened and was a foreboding mixture of dark blue and grey. The winds blew strongly. The waves rose and fell. I let the echoes of that elusive symphony of the ocean fill my being and I prayed loudly for joy, strength, and grace.

A few birds still flew about the shore. I began to walk the length of the beach, home. I did not want to stay too long. Being at the beach was in a way like drinking. If you take a little you'll want more. If you take too much you'll get drunk and miss the real fun.

I wanted just enough of the feeling of attunement to carry the glow into my daily life. So that when I struggle for a bus to work tomorrow or when I wearily trudge back home late in the evening I would not lose sight of the fact that the whole of my life was like a big bad joke. And that I needed a positive outlook and a steady vision to make the joke become a good one.

As I walked over the sands and went to the bus-stop, night fell. All around me, the high life was booming. I could make out the heady lights of the big hotels nearby. The large ornamented houses that stood on the other side of the road reminded me of another life.

The tall trees cast sombre shadows on the dark, neat road. Cars, big and expensive, drove up and down. One had some boys and girls in it who were shouting and sounded drunk.

Some beggars passed by. There was a small girl among them. She was blind. I gave her a ten-kobo coin.

The night before my birthday Mother told me about her being an orphan and that nobody knew what had happened to her parents. And how later she had been taken from the orphanage by a rich, barren widow who used her as a servant and housegirl.

When Mum told me this, many things about her that formerly perplexed me fell into place. I began to see her differently. My knowledge of psychology is limited but I have a feeling that's one of the reasons why Mum was the person she was, why she always seemed to expect disasters to befall her, why she was always afraid of the future, always seemed to be holding her breath.

I began to open up to her and love her as I never have before.

Soon a bus came and there was the usual struggle to embark. I managed to get in. I changed buses three times before I could finally reach home.

When I got home I found Mum painting. I looked over her shoulder. She was putting finishing touches to the painting of the flowers in the shadow. She had been working on that painting, on and off, for a long time. I kissed her cheek and went to my room and changed. Tomorrow is Monday, and I would need to wake up early.

'Jeffia! Come and see this,' my mother called excitedly. I went and looked at the finished painting.

'Looks surrealist, Mum. I like those shades of colour you gave the flowers. The vase looks strange and beautiful. The shadows look mournful.'

She didn't say anything. She just stared at the painting, at the symbol she had created. Then I remembered what she had told me a long time ago: that we are all little flowers in the shadow.

Her face had clouded. I wondered if she was thinking the same thing.

Epilogue

It was another bright Saturday morning.

I was returning from an early walk. I didn't feel like going to work that day. The streets were dusty and dirty. Children were playing about, some of them naked. I could hear the vendor's horn announcing his arrival with the daily stock of newspapers.

I passed a number of men who stood in front of their houses masticating their chewing sticks with a dog-like verve. Most of them had wrappers tied round their black, hairy waists. The record shops were already open and had begun blaring their discordant mixtures of music into the street. In front of one of the record shops a few men danced to Apala music, swaying in exotic and apparently drunken movements.

The women who sold cooked rice by the side of the streets had come out and were chanting 'Oni rice re – O!' Some children, their stomachs shrunken, their faces eager, had already lined up with their empty plates.

I walked past the stagnant pool of greenish water that had refused to dry up even in the terrible heat of the dry season. A woman with nothing on the upper part of her body but a piece of cloth covering her fallen breasts, walked in front of me carrying a small pot. She poured her baby's excreta into the stagnant, greenish water. I avoided a filthy dog that was licking someone's excreta at the corner of the scum.

Alaba is a dirty place but it shows a bit of how people lived in the sad crude simplicities of poverty. On another dimension it reminded me of what I had read about Harlem. For dirty as the place is and uncared for as the roads were, the lives of the people are a heart-breaking celebration of the strength of the human spirit, its adaptability.

I branched into our street and noticed that someone was pointing at me from among a group of boys. I ignored them and walked on. I didn't mix with the ruffians in the area.

I had got to the front of our house when I heard from behind me, 'Excuse me, mister ... excuse me, sir ...' I stopped and turned to see who it was calling me so early in the morning. A boy came running to me. He looked rather familiar.

'Yes?' I said to him. 'What do you want?'

He was panting. I had seen him somewhere before. I was sure of that. He came forward and put his hands on his chest.

'Have you forgotten me, sir?'

'Not really. But I can't remember exactly where I met you.'

He looked at me and smiled. He was holding something wrapped-up in leaves. I guessed it was food of some sort, maybe eba or fufu that he had bought from a bukka.

Then he spoke again.

'I was the boy you gave two Naira that time at Ikoyi when me and my brother was beating up a dog.'

Then I remembered. He had grown up a bit and was better dressed.

I smiled at him.

'How are you?'

'I'm fine, sir.'

'What about your brother?'

'Oh, he's at home. He's got malaria.'

'I hope you don't still beat up dogs?' I said, smiling. He laughed.

'No, sir. Things are better now, sir.'

'Well, that's nice. So what do you do now?'

He changed the wrapped food from one hand to the other.

'I'm now in the government school. I am in primary six. My brother is a messenger in a canteen at Tinubu.'

I nodded.

'Why isn't he going to school?'

'Ah, he doesn't want to go to school. He said he wants to be a mechanic but my mama won't let him. He went to even be a bus conductor but my mama bring him back again.'

'So how is your mama?'

'All right. She's a cook now at the canteen where my brother with big head works.'

'So where are you coming from?'

'My mama send me to our grannie's place to go and give her these kola-nuts. The place is not far from here.'

My guess about the food was wrong. It made me smile.

After a brief silence he spoke again.

'I want to say thank you for that money you gave us the other time. Our mother told us that if we see you again we should greet you for her. At first she even think we thief it.'

I said, 'Don't worry.'

'So you stay around here now?' the boy asked me sceptically. I looked at him.

'Yes,' I said slowly. 'I stay around here now.'

I pointed to the house where I lived.

He looked at me, then back at the house. I know he wanted to ask me something further, but he just said, 'Okay, sir . . . I think I want to be going now or my mama will worry why I am so late. Thank you again . . .'

I nodded and put my hands into my breast pocket and brought out a fifty-kobo note. I offered it to him. He said he didn't want money. But I insisted.

'Have it,' I told him. 'I like people who know the meaning of appreciation. Come on, have it.'

Finally he took it from me, thanked me again and went in the direction he came. In the distance he turned and waved to me. I waved back.

He didn't know it but he had brought a dimension of joy into my life. I felt light. I sang as I went upstairs to our apartment.

'Jeff, is that you?' my mother called.

'Yes, it is, Mum.' I went on singing.

'You sound happy, Jeff.'

I looked at her face. It was flushed with the sun and looked lighter.

'Yes, Mum, I am happy.'

'Is it because Cynthia is coming today?' she said smiling suggestively as she brought the food to the dining table.

'This is one guess you are not going to get right, Mum.'

We both sat down at the table and had our breakfast. As I ate I noticed that she kept glancing up at me. I knew she was still trying to guess why I was happy.

I looked at the framed painting that hung on the wall behind her, then I looked back at her.

I smiled, mysteriously. She smiled back at me, puzzled.

I looked out of the window. It was going to be a beautiful day: I could see the sun breaking out from behind a mass of clouds.

I went on eating.